THE Signs AND Wonders OF TUNA RASHAD

NATASHA DEEN

RP|TEENS
PHILADELPHIA

Running Press Teens
Hachette Book Group
1290 Avenue of the Americas,
New York, NY 10104
www.runningpress.com/rpkids
@RP_Kids

Printed in the United States of America

First Edition: June 2022

Published by Running Press Teens, an imprint of Perseus Books, LLC,
a subsidiary of Hachette Book Group, Inc. The Running Press Teens
name and logo is a trademark of the Hachette Book Group.

The Hachette Speakers Bureau provides a wide range of authors for speaking events.
To find out more, go to www.hachettespeakersbureau.com or call (866) 376-6591.

The publisher is not responsible for websites (or their content)
that are not owned by the publisher.

Print book cover and interior design by Marissa Raybuck.

Library of Congress Cataloging-in-Publication Data
Names: Deen, Natasha, author.
Title: The signs and wonders of Tuna Rashad / Natasha Deen.
Description: First edition. | Philadelphia : Running Press Teens, 2022.
Identifiers: LCCN 2021035638 | ISBN 9780762478682 (hardcover) |
ISBN 9780762478705 (ebook) Subjects: LCSH: Caribbean Americans—
Juvenile fiction. | Caribbean Americans—Social life and customs—Juvenile fiction. |
Brothers and sisters—Juvenile fiction. | Families—Juvenile fiction. |
Bereavement—Juvenile fiction. | Interpersonal relations—Juvenile fiction. |
Ontario (Calif.)—Juvenile fiction. | CYAC: Caribbean Americans—Fiction. |
Brothers and sisters—Fiction. | Family life—California—Fiction. |
Love—Fiction. | Grief—Fiction. | Ontario (Calif.)—Fiction.
Classification: LCC PZ7.1.D446 Si 2022 | DDC 813.6 [Fic]—dc23
LC record available at https://lccn.loc.gov/2021035638

ISBNs: 978-0-7624-7868-2 (hardcover); 978-0-7624-7870-5 (ebook)

LSC-C

Printing 1, 2022

For my Elders and Ancestors,
who keep my eyes on the Heavens
and my Heart in the stars.

CHAPTER ONE

It Starts with a Pink Sweater

THE PLANETS ARE IN PRECISE ALIGNMENT, THE MOONS are in their proper houses, and the auspicious signs can't be denied. Okay, okay. So maybe a five-year-old student pooping in the pool during my swimming class at the Ontario Rec Center isn't the most glamorous—or attractive—good omen. But—BUT—class ended early (thank you, ancestors!), which meant my shift ended early. Which means I have *just* enough time to oh-so-casually get to the soccer field behind the building for a "goodness, what a coincidence" meet-cute with the future Mr. Altuna Kashmir Rashad, aka Tristan Dangerfield.

Don't let his last name mislead you. Tristan's not dangerous or a bad boy, or anything like that. Actually, he's this kind, double helping of boy-treat who loves science and math, and who's been lighting up my days since freshman year at Woodbine High.

He's practical, logical, and level-headed, with just the right mix of sexy and intriguing. In other words, he's perfect for me, and I for him. And I have this summer to get us together, because come fall, it's off to Georgia for college before beginning my glamorous Hollywood life as a screenwriter. But first, I have to get my admittedly flat—but still cute— derrière out of the center. I've got the glass doors in my sights, my canvas bag on my shoulder, and my flip-flops are flip-flopping their way to the exit.

"Tuna! Tuna!"

No. Just NO. Ignoring the call of my manager, Penny, is a skill in itself. She has the voice of a cartoon character—high pitched, piercing, and from the chest.

"Tuna! Sweetie!"

Nnnnnnoooo, why is she still calling my name? And adding the "sweetie"? I contemplate running, then give up the idea. Penny is small but feisty. I could see her doing a blind-side tackle and bringing me to the ground. I pivot, which makes my maxi dress swirl around my ankles—and geez, why is Tristan not here for this slo-mo Hollywood moment? Then I give a quick wave and point at the door as though my life and liberty depend on my exit. Which they don't, *but* my heart depends on the exit.

My pointing and waving and fleeing like a convict running from the prison grounds does not deter Penny. Which shouldn't surprise me. She's relentless. The Terminator could take lessons from her. The woman was hired as a last-ditch effort to save the center. In less than two years, she's made it the place to be in the neighborhood—maybe in all of Ontario, California—and there are waiting lists for the classes. She's done so well, the center's actually in the midst of upgrades. Penny comes at me in a flurry of athletic sneakers, cotton t-shirt, and cargoes.

"Darling, I heard." She sweeps me into a black-cherry-scented hug, then steps back. "How *are* you?"

Bless her heart. Only Penny can turn a poop moment into an emotional story beat worthy of a multimillion-dollar movie, with orchestral soundtrack and all.

"All good." I clutch the four-leaf clover key chain in one hand, hoping it'll bring me some luck and get me out of the center. With the other hand, I jerk my thumb at the door. "I should head—"

"Did you take the proper precautions?"

For a woman who spends her days surrounded by sweat, wet towels, and athletic cups, Penny's a little high-strung about hygiene and cleanliness. "It's all good," I tell her. "My hands are sanitized. Everyone's good. I should go."

"What about you? How are you after the incident? Do you want to talk?"

The sweep of the clock's second hand feels like the final countdown. Normally, I'm all for ticking clocks. As a soon-to-be famous Hollywood (and indie because, you know, artistic freedoms and all) screenwriter, I know a ticking clock is vital to the story. It adds intensity, movement, and tension. Except now, when all it's adding is anxiety because I'm about to lose my chance with Tristan. "I'm so good, I don't need to talk. However, I really need to go. Like, *really*."

"Oh." Her brown eyes widen behind her glasses. "*Oh.* Of course. Yes, yes. Run along, sweetheart. We can talk later."

From the tone and sympathy, she's misunderstood the motivation behind why I want to leave, but now isn't the time to correct her. This isn't about grief. This is about love.

I have T-minus three minutes to catch up to Tristan, and I'm not about to waste it. "See you!" I dash into the June sunshine, blink to adjust to the light, and hang a left to speed for the field. There's some zigging and zagging to get around the construction guys and scaffolding, but I'm an athlete. An athlete in almost-love. Cement mixers and hard hat areas don't stand a chance against me.

"Tuna!"

Nnnnnnnnnnooooooooo to yet another detour in my plan. I get that the universe likes to test us mortals, make us question how badly we want our goals, and throw obstacles into our paths, but why, *why* is it throwing me my adorable little swimmer? I can't ignore him. Not just because he's a kid, but because he's the kid who had the accident, and I know it'll keep him awake tonight. I can't have that baby face losing sleep. "Hey, Mitchell. How are you doing, bud?"

He's clutching the hand of his mom, and his face is redder than his hair. "I'm sorry about the accident. I didn't mean to."

I send up a prayer to the ancestors and screenwriting gods that the soon-to-be love between Tristan and me can handle a delay. "I know, little man, you're good."

Brown eyes well up and time stops.

I squat in front of him, let my bag flop to the ground, and take his hand. "You are so good, and no one's going to remember what happened next class." So not true. It's eight kindergarten kids. They're going to remember this story until they die.

"See?" His mom rubs his shoulders. "I told you. No one is mad at you. Accidents happen." She smiles my way and mouths, *Thank you.*

They head to the parking lot. I check my watch. If I sprint, I can do this. The Savannah College of Art and Design in Georgia may have thwarted one dream by not giving me a swimming scholarship, but my second dream is on the field, and if I don't hurry I'm going to miss him.

I grab hold of my bag handles and run for it. The wind is cold on my wet scalp, and tendrils are sticking to my face, but I'm not letting a lack of foot support in my flip-flops deter me from pursuing love. Nor will I slow down for the stitch in my side.

Okay, the bug I just swallowed may have slowed my roll, but just for a second. I put on an extra burst of speed and swing around the corner.

Ah, yes, *yes*, to signs and omens. It's Friday, which means all the Littles are losing their minds and delaying Tristan's schedule. They're a group of ten kids, all eight-years-old, and they're in various states of chaotic energy, zooming around the field. Tristan is doing his dreamboat best to corral them, but let's face it: one super hottie with a heart of gold is no match for a bunch of kids hopped up on vitamin D, courtesy of the sunshine, and the promise of Saturday cartoons in the morning.

And okay, okay, silently cheering on the kids to ignore him is not my *highest* moment, but yo, man, this is *my* moment, and I can feel it in my multiracial, chocolate-vanilla girl bones. Maybe one of the Littles will trip and fall, and I'll be there with a soft word and a kind touch that will prove my big heart and love of—no. No. NO. Scratch that. Oh, my ancestors, DELETE AND REWRITE! I'm not up for any kid hurting themself just so my heart can score a victory or so I can showcase how caring I am.

I cross the field, scanning for a way to subtly shove myself into Tristan's life. I've been drooling over him since, you know, *forever*—but either he's been dating or I've been dating. Except for last year and a bit, but that doesn't count. My world was detonated in a *Superman*-esque explosion that would have wowed the special effects guys at the Warner Bros. Studio.

My universe is rebuilt now. At least the foundations are in place. Tristan is unattached and this is the first time we're both in a place to date each other. We've been in each other's orbit because we have mutual friends, and it's practically in the stars for our romance to happen.

Tristan's the proverbial flame, and the kids at Woodbine were the moths. Except instead of burning or destroying, Tristan's flame lit us up and warmed our fingers. I've never known anyone with as many friends as he has.

Last semester, we were finally in the same class—English—together. For group projects, the teacher ended up having to assign kids because *everyone* wanted to work with him. All of this is good news. If I ask him out and he says no, I know he'll be nice about it. Other people's DNA may consist of nucleotides, but Tristan's is pure kindness. Honestly, how can my heart not melt for a guy who stops in the middle of gym class to pick up a disoriented butterfly from the track and put it in a tree, safe from sneakers and stomping? Butterflies, man. That's a *sign*. So, yeah, I can totally do the asking out. Easy-peasy lemon squeezy. How hard can it be?

One of the kids kicks a soccer ball and snaps me back to attention. It curves toward me and rolls to a stop. Bingo. I'll bring Tristan the ball, we'll share a laugh over the hijinks of tiny ones, and I'll have the perfect segue into an invitation to some kind of casual group date thing, so, you know, he doesn't feel too much pressure.

The kids are running zig-zag, a few with arms outstretched in plane mode. A few more balls rain my way. I don't know what the game is, but apparently it involves seeing who can make the ball curve the most. I'm hoping that's the game. I'd hate to think the objective is to hit me. The grass tickles my feet as I kick the balls back and run closer to the group.

This gets me squeals of delight and immediate inclusion into the game.

"Hey, guys, leave the lady alone," Tristan's deep voice booms. He may as well be whispering for all the good it's doing.

I shoot him a grin. Then I toss the ball at a Little with cheeks so chubby and cute, she looks like she's storing nuts for the coming winter. "It's all good."

He smiles my way.

I don't have a chance to acknowledge or respond to the smile because the kids are kicking balls my way. More than kicking. Booting. Blasting. Rocketing. Oh, dang. I may have seriously underestimated the energy of these kids.

I find myself flicking off my flip-flops and suddenly playing goalie, diving and catching, kicking back to them. And let me just say, this is not the easiest thing to do while barefoot in a maxi dress. Although, I bet the printed flowers, along with the wind and sun, are casting a summertime romance vibe.

Tristan runs in my direction, but I don't have time to even nod his way. Balls are coming at me from all directions—cue wildly inappropriate joke, with a punchline about balls and Tristan. I'd think of it myself, except I can't come up with it right now because, you know, balls coming at my face. Oh, dang. There's a joke in there. I'll have to remember it for later, to share with Tristan—as long as the vibe says he'd find it funny and not uncool.

My coach brain kicks in and reminds me that I don't have to do anything other than catch the soccer balls. I collect them and put them in a pile.

This is the wrong thing to do.

A roar of dissent and rebellion comes from the kids. They are not ready for the day to be done. I'm not a small person—I'm five-ten, built solid and strong—but something about a horde of ticked-off, hyper Littles coming at me is all kinds of horror-movie *Children of the Corn* wrong. And I belatedly recognize the difference between my Littles and his Littles. My kids have a built-in behavior guard—the water. There's nothing like the risk of drowning or getting chlorine water up the nose to keep them in line. Tristan's kids have no such restraint.

One of the kids—dark hair, and in a red-and-white striped t-shirt—grabs one of the balls from the pile. I catch hold of the ball, tug it away, and hold it over my head. Which, good move, because authority and consequences.

But also bad move, because the game has shifted. I now have tiny humans trying to scale me, which would kind of be okay in most cases, but not today, when I'm wearing a dress that's made of stretchy fabric and is pull-on. If I don't get a handle on this soon, Tristan's soccer class is about to learn a wildly inappropriate biology lesson.

Luckily, Tristan swoops in like the next story beat in a rom-com screenplay. He's got the bag for the balls. Tristan steps close, leaving me with the warmth of his skin and the smell of sunshine, scooping the ball from my hands, and tossing it in the bag.

This gets a chorus of boos and hisses, and I'm debating which of my limbs they're going to dismember first when Tristan says, "Balls in bag, crisscross applesauce, or no goodbye Popsicle."

Nothing gets Littles to cooperate like sugar. Come to think of it, nothing gets teenagers to cooperate like sugar. The kids scatter and drop into a line. Tristan pulls a bottle of sanitizer from his pocket and washes his hands.

I smile his way and take a moment to admire his perfection. Technically, he's not perfect. He's taller than me. Not that it matters. If he were pocket-sized, I'd carry him in my purse, he's that delightful. He has dark brown hair that's always a little too long and unruly, a nose that healed crooked after a run-in with a soccer ball, an off-center smile, and his build is lean to the point of scrawny.

In other words, he's *interesting*. His face calls you to constantly contemplate it because you uncover something unique every time. Like now, when I notice one of his incisors has a small chip in it. Plus, he's got this inner brilliance—smart mixed with fun—that makes him more beautiful every time I see him, and if that doesn't make him perfect, I don't know what does.

I catch myself staring and say, "Thanks for the save. I thought it was going to be *Lord of the Flies* for a minute."

"Oh, a classic reference," he says. "Very nice. I would have gone with *Hunger Games*."

"Maybe, but I was giving off a Piggy vibe when the horde came near." I take a couple of balls and put them away.

"I'm sorry they came after you like that. Usually, they're better about respecting people's space when they're crossing the field."

"No worries. It's Friday and something's in the air. My class got called early on account of a submarine incident. Penny's on shift," I say, even though he's aware of this. "She always shuts the pool down after an incident."

"Yikes! Poor kid. I hope they come back to class."

See? How can you not love a guy who's first reaction is sympathy for a Small One who pooped in a pool?

He puts the last ball in the bag. "I should get the kids back to the center. It was nice seeing you, Tuna."

"Oh, yeah, you too." This is my moment. Time to take out my shield and sword and slay for love. But instead of a super suave, "Hey, we should do a group hang," all that comes out is an awkward, "Catch you around."

It's a blow to the signs, omens, and auspiciousness the heavens gifted me with, and I imagine my ancestors in the celestial planes shaking their heads at their cowardly *nu-nu* of a descendant. I offer them a silent "sorry" and ask for another chance to show the worthiness of both my heart and intention.

He hoists the bag over his shoulder. "I'll let you clear the field before I let loose the galloping horde."

And the signs are back in my corner. Thank you, ancestors. I say, "Oh, my car's in the lot." I'm about to connect that sentence with, "We can walk back together," but confusion clouds his face.

"If you're parked in the lot, why are you here?"

The world stops so suddenly, I feel its antilock brakes engage and the seatbelt snap across my chest. It's painfully obvious from the tilt of his head that now is not the time to confess that I came racing out here to meet him. Even in my head, that's solidly in the "creepy girl" section of behavior.

"I thought I'd left my sweater out here." The lie is out of my mouth so fast, I'm amazed my tongue was able to form the syllables. Up in the heavens, I'm sure the ancestors are doing rum shots and shaking their heads at how I waste the chances they send my way.

"What color is it?" He turns to the kids. "Did anyone see a sweater? It's—" He spins my way. "Color?"

Okay, I've studied enough screenplays and movies to know this could be one of those small moments that snowball into wild hijinks, slapstick, and misunderstanding. Fine, but I'm more of a regular rom-com kind of person, and I think Tristan is, too. Under no circumstances am I going to allow for any off-the-grid shenanigans. "It's fine. I don't see it out here. If anything, I'm sure it's in the lost-and-found bin."

A cute Little with braids puts up her hand, then points in the distance. "I saw a sweater over there."

"You did not!" I adjust my tone from *liar, liar, pants on fire* to *you're so amazing* and try again. "You did not!"

"I did," she says. "It was pink."

"Was your sweater pink?" Tristan asks.

It's an easy "no." Not only am I decidedly not missing a sweater, even if I were, it wouldn't be pink. I can't stand that color. So why do I suddenly hear myself saying, "Yes, it was," as though I'm in a remake of the *Body Snatchers*?

"Me too!" says another Little. "I saw it!"

"Me too!"

Suddenly, EVERYONE'S seen the nonexistent sweater.

"I'll get it." The little girl jumps up.

Shenanigan alert! Shenanigan alert! "No! No! Everyone sit. *I'll* go and look for it," I say. "But this is a good moment for all of us, right? About paying attention to where we leave our stuff?"

That gets me serious nods.

Bless little kids and their default programming that makes them think anyone older somehow possesses the wisdom of the ages.

I turn to Tristan. "Sorry, I'll let you guys go." My haste in leaving has less to do with manners and more from worry that he's going to ask about the sweater.

"Sure, thanks."

I spin from him, looking for my flip-flops, get my feet caught in the hem of my dress, and pitch forward. There's a moment of stumble, then his arm is around my waist, pulling me upright.

Our eyes lock.

"You okay?" he asks.

I nod, and a few of the kids giggle.

Tristan and I exchange a smile. And there's something in his eyes— a flicker? A twinkle?

A chance.

I have a chance with this guy. And sure, the heroine falling and being caught by the hero is both cliché and overused in movies, but sometimes you gotta go with the trope to move the story forward. Especially because this is life and not art. If this were a movie, for sure I'd have on makeup, and there'd be way better lighting.

Plus, there's a good chance my ancestors have given up on giving me any chances that are truly unique. Knowing them, knowing me, they've probably opted for the tried-and-true clichés until I prove myself worthy of creative opportunities.

I'll take it, both their watching over me and getting another chance with Tristan. So let the word go forth that I, Altuna Kashmir Rashad, am stating the theme of my story is love, love, love, specifically Tristan love, love, love. (And, okay, I know technically that's not really how a screenwriter states the story's theme. Even more technically, it's not for the main character to state said theme. But, may it please the court, story is about playing with templates.) I steal a peek at Tristan and contemplate how much I'd love to play with his templates.

I gently push away from him and slide into my flip-flops. After a quick wave at the kids, I walk away, and I don't look back. My meet-cute has been accomplished. Now for the second part of my grand plan: asking him out.

It's going to be creative, inventive; I'll show my ancestors that their efforts aren't wasted on me . . . at least, *as soon as I think of it*, it's going to be creative, inventive, and show my ancestors that their efforts aren't wasted on me. I head to the spot where the nonexistent sweater was totally not spotted by anyone and plot out the next story beat in my plan to win over Tristan.

CHAPTER TWO

The Tyrant Cometh

I LEAVE THE WARMTH OF THE WEST COAST SUN BEHIND ME as I place my flip-flops on the outdoor mat, then step backward into the cool of our house. The braided rope that hangs on the handle gets caught in the door. I shove it aside and engage the lock.

The mirrored closet doors cast the reflection of the living room and the horseshoe that hangs on the wall. I spot Mom, on her hands and knees, crouched in the corner by the picture window. Either she has mixed up both the time and direction for afternoon prayers or she's in the midst of creating another picture-book character. Judging by her movements, I'm guessing a story premise based on an adorable robotic vacuum who's trapped by his lack of directional circuits.

"I'm just saying, at the next book launch, if you get Dad to make me coffee-flavored cupcakes, I promise not to bring up this moment as an example of how your creative mind works," I tell her as I head over. I catch sight of her hands. "What! No! No, Mom!"

"Honey, I'm sorry . . ." She pushes a blond hair off her face. Mom unfolds herself from the corner and it's a sight to behold. Before she was an illustrator, she was a ballerina, and it shows in her long limbs and graceful air. She says she quit dance because art was her true love. I wonder sometimes, though, if she quit because the world wasn't ready or open for a Caucasian-Caribbean prima ballerina.

"You promised, *promised*, it was just you, me, and Dad tonight. It's Friday—I had a submarine incident—"

"That red-headed kid again? What is it with his bowels and chlorine?"

I flop onto the couch and let the micro suede take me to a better place. "We were supposed to have pizza and movies tonight."

"We're still having pizza and movies."

I level an accusing finger at the wet rag in her hand. "No, we're not. You're washing the baseboards. That can only mean one thing. The Tyrant is returning for an encore performance."

"Don't call him that."

"The Tryant. Now, we're going to have to eat some crappy pizza that will taste like cardboard and watch a foreign film with subtitles."

"You love foreign films with subtitles."

"When they have a story, not when they're these weird, esoteric, surreal, go-nowhere movies where all the character does is stare out the flipping window!"

"That was one film, and in the character's defense, the window was a symbol of . . ." She trails off because she, like Dad and me, fell asleep five minutes into the movie. "It was a symbol."

I rise from my chair and do a head toss with all the hutzpah and fierceness of Alice Guy-Blaché, the first woman to direct a film. "One day, when I'm a rich and powerful screenwriter, beloved by the masses and on the cover of all the hippest holographic magazines, I hope you remember this moment as the reason why you're only getting face towels at Christmas."

"Trauma, antagonists, and obstacles are the bedrock of storytelling. I'll be the reason that you're rich and powerful," she says. "And I'll expect those face towels to be monogramed, Little Fish."

"Fine, but they'll be poorly done and the thread will unravel within weeks."

"Too bad I can't say the same of your overly dramatic ways." She goes back to wiping the baseboards.

"I'm going to my room."

"Your dad made cheesecake. It's in the fridge."

"I'm going to the kitchen."

"Eat enough to ruin your dinner. Your brother's in charge of the meal. It's going to be something made—badly—with spelt flour."

"If that's not a logline for Robby—"

"Little Fish, let's not bring screenplay fundamentals into this."

"Fine. But I'm not leaving you any pieces of cheesecake."

"Yes, you are, because we're in this together and you love me."

She's got me there. "I'm not leaving you any good pieces of cheesecake."

"Move the photos, Tuna."

"I know the protocol for when Himself visits." I flounce (clearly my brother brings out the overly dramatic in me) to the kitchen. Ugh. The Tyrant is such a buzzkill.

He arrives on the doorstep a half-hour later.

I stand on the other side of the wooden door and debate pretending we're not home.

"Tuna, you ninny! Open up!"

"How do you know it's me on the other side?"

"Because Mom and Dad would have opened the door by now."

"No! You're the worst brother in the world, and I'm not surrendering to whatever weird thing you're going to make us eat tonight."

"Look at the video monitor."

On the screen to my left, he shifts toward the camera.

I open the door and take hold of the cake box. "You're still the worst brother in existence, but you may enter."

He grins and steps inside.

"Backward!" I shove him out the door.

"Tuna! Don't be so stupidstitious!"

"Robby, respect the rules of the house."

He groans, but steps backward into the house, then spins and smiles at me.

The worst thing, the very *worst* thing, about my brother The Tyrant (aka Robby Hosea Rashad) is how very, very much I love and adore him.

Robby wraps me in a tight hug and, typical sibling, puts just enough pressure into it that I'm certain I hear the faint crackling of hairline fractures forming along my ribs.

"Mom was cleaning the baseboards because of you."

"She was not." He kicks off his sneakers and hangs his jacket in the closet. "But it's good for her to do small chores and stay active."

"Robby! You know the rules! Shoes are outside!" Our folks are big on respecting the old ways. They're also big on respecting the new ways. It's an interesting mix of ropes to keep out bad spirits and not looking at people's food so you don't Bad-Eye their meals. But also keeping up on math and science, and weaving all of it together. Old ways meets common sense. I like it. Robby used to like it, too.

He rolls his eyes but throws the shoes on the outdoor mat. "If any *jumbee* come in tonight and harm you, I'll apologize for the shoes."

"Facing out—" *Why do I bother?* I step out, arrange them so the toes point away from the door. "Anyway, you're the only poltergeist around here."

"Nice, Tuna, really nice."

"Like it's my fault you dress like a ghost thrown forward in time from the nineties."

"The nineties are inspiration for today's fashions."

"Not the way you wear them." When I step back inside, I see Robby being typical Robby. That is, my brother can't resist giving himself an appraising and approving once-over in the mirror.

I'm not the best judge of whether my brother is good-looking, what with him being my sibling. But based on the number of people whose gazes snap his way, and that he fits the tall, broad, mocha skin with the twist of blue eyes, it's a safe bet to say he lands in the gorgeous range.

"Yes, she was."

He gives his reflection a confused look and (I swear) a lip pucker. "What?"

"Mom. Wiping down the baseboards. You were over last night— like you're over *every night*—and you freaked her out about the dust mites."

"All I said was that the baseboards were a little—"

"A lot—"

"—dusty and it can be a health concern."

"You basically told her that she's in line for asthma and respiratory problems because the mites were going to breed and take over the world. And then you made her feel like a bad wife and mother by saying we'd get sick, too."

"I would never say that."

"Yes, you would. You're a tyrant."

"Benevolent tyrant."

"That's what they all say."

"I'm only pointing out the things they need to change in order to keep them healthy and happy."

"That's what all tyrants say." I take the box into the kitchen. "What kind of cake?"

"Look."

There's a lift in his word, and from eighteen years of being his sister I know it's going to be very good cake or he's about to pull some nimrod prank. I set the box on the countertop and lift the pink lid with cautious fingers. When nothing jumps out at me, I lift it the rest of the way.

Inside is a cake decorated with a tuna fish swimming underwater. Above the waves are a trio of butterflies: pink, purple, and orange. No blue ones. That's not an oversight, and it breaks my heart, just a little.

"Tuna for the Little Fish, butterflies because she loves them. It's chocolate on the inside." He gives me a kiss on the top of my head.

"You are the worst kind of tyrant."

"What kind is that?"

"A loving one." I help myself to a swipe of buttercream frosting. "I'm still not eating whatever hideous pizza you have in mind, but I will agree to whatever hideous foreign film you're going to inflict on us."

He grins. "Great. Because this is from an up-and-coming director—"

"Stop. I don't want to hear it."

"You want it to be a surprise?"

"I want to not throw up the frosting." I text Dad at work and tell him to get our usual deep-dish, billion-calorie pizza from the place down the street.

Thank god, he texts back. I was going to sneak a
burger on the way home.

Without getting one for me?

All's fair in love and war and Robby's "food,"
Little Fish.

I'm eating all of your cheesecake and the
chocolate cake Robby brought, too.

Ouch! No! Save a piece for me.

All's fair in love and war and Robby's "food."
I set down the phone and dig into the cake.

Robby's in the office with Mom going through her sketches for her new book when Dad comes in the door. I inherit my sturdy, strong build from him, as well as the darker skin tones of his African-Caribbean descent. Right now, though, I'm less interested in our physical similarities and more interested in the culinary tastes that make us family. Specifically, the melted cheese, peppers, mushrooms, onions, and salami pizza that herald his entry into the kitchen.

"The pizza stone's already heated." I hold out my hands. "Hand over the food and no one gets hurt."

"Where's the rest of them?" Dad takes a beer from fridge and runs a hand through his curly hair. His tie's already unknotted, and he drops his jacket onto the back of the bar stool.

"In the office." I open the oven, slide the pizza from the box to the stone, and close the door. "Did you guys make a decision yet?"

Dad's beard, black-shifting-to-gray, hides his mouth as he presses his lips together. "It's a big ask."

"It's not that big of an ask. A week. You guys go away for a week, leave me alone in the house."

"Honey, you don't think it's a long time, but being alone when you've always had people around you—"

"But in two months I'm going to SCAD, and I'll be living alone, off campus. Now is a great time for me to practice." Mmm, SCAD. The Savannah College of Art and Design. One day, I will be one of SCAD's shining screenwriting alumni whose works delight both viewers and critics. "Come on, Dad," I say. "A few days is good rehearsal time." Plus, a week without them around holds promise for me and Tristan, but he doesn't need to know that.

"A week with you alone in the house is a long time—"

"Why is Tuna going to be alone?" Robby appears in the kitchen like a poltergeist.

"What the—!" I'm not the only one surprised by his sudden appearance.

Dad jumps and does an arm jerk that sends beer and foam splattering on the floor.

"How can a guy as big as you make so little noise?" I ask Robby as I hand Dad a towel.

"Someone explain why a teenager is going to be alone?" Robby takes the cloth and wipes the spill.

"First, not a teenager—legal adult," I say.

"And second," says Dad, "she's not staying at home alone for a week."

"Good." Robby heads to the sink to rinse the cloth. "The security system's—"

"Don't," I tell him. "Don't even start with all the horrible things that can happen in the house."

"I'm just trying to protect you," he says.

"Robby, I'm going to college in six weeks. I have to learn to be alone." It's the truth, but it's not the right way to say it, because his face tightens.

"No one should ever have to be alone," he says. "I should get this in the laundry." He disappears down the stairs.

Dad squeezes my shoulder. "You didn't say anything wrong."

"I know." And I do know. But I also punched my brother's already broken heart, and I know this, too.

By the time he comes upstairs, he's back to normal. At least, as normal as The Tyrant can ever be. We sit down to a family dinner that's light and airy. Dessert for three of us. Not Robby, because, "I'm past thirty and a man's metabolism can change as they age. I have to be good about the processed foods I'm putting in my body." After the dishes are put away, I head to the theater room for whatever torture Robby has in store.

"Where's Grandma's quilt?" he asks as we head inside.

"In my room," I say.

"I'll get it."

"No!"

He freezes at the volume in my voice.

"Uh—I was running late," I lie. "I left a bunch of my pads and tampons on the bed. I'll get it for you. The quilt, not the feminine hygiene products." I scramble for the door.

"See? This is why I think we should be doing a family book club instead of family movie night. Film media sends terrible messages to young women. You shouldn't be ashamed of having a uterus."

I don't know what's worse. My brother, the feminist, or what'll happen if he gets to my room before I do. "I'm not ashamed. I'm just—private. Very private." I dash up the basement steps, but I can hear him behind me. How is an almost-middle-aged man able to keep up with me, an almost-elite-athlete?

"Little Fish, I used to change your diapers."

"Don't remind me!"

"I'm just saying, the human body, in all of its forms and permutations is beautiful. Don't let society dictate your self-image."

Spoken like Ontario General Hospital's favorite surgeon. "And I'm just saying, privacy!" I toss dignity aside, drop on all fours, and lope my way up the stairs from the main floor to the second story.

"Don't internalize society's misogyny."

"This is a wildly inappropriate conversation. In the name of all our ancestors, stop!"

"I'm supporting you! Celebrating you!"

My god. For a way past twenty-year-old man, he can move. I can almost feel him on my heels.

"Do you know how many people would kill to have a brother like me?"

"Do you know how many people would kill if they had a brother like you?" Breathing hard, I burst into my bedroom. My pristine, never cluttered or dirty bedroom. I'd read once that the tidier the space, the better for creatives to create. Okay, chances are that Mom put that article on my plate when I was ten as a way to influence my pigsty ways. But it worked. My room is so clean, Robby could do surgery on any surface.

The bed has hospital corners, my laptop sits precisely in the middle of my desk, and two small faux Tiffany lamps border it. There's a bowl with a mix of red and green grapes on the credenza that sits under my window. They're an offering to the screenwriting muses. Of course, I'm not for wasting food. So the muses get one or two days to smell and enjoy the grapes' essence. Then I inhale them—the grapes, not the muses—until it's time for the next offering. Side note: grapes warmed by the sun taste extra good. A host of other decorations and accessories turn my room into a creative and spa-like haven.

Which means the thing he must not ever—in any way, shape, or form— see is on prominent display. Which also means it's super easy to get. I leap over the mattress, grab it, and slide it under the bed just as Robby walks in the door.

He does a quick surveillance. "You hid your stuff under the bed?"

I shrug, too winded to speak.

He takes Grandma's quilt off the bottom of the bed. "I was the one that bought you the first box of pads, remember?"

I nod. It wasn't *him*. It was *them*, because Mom and Dad were at work, but now's not the time to correct Robby on a technicality.

Robby heads to the door, then pauses in the threshold. "You're a good person, Tuna. Don't settle for anyone who won't embrace all of you."

I blink back tears. "I won't." I pull the duvet over the edge of the bed for extra cover for The Thing He Must Not See and follow him out the door.

CHAPTER THREE

A Sign That the Time Is Now

THE MOVIE IS MORE TERRIBLE THAN I IMAGINED, AND that's saying a lot, because my whole life is imagination, and my professional career will be about imagination. I sit watching a screenplay that shoves characters into scenarios for the sake of driving the plot forward, and a main character who is so stereotypical and cardboard, she takes my breath away.

Okay, okay, so it's entirely possible that my anxiety over the picture frame hidden under my bed is affecting my ability to judge the movie properly. And also, I feel bad judging the movie negatively. Screenplays and films are no easy task. This is someone's dream come true, and I shouldn't be tossing sewage on it.

I count down the minutes until the credits roll and spend most of my time thinking of all the things I do to listen to and follow the ancestors. Am I honoring my heritage, or is Robby right, and I'm just a superstitious loon? But as I scroll through the mental list, everything seems solidly in the "respect your heritage" pile.

Don't step over people who are sitting on the floor, broken mirrors bring seven years of bad luck, when stacking books always ensure the religious texts are at the top, careful how you speak of the dead because they will hear and come to you, honor the images and possessions of those who have gone before you. Which, dang it, triggers the anxiety and wild guilt over the frame.

As soon as the screen fades to black, I hop from the chair, babble something about needing a bathroom, and race upstairs. I close the bedroom door, then I'm on the floor, lifting my duvet and gently pulling out the frame that holds the collage.

Along the edges are butterflies made of metallic paper and paint, and even under the ceiling light, they glow with intricate beauty. The most gorgeous are the ones Mom made, but mine aren't too bad. I check each of them, from the monarchs to the multicolored brush-foots to the bright blue morphos. I double-check each, ensuring their wings didn't suffer.

Butterflies. Did I love them first, or did he make me love them?

I wipe the glass with the hem of my dress and make eye contact with the image of David. Strong, wonderful, gentle David, with the black hair and the smile. "Sorry, bro," I say. "But you of all people know how he can get. He's barely keeping it together. Seeing you—" I stop because seeing David's photo is one thing. Seeing David and thinking of him in connection with Robby is another thing entirely.

I hold the frame and take in the photos, one at a time. The two of them on their first day in pre-kindergarten, where, Robby told me, "it was love at first sight. I saw him over the snack table, drinking a juice box, and I knew." And I take in the photos of the three of us, me always in the middle, them never minding that I tagged along on everything. And I trace the image of their wedding day, their matching rings, and how it was so weird to have a couple of kids marry right after high school, but how it seemed totally fitting because it was David and Robby, and they would be together forever because they were one of the great love stories of all time.

"He's struggling," I say. "And I don't know how to help him. None of us knows. He's over all the time, and that's great, but—" I hear David finish the thought. *But he's over for the wrong reasons.* "I have to do something."

I put the picture back on the dresser and open the window to let in the evening air. The leaves of the tree outside rustle, and as I start to turn away, I see it. A monarch butterfly flitting between the branches. I hold my breath, then exhale as it comes to rest on the windowsill. "Hey. You're my confirmation, huh? David agrees?"

The butterfly does a slow flap of its wings, then disappears among the leaves.

I go back downstairs, take the empty popcorn bowls and candy packages upstairs.

Robby's loading the dishwasher. "Do you need a heating pad?"

I shift around Dad and hand Mom the candy. To Robby, I say, "I will give you the rest of Dad's cheesecake if you never again bring up my uterus."

"Hey," says Mom. "I haven't even gotten a piece yet!"

"It's called maternal sacrifice," I say. "Like not eating sushi when you're pregnant."

"Shows what you know. I ate raw sushi when I was pregnant with you."

Robby laughs. "That explains everything."

"About you, maybe." I elbow him out of the way and put the popcorn bowl in the dishwasher.

It's a few minutes more, then everything's sorted, and we're at the door, hugging Robby goodbye.

"There's a full moon," says Mom. "Close your curtains."

He makes a production out of rolling his eyes. "How can I be alive at the height of the modern age, yet born to the most superstitious family in existence?"

It almost slips out, for me to volley back the joke, and say, *You should be thankful. You're only alive because you're part of the most superstitious family.* I don't say it, because of David.

"A full moon shining on my face won't cause wrinkles," he says.

"No kidding." I poke his temple. "They're already there."

"Stop it!" He massages the corner of his eye. "I don't have wrinkles."

"Do cashiers try to offer you senior discounts when you go out?"

"I'm leaving now."

"I hear white hair really gives men a distinguished air."

Dad's chest puffs out. "I can attest to that."

"Hmm," I say. "I hear white hair really gives *most* men a distinguished air."

"You're grounded," says Dad. "For eternity."

After Robby leaves, I head to my room, then freeze in the doorway. Grandma's quilt is back on the bed. "Did you bring up the quilt?" I yell the question down the stairway.

"No." Mom's voice comes my way. "Robby must have left it downstairs."

But he didn't. He came into my room to put it back. My gaze lifts from the bed to the dresser. Which means he saw the collage. I step into my room, positive I'll hear the echoes of his wailing grief, but meet only the soft swish of my bare feet on carpet.

The frame's been moved. Not a lot, but enough to confirm that Robby touched it. Robby touched something that held an image of David.

If that's not an omen, then omens don't exist.

I set the frame back to its original position and acknowledge the sign to my ancestors and David. And I promise them and myself that I will do all I can to help Robby remember how to smile, and laugh, and maybe love again.

CHAPTER FOUR

Okay, the Time May Not Be Now, but It's GOT To Be Nigh, Right?

SIX IN THE MORNING COMES EARLY. OKAY, SO IT COMES at the same time every twenty-four hours, but pizza and last night's movie makes it feel like it's coming early. My bleary, gritty eyes and tangled pajamas may also have a lot to do with worrying about my brother.

I hoist myself out of bed, do a zombie-shuffle to the kitchen for coffee, then get ready for the pool. I'm hoping my partner in crime, life, and sports, Fiona, will be there, but I doubt it. Fi's heading to NYU in fall. She didn't get any gymnastic scholarships, and with the injuries she's had, plus the back surgery, she said she was done.

Typical Fi, to be so chill about the hard pivot of her life. She could have made it to the Olympics, she was that good. Surgeries, rehab—

she was a media sensation for a while because she worked so hard to return to competition.

I watched with wistful envy about her focus and determination. She threw everything at her comeback. Meanwhile, when I didn't get the swimming scholarship, I was disappointed but not devastated. The competition for getting on the team was fierce, and truth is, I didn't want it enough. What I really want, dream, breathe, and eat is movies and TV. But Fi, man, she *was* gymnastics, which makes her Zen attitude to dropping it another reason I'm in perpetual wistful envy of her.

"I'm an old eighteen," she said. "My knees hurt, my hips hurt. What am I supposed to do when I'm done? Mainline painkiller injections and feel like I'm eighty when I'm twenty? No thanks. I'm going to let this body rest and catch up on all the sleep I've lost."

I put her from my mind as I drive to the pool. Two hours of laps, drills, and more laps and drills—because swimming clears my head, then I heave my tired limbs from the water. A soak, a shower, and I'm back at the house by nine.

I'm pulling my gym bag out of the sedan when my phone bings. Fi.

I woke up early just to rub it in your face that I no longer have to wake up early.

> More like, woke up jealous 'cause I have more grit than you do.

You're right. I have no grits. A bing and the image of Fi, hair in a kerchief, sitting in her kitchen with a stack of pancakes, lights up my screen. **But I do have pancakes. Get it? Grits. Pancakes.**

I send her an eye-roll GIF.

Wanna head over? I'll share.

> **Nice try. You stabbed me with a fork the
> last time.**

Clarification: I'll share until the LAST pancake.
Then it's everyone for themselves.

> **Let me drop my stuff at my house and I'll
> head over. Need your help with Mr. T.**

It's silly to keep Tristan as an initial, but why challenge the negative forces in the universe by using his full name? And okay, okay, probably the negative forces already know who I'm talking about, but I feel like using initials give me plausible deniability.

The smell of chives, fried tomatoes, and egg greets me as I walk backward into my house. I head to the kitchen, amazed my parents are up at nine on a Saturday morning. I'm surprised but not shocked to see it's not them. It's Robby, in sweats and socks, cooking an omelet.

I'd like to argue that my brother showing up at the house less than twelve hours after I promised the ancestors I'd step in for him isn't a sign, because he's always here. But who am I kidding? I just wish they'd send me omens after I've eaten, because this boy should be tackled on a full stomach.

You know what I mean. Not tackled with a literal full stomach, but figurative full stomach.

"I thought you'd be hungry after the workout."

I take a seat at the counter. "Have you moved back home and no one told me?"

"Ha ha. I went for a run, then thought it would be nice to have breakfast with my family."

"You know what would be really nice?" I wade into the fray, hoping the moment will have a nostalgic filter and not a harsh, inverse light. "Theater tickets."

"You want theater tickets for a gift?"

"No, I mean, you used to do all that artsy stuff, ballet, plays. We haven't gone for a while—" *Sixteen months, to be exact.* "—but you had fun, right?"

He's turned away from me, so I can't see his face. But I hear the guarded, "Yeah, it used to be fun." Robby slides the omelet onto a plate and hands it to me. "I've been busy lately."

"Unearthing the worst indie movies known to man? You know, there's nothing wrong with enjoying Hollywood movies."

"Someone has to do it." He flexes a bicep, and for a second—a split-second—there's a ghost of the old Robby on his face. "Maybe when things settle. Summer means surgery. Boating accidents, motorcycle crashes—"

I wait for the rise of Factoid Robby, who'll tell me the number of boating deaths per year, and how often booze is involved. But that Robby's in a grief-coma. So I say, "Stop, I'm trying to eat."

"It's good, right?"

And the way he says it makes me push away the plate. "Ugh, nimrod! What vile thing did you put in my food to sully my breakfast?"

"Nothing. It's all good."

"Gross, it is not! What did you put in it? It's not ground-up grasshopper again, is it?"

He grins. "You're so easy to mess with." Robby takes a pull of his coffee. "Don't you trust me? It's fine to eat."

"I'm waiting for Mom and Dad. If you let them eat it, then I know there's nothing gross."

He shrugs. "Maybe. Or maybe I've gone fully into the dark side and there's gross stuff in there for everyone." He takes my fork and takes a bite.

"That doesn't help. You've eaten chocolate-covered ants."

"They're a good source of protein. Insects are both sustainable and environmentally friendly."

I wait, again, for a factoid that never comes. "Locusts are not environmentally friendly." I push the food around and look hard for insectile legs or antennae. If there are grasshoppers, I can't taste them. And Robby's eggs are drool-worthy. They should be. David taught him how to make them. I eat my breakfast but maintain aggressive eye contact.

Mom and Dad are down by the time I'm finished, and Robby makes them omelets—sans ground-up anything. While they eat, I take my chance and head over to Fi's.

She answers the door, dressed in a lime-green jumpsuit, hot pink lip gloss, and she's rocking a natural look for her hair. "You're going to love me."

"I already love you."

"Put-me-as-the-sole-beneficiary-in-your-will love me." She grabs her macramé bag and closes the door. Fi moves past me, leaving a delicate tendril of cocoa butter and vanilla in her wake. "Come on. We need to go shopping."

"Why? And why do I love you so much?"

"Tanisha's spending the day tomorrow. I promised I'd do cornrows for her; I need supplies."

"That's love." I tried to help with the braiding one time, and the kindest thing to say was that I got an A for effort. It was a hot mess, the braids were a disaster, and my fingers still hurt. But Fi's mom owns the best hair salon in the world—my humble opinion—and Fi can braid the devil under the table.

"I do love my cousin," she says.

"And I love you because—"

"Because I rocked and rolled my connections, and guess who's having a summer thing tonight? Amelia."

"Cool." I mean, it's cool. Amelia and I get along. We're not super best friends or even acquaintances, but she's fun to hang out with.

"Yeah, but guess who I made sure was going to be there?"

I stop at the passenger's side door of her cherry-red Jeep. "No!"

"Mr. T himself!" She gestures at her soft top. "Thank me by helping roll this off."

"We need a plan."

Fi moves to the other side of the Jeep, but I give her the Stern Eye. I love my badass friend and her kick-butt force of will, but her back is delicate. For all her strength, there are days when sitting upright can take it out of her.

"Today's a good day," she says. "I can do this."

"I'll do it, as thanks for arranging the party invite. Now, what about a plan?"

"We don't need a plan. You just need to be yourself," says Fi. "Maybe a less signs-and-omens version of yourself. You know Tristan's a science and logic guy."

"I don't know." I climb into the seat and belt in. "That's core to my character and personality. Is it really a good idea to pretend I'm something I'm not, just for the sake of a cute guy?"

"You're not pretending." Fi belts in and reverses out of the driveway. "You're simmering instead of boiling."

"I don't know if I like the message it sends, and for this romantic install-ment of my existence, it's too near shenanigan territory."

"Shenanigan territory? Is that by the Chino Airport?"

"Ha ha. I told you about the pink sweater."

That gets a double take before she turns back to the traffic. "No. Pink? You hate pink. What happened?"

I tell her about the meet-cute setup (and now that I'm thinking about it, kinda totally cringing at the scheme) and the kids.

Fi shudders. "Gross. I don't know how you hang out with kids all the time. They always have their fingers up their noses." She shudders again. "Or out of their noses and in their mouths.

"How can you *not* like kids? You would set the world on fire for Tanisha."

"That's different." She pulls to a stop and tosses a dazzling smile at a group of dudes that leaves them blinded. "That's *my* family. I like kids in my family. I like kids in my friends' families. But rando little clowns with scraggly bodies and whiny voices?" She shudders. "Nope, no, and nada."

"A butterfly landed on my window last night," I tell her. "I was talking to David about Robby, and it flew onto the sill."

"You think your dead brother-in-law came back as a winged creature? That boy had a big ass head. Imagine that mash-up."

I laugh at the image of a butterfly with David's face.

Fi laughs too. "I tell you what, though, if there was ever a guy who could fly, it would've been David. He was light as love." She closes her eyes for a second. "And his mac and cheese was bliss."

"There's a reason every hoi-polloi restaurant wanted him as their head chef." I'm glad the top's down on the Jeep, because the wind burns my eyes and lets me pretend that's why tears are falling down my cheeks. "I know you don't buy into the whole 'dead relatives talk to you through nature,' but I'm sure it was him."

"Look, Tuna Fish, you give me any kind of 'ology' that can back it up—psychology, biology. Hell, I'll even take *ge*ology, and that's barely a science. Until then, I'm going to respect your beliefs, but hold to my own."

"What about paranormal-psychology?"

"Nuh, girl. If you got to hyphenate it, then, no, it ain't a real 'ology.'"

We get to the mall and Fi finds a handicapped spot. The errand for the braiding supplies is quick and easy. But, of course, we *have* to stop for frozen yogurt.

"Why are you looking at the menu, fool?" Fi eyes me up. "You get the same thing, every time."

"I do not. Okay, I do. But maybe, this time, I'll get something different."

While I twist myself over the choice of twenty flavors, Fi does the smart thing and requests three one-ounce sample cups. The strawberry shortcake flavor seems to have her attention.

"Excuse me."

We turn to the woman behind us, and I have to put my hands over my mouth to stop from shrieking. The woman has the archetypal "I want to talk to your manager" hair. I'm staring in fascination, wondering if she knows her haircut is both from the '90s and an online punchline. I'm also telling myself that whatever will come out of her mouth next will violate the stereotype of her appearance because, you know, cliché and not judging a book by its cover, and all that.

But then, THEN, she turns to Fi and—I kid you not—says, "Could you please move out of the way? I can't see over your hair to the choices."

And I'm stunned, amazed, and inscribing the moment in my synapses for future writing fodder. The *irony* of her commenting on anyone's hair when she's got *that* hair (and okay, okay, maybe it's not irony, but still, it's iconic AND ironic in my book) is shriek-inducing. But also, WE WERE HERE FIRST. *WE'RE IN FRONT OF YOU. WAIT YOUR TURN.*

Fi and I give each other a long look, gauging which of us handles this middle-aged nightmare and which of us storyboards it for later telling to everyone we know.

"Girls," says the woman, and I swear the snottiness in her voice ratchets up. "Your hair is blocking my view."

"Your privilege is blocking my progress," says Fi, "but you don't see me pitching a fit." Then—and this is why I will love her forever—she does a slow-motion turn, smiles at the person behind the counter (who's trying not to laugh), and says, "I'd *love* to have some more sample cups."

"Of course," they say. "Take your time."

It takes three more samples before the lady takes off.

"Tonight," I say to Fi. "We're going to laugh about her and tell everyone how unreal she was. But I bet she'll be doing the same thing."

"No, she won't," says Fi. "That woman? She'll be rage drinking, crying, and risking her Botox injections."

"Another sample cup?" The frozen yogurt person asks.

"I'll take a medium birthday cake," I tell them, "with nuts."

Fi does a combination of raspberry and orange, then gives me a raised eyebrow at my choice.

"The omens weren't there," I say. "I took that as a sign to stick with what I know."

She rolls her eyes, pays for both of us, and grins when she sees the total.

"That woman's in all the time," the server says, "and she picks a fight with everyone. Moms, singles, couples. I swear, she lurks near the washrooms and waits for someone to come in line. I give a ten percent discount to anyone who holds their own. You were a delight, so you get the employee discount."

Fi flips the receipt over, pulls a pen from her bag, and scribbles her number. "For coffee, friendship, more than friendship, whatever. I appreciate your support." She smiles, then leads the way to the food court.

"Maybe it's intuition," she says, picking up the conversation of signs, Robby, and the butterfly from back at the Jeep. "You're calling it help from on high, but maybe it's just intuition."

"What 'ology' does that fall under?"

"Neurology," she says. "It's as simple as your brain wading through history, sensory information, reading the clues and signals during conversations, and then directing your actions and thoughts a certain way."

"Spoken like the next surgical star at Ontario General."

"Huh, only if your brother leaves the city." She swirls her frozen yogurt.

"I don't think it's a bad thing to listen for the ancestors," I say. "My elders did, and their lives turned out great."

Fi rolls her eyes.

She does that a lot with me.

"I miss hearing Robby laughing," she says, "and the pranks. I was so sick of all his jokes and puns and pranks. And Lord, the never-ending facts. Now, I'd pay money to have him do something nerdy and useless."

"I miss Factoid Robby, too. These days, he's all about health care— eating right, sleeping—the other day, I caught him trying to low-key run a dementia test on Dad."

"Did your pops know?"

"Yeah, and he messed with Robby by acting confused and giving the wrong answers, which just made my brother mad, which ticked Dad off. It was not the most raucous of our family dinners."

"Your brother's in cement. Whether it's your intuition or the spirits reaching through the veil, he needs help." She nudges my shoulder. "Good thing he's got you."

"And you."

"Whoa. What?"

"You're going to help me."

"No, no way. I love you, Tuna, but you scheme like your mom."

"What does that mean?" I don't tell her about a plan that's been form- ing in my head involving Robby and the Eros and Agape website. It's an out-there scheme, even for me. (Don't tell Fi that I know exactly what she means about my family and our scheming ways.) I need to verify the logis- tics before I share the plan.

"Your mom blew out the circuits in the house when she was experi- menting with surround-sound speakers throughout the house."

"Almost."

Fi stands and moves to the garbage bin. "Forget it."

"Please. Two heads are better than one."

"Isn't this in that shenanigan territory?"

"Shenanigans only happen when you're planning your own life," I tell her. "Do you not pay attention when we're watching movies and I'm pointing out the beats and tropes?"

"I'm usually just wishing you'd shut up so I can watch the movie in peace."

"Everyone's a critic."

We leave the food court and thread ourselves through the mass of humanity getting their Saturday shop on.

"What's your plan, anyway?" she asks.

"I don't have one yet," I say, insecure about sharing my idea. "I'm waiting for a sign. I tried to get him to go to the theater, but he wasn't feeling it."

She sighs. "I feel that. I went by our old elementary to drop off some stuff for Mrs. Smith."

"She is *not* still there!"

"A hundred years from now, archaeologists will unearth her body, seated behind the desk."

"They're probably the only ones who'll ever be able to get into her contraband drawer. You know, she never gave me back that puffy dragon she took."

"I'll get it for you next time. For sure, she's still got it in the drawer." Fi fiddles with the handles of her cloth bag. "I saw the playground and I went to pieces. Remember when they'd take us there and David would push us on the swings? I can't fault Robby for being stuck in cement. You can't, either."

"I don't! I don't—" *How do I even explain it?* "If he wants to be in cement, cool. I just want to hand him a jackhammer, in case he wants it."

She lifts her face to the sun and smiles into the warmth. "I feel that." She opens her eyes. "I'll help you with Robby, too, shenanigans or not."

"No shenanigans. No complications. The plan will be clever, simple, and easy. Just like tonight with Tristan. Casual, smooth, no hiccups."

Trust my brother to send me a text five minutes before I'm supposed to leave for Amelia's and blow up my plans for the night.

CHAPTER FIVE

Where Even Monks Fear to Tread

THE TEXT COMES IN JUST AS I'M PULLING ON MY ESPADRILLES.

Look.

Robby follows the text with a pic of theater tickets.

I enlarge the image, check the details.

Look, indeed! Robin Hood? A group of grown men frolicking in a forest. Right up your alley.

In tights. They frolic in tights.

Leave me out of your fetishes. PUH-LEASE!!!

Pick you up at 7? We can get ice cream after.

Okay, what is going on here? **What? Why are**
you picking me up?

You want to meet me there instead?

No. Why me for the second ticket?

You suggested it, numbnuts. Why wouldn't
I get you a ticket?

"Mmmmmoooooom!!!!" I sprint to her office. "I have troubles."

"Don't we all?" She holds up her sketch pad. "These ears are too big. Floppy is one thing, but these will suffocate him. Or make him airborne in a stiff wind."

"Don't worry about the rabbit," I say. "Worry about your fish." I show her the text.

"Wow." She pushes her red-framed glasses onto her forehead. "He's actually going out? And to a play?"

"An outdoor play," I say miserably. "It's a bigger step than I thought."

"Way to go, honey." The glasses are moved to her nose, a sure sign of dismissal. "You're a good sister."

"No, I'm not. I didn't think he was going to spring tickets on me. I'm supposed to go out with Fi tonight."

"I'm sure you can get an extra ticket."

"No, *Mom*, going with Fi to Amelia's, where a certain soon-to-be Mr. Rashad will be lounging in all his demigod glory."

"Oh." She stops mid-sketch. *"Oh. Tristan."*

Full confession, my adoration of Tristan and genetic need to speak his name may have resulted in me telling my folks about him, again and again, like the girl-crush version of *Groundhog Day*.

Mom moves her glasses to their off position. "Tell your brother. I'm sure he'll understand."

"Of course he'll understand. That's not the problem, is it?" I flop into one of the office chairs. "What am I going to do? He'll be all, 'Sure, Little Fish, I get it. No prob.' But will he still go to the play? Probably not. Will he buy another set of tickets to another play? Probably not. This is the first time in over a year that he's been willing to do anything, save come over and hang. What am I supposed to do? Help my brother or help myself?"

"Tuna," Mom says, her voice soft. "You can't stop your life for him."

Maybe not stop. Maybe I just press pause. In the weighing of outcomes and the forecasting of decisions, if we—I—don't get Robby moving back to his life, it's only going to get worse. And also, I only have one brother.

If Tristan and I are meant to be—no, edit. *Since* Tristan and I are meant to be, then this is a blip. A twist in the plotline of our romance.

Right.

So why, though the problem is easily remedied and intellectually solved, do I feel this bubbling resentment inside me? And why is the anger illogically creeping toward David and his untimely and unauthorized exit from our lives?

"Tuna."

Mom's voice brings me back from the brink.

"If you can't do this joyfully for your brother, don't do it. I can go."

I point at her sketch pad. "The ears."

"The ears can wait," she says. "We're in all of this together. You got your brother to stick his head out of his den. I can take him for the play and ice cream."

I kiss her cheek. "You're the best."

"Don't you forget it."

I go to the front door to get the car keys and call Robby on a video chat.

"Hey. You look nice!"

"Thanks, I'm going out with Fi tonight."

The look on his face is the same one (I'm sure) the kiddos get when they find out Santa Claus isn't real and the Tooth Fairy probably just dumps their baby teeth.

"No worries," he says. "I sprung this on you, anyway. Next time, right?"

"Mom says she'll go with you. She's just shutting down the office, then she'll get ready."

Panic tightens his face.

"What?"

"This isn't *that kind* of Robin Hood," he says. "It's not really parent-friendly, or really take-your-parent-as-your-guest friendly."

"*Oh.*"

"I thought you'd find it funny."

And there's an extra knife to my heart. Not only did he buy tickets, he bought tickets with me specifically in mind. Why oh why did the universe shackle me with this loving tyrant?

"It's no problem," he says. "I can sell them online. Tell Mom I'll swing by in a bit and we can go for ice cream."

"I'll go with you." The words, spoken by my heart, are out before my brain even considers them.

"No, Little Fish—"

"I'll get you, but we just have to drop Fi at Amelia's."

"Tuna—"

"I'd rather hang with you," I say and smile into the lie.

"Are you sure?" He's asking the question, but I know the answer he wants.

"Positive." I shut down the call, kill the negativity swirling inside me, and text Fi the update.

Seriously? she texts back.

You're opting for bro over dude?

Family.

Signs?

Does his face and the sound of his breaking
heart count?

... 😔 🤍 Yeah.

I'll let you know how the night goes. Have fun
with Amelia.

🤍

Will also buffer anyone trying to get to Mr. T.

Ha! Thanks!

I opt for picking Robby up, and boy, my brother was right. This play
is definitely not bring-your-mom appropriate. I'm not even sure I'm comfortable with the thought of my ancestors looking down and seeing me
watching this. Still, it's funny and raunchy, with the right twist on the
Robin Hood archetype to make it fresh and funny.

We're at intermission when I get Fi's text.

Guess who's asking about you?

Don't even joke about that!

She sends me a pseudo-selfie. It's a shot of her eyeball, because really,
it's a shot of Tristan in the background. And bbbooooyyyy, he is delicious. Pink-checked shirt, adorably floofy hair, head thrown back 'cause
he's laughing at something.

What did he want to know?

I tap the edge of the phone and wait for the text bubble to resolve into actual words.

(...)

Uh. Fi?

(...)

She's messing with me. I bet she's just typing in random letters then erasing them. **FFFFIIIII!!!!!**

LOL

OMG. Fi. FI! FFFFIIIII!!!!

Fi-Fie-Foe-Fum. Who wants information on the Tristan?

Don't type his name! That's bad luck!

He wants your number. Still bad luck?

Oh, my heavens. We've never exchanged numbers, because you know, attraction vibes and one of us always dating someone else. **!!!!!!!!!!!GIVE IT TO HIM! GIVE HIM ALL THE NUMBERS!!!!!**

"What's going on?"

Robby's appearance startles me and I juggle the phone.

He hands me a cherry ice.

"Fi, giving me an update on the party." I want to tell him about what's going on. I used to tell him almost everything, whether he wanted to hear it or not. But now, I'm not sure if talking to my brother about a love match is the kind thing to do.

He bumps my shoulder. "Thanks for choosing me over them." He shoots the rest of his ice. "Come on, let's go."

"We have five minutes before the end of intermission. I still have to wait in line for the bathroom, and question both my existence and the strength of my bladder."

"Not back to the play. Let's get you to the party."

"What? What about the play?"

"Meh, you see one saucy Robin Hood, you've seen them all." He helps himself to my ice. "This was nice, but I've had enough. Besides, this is your last summer before college. You should be out with your friends, not hanging out with your elderly brother."

It's then I notice the tired lines around his eyes, the fatigue that sags his skin. "Was this too much?"

He shrugs. "I want home."

We head to the car. On the return trip to his condo, I swing by a food truck and get us a snack of fish tacos.

"Give me a second," Robby says when I pull to the curb at his high-rise condo. "I have some pamphlets for Dad about heart health."

"Robby, they're not that old. It's rude to keep bringing up them aging."

"And if they take care of their health, they'll age beautifully."

I pull away from the curb and take a visitor's spot. "If you're running upstairs, I'm running to the bathroom. My bladder has had all the strength training it can take."

"Did you know there was a guy who died from an exploding bladder?"

"This is your choice of conversation?" The seatbelt slithers into its holder and I'm out of the seat.

"I'm just saying. Tycho Brahe. He was at a royal dinner, wouldn't go to the bathroom because it would have been a breach of protocol. And boom! Burst bladder."

"I can't believe this is the story you're telling me." I'm basically dancing through the lobby, trying to keep from having an accident. Also, there's a bit of a jig because I hardly see Factoid Robby anymore. It's glee-inducing that he came out to play, even if his timing stinks.

"The moral of the lesson—"

"Brothers suck?"

"That being polite should never take priority over your health."

I roll my eyes and mutter something about wishing I was an only child. Truth is, Factoid Robby is a facet in the kaleidoscope of Old Robby, and I'll take it.

The elevator takes five years to get to the main floor and another seventeen decades to reach the twenty-third floor. As soon as the doors open, I explode past my brother—all while hoping my bladder doesn't also explode—and race for his door. I'm doing a jump, jive, and trying *not* to wail, as I stick my spare key into the lock.

I kick off my shoes as I push open the door and run onto the hardwood floor. And almost have an accident, right there. Not because of any organ failure, but because of what Robby's done to the condo.

Every indication of David is gone. From the abstract oil paintings, the hand-blown vases, the textured rugs and throw pillows, it's disappeared. Even the kitchen table—Robby's moved the chairs to the wall, so there's only one seat. There's no smell of onions or spices, no indication of the love, laughter, and food that defined David's existence. The condo would make a monastic monk weep at its sterile aesthetic.

My bladder shouts and I answer its call. Dang, even the bathroom lost the David touch. No soft towels. No delicately scented soap. When I come out, Robby's in the gray and white kitchen, pamphlets in hand.

"Here. He doesn't have to do a lot to change his lifestyle. More cardio, less red meat."

I take the brochures. "The house looks different."

"Purged," he says. "I realized I was hanging onto every—there was a gum wrapper from the last time we went to the movies—" He blows out a breath, hard and fast. "—Go to your party. I've got some reading on surgery procedures I should do."

But I can't leave, because his house is empty and lonely, and our voices echo because there are no soft objects to absorb the auditory vibrations. I *should* go, though, because Mom says I'm not supposed to stop my life for Robby.

Robby, who helped me learn how to read.

Robby, who's been to every swim event since I convinced him I was a reincarnated dolphin when I was five.

Robby, who—whether I want it or not—cheers and encourages me on in matters of life, love, and, god help me, womanhood.

"Those tacos were good," I say, "but I'm still hungry. You up for something substantial?"

"What about your party?"

"No one's expecting me. Why bother?" I have no clue if this is the right decision or not, but something about leaving Robby alone feels like abandoning a puppy in the rain. And something about leaving my brother to a kitchen table with only one chair seems inordinately cruel.

"There's a great vegan Indian place that just opened."

Just opened? I'm regretting this offer already. "How 'just opened'?"

"Stop worrying," he says. "It's been around long enough to convince me that the food is great." He pats his stomach. "Give me a sec to change. I need sweats for this."

He disappears into his room and I text Fi.

Send pics.

She must have been hoarding, 'cause a bunch of them pop up. In all of the images, Tristan's smiling or mugging for the camera. I really hope I made the right choice, opting for valve repair for my brother's heart instead of pumping blood and life into the Tristan chambers of mine.

I try to stick my phone back in my bag, but it slips past and clatters to the floor. Luckily, it's got a smash-proof cover, so I'm not worried as I bend and pick it up. Something under the couch catches the light and glitters with quiet mystery.

I grope for the object of unknown origin. My fingers close around something metallic. I pull out a small gold butterfly, the kind that attaches to walls with magnets. A trademark David decoration if there ever was one.

"Fine," I tell the object-sending-messages-on-behalf-of-David. "I'm good with losing tonight with Tristan. But you have to do your part. Tell me what the plan is, because our boy cannot live in this plain, white cave. I've been here for five minutes and I'm already going stir-crazy."

"Ready." Robby comes out of his room. "Why are you on the floor? Are you feeling dizzy? Light-headed?" He rushes forward in a panic.

"Slow it down, Dr. Doom." I wave him back, feeling guilty for scaring him. "I dropped my phone. It's all good." I hold the butterfly close, certain I can feel the spiritual energy and the psychic bond connecting me to David, and head out the door.

We're in the elevator when I feel the butterfly vibrate against my skin. Maybe it's the hum of the elevator causing its delicate wings to flutter. Maybe it's David, telling me he has a plan. Either way, it's a sign of good things to come.

CHAPTER SIX

Pink Could Be My Color

SHENANIGAN ALERT. SERIOUS SHENANIGAN ALERT. I
read Tristan's text for the four billionth time and curse my lying lips.

Think I found your pink sweater.

Now would be a great time to come clean. I can text and say, *Mixed
up the clothing. No pink sweater lost.* Except, what kind of fool forgets what
she's wearing?

I can text him and *really* come clean, admit that the sweater was a ploy
to see him. Except it's a text, so he can't tell intonation, or tone, or see
me awkwardly smiling and hoping he'll find the subterfuge adorable. So
chances are good he reads that text and instead of clumsy but endearing,
he's seeing shades of Norman Bates or Annie Wilkes.

Also, I don't know him well enough to know how he'll view the work he put in to getting my so-called pink sweater. Is he going to be ticked that he wasted his time holding on to it for me? Slightly weirded out that he's got the clothing of a total stranger in his bag?

I take a bowl of grapes from the fridge and assembly line them into my mouth. There are ten thousand stop-starts to my reply. Thankfully, they're all with hovering fingers over the keyboard, so Tristan remains ignorant of my psychic torment.

In the end, I opt for the super-pathetic

Are you sure?

Did you find yours?

Not exactly.

This one might be it. One of the kids found it around where you lost yours.

Send a pic?

Running errands for my mom. I can drop it by.

I'm about to text, *No, no, just send the pic*, when my ancestors intercede. Okay, so it's a flash of sunlight through the window that momentarily blinds me. But as I squint and turn from the screen, I catch the subtext of what he's saying. Not "I can drop it by," but "I'd like to see you." I give myself a mental pat on the back and preen in smug self-satisfaction for all the years spent watching movies and listening for dialog gaps.

"Thank you, ancestors." But wait. Would my ancestors allow this wading into shenanigan territory? All of the grandparents are up in their heavenly abode. No way would they allow for me to make a fool of myself. Then again, they're outnumbered by the great-aunts, who would gleefully strike me with lightning or bird poop for laughs and cackles.

I opt for classy restraint in my text. **Are you sure?
I'd hate for you to waste a trip out if it's not mine.**
There. Not only classy, but a chance for him
to jump in with a romantic reply, like, *Never a
waste of time for you.*

**No worries! My mom's paying me by the hour
to do the errands.** 😊

So. Not romantic or chivalrous. More of a money grab. Suddenly I'm less
about the subtext and more about the petty need to rob him of the wages
he'd make for a trip my way.

**Anyway, summer'll be over soon. It's good to catch up
as much as we can.**

That mitigates the pettiness. I text him my address
and follow it with, **Let me buy you a coffee or
something for your time?**

You don't have to.

Consider it a bonus? C'mon, c'mon, I psychically
urge him on, take the opportunity for the subtext
and cute reply. *Any time with you is a bonus.*

OK.

Gack. Boys. Thank god they're cute or else what's the use for them?
Tristan texts he'll be over in fifteen minutes. I set down my phone and run
to get ready so I can look like, you know, I just wake up looking hot.

"Hey." Tristan points at his sneakers as I open the door. "Do you want me
to leave them outside with the other shoes?"

"No, it's cool."

He hesitates and glances at the shoes.

"It's a cultural thing," I say. "Don't worry about it."

"Oh, okay." He kicks off his sneakers, places them in line with the other shoes, and makes sure the toes point out toward the steps.

And my heart does a happy-tappity. You've got to cheer for a boy who slides into acknowledging your culture even when he doesn't know what he's doing or why he's doing it.

"Your sweater—hopefully," he says, pushing his sunglasses onto his head and pulling out an adorable baby pink cardigan with pearl buttons.

"It's beautiful," I say, "but it's not mine."

"Shoot." He does a long take of the sweater, then in a worried tone says, "Whose sweater am I holding?"

Yeah, definitely not the time to tell him that his kindness has been corrupted by my white lie. Tristan's personality wheel includes a hyper-awareness of germs and dirt. It was one of the first things I learned about him. He saved the disoriented butterfly on the track, then promptly washed his hands. Twice. Telling him that I fudged the truth to get closer to him might get me sprayed with sanitizer. "So. Coffee?"

"Sure. You mind if I drop this off at the rec center's lost and found? I feel super weird holding on to some stranger's sweater."

"Makes you wonder how they lost it in the woods, right?"

That gets me a double take from him and a mental kick from my brain. "I'm sure it wasn't anything creepy or pervy," I say, trying to right the wrong, and instead making the wrong even wronger.

"Uh. Yeah." He shoves the sweater in the bag. "Do you mind if I wash my hands before we go?"

I show him the bathroom, do a quick check on my makeup while I wait. We climb into his truck and head to the center.

"I heard you got in to your first school of choice, right?" he says. "That's cool."

"Cool and lucky. You?"

He nods. "Kind of. My parents own a real estate firm, so I'm going to work part-time with them this summer, and then go for a business administration degree in fall. It's not 'follow your dreams,' like you and your screenwriting, but it's solid." He shrugs, like he's offering an apology. "Follow what you're good at."

"Hey, I'll need someone to sell me that dream McMansion when I make it big."

He laughs. "I'll even take a discount on my commission, for old time's sake."

"Shoot. I was going to give you double commission to show how successful and powerful I'd become—that I'm happy to throw coins like a queen."

"Screenwriting, huh?"

There's something about the way he says it, but I can't tell if his vibe about my chosen profession ranks alongside pond scum or if it's such an odd life choice, he's just confused.

"Yeah. Screenwriting." I do my best to match his tone and see where it takes me.

"That's a lot of writing, isn't it?" His face crinkles. "I can't imagine sitting around, staring at a page, and writing."

"That's where you've gone wrong," I say. "It's not writing. It's life! Joy! Hope! Heartbreak! It's every good and bad thing within the human heart!" Okay, my passion and excitement might be overly exuberant because he's looking at me like I'm about to sacrifice him and offer his still-beating heart to the screenwriting gods. Which I'd never do. Everyone knows the screenwriting gods prefer alcohol. I'm too young to buy booze, which is why I offer them grapes instead.

"It still feels like creative writing for Mrs. Barry's English class."

"The core stuff's the same," I admit. "You have a main character who wants something, but stuff gets in her way. And she's got to have emotional growth, too." I'm trying not to talk too much about this because Fi says I'm overbearing and will get into the weeds of storytelling, to the point of not seeing when people's eyes glaze over.

"So, what's different?"

Nnnnnooooo. He's *so* tempting with that question and the cute way his head tilts when he asks it. "The story beats, for one thing," I say. "The industry standard is one minute of screen time is about a page, so in a ninety-minute movie—"

"You have ninety pages," he says, and I bless his mathlete heart. (I realize it's simple math, but I'll take any chance to bless that awesome heart of his.)

"Yep. Plus, film is mostly visual scenes and dialog. So every word counts. It's not like a book, where an author can go hard with description."

He nods. "Beats?"

"The moments where things happen for your character," I say. "I can go on—Fi tells me I tend to go on and on and on, so . . . do you want me to keep going?"

"Yeah, I like listening to you." He relaxes into his seat. "You were always the most interesting part of English class."

Mmm. I can see the great-aunties on their clouds, fanning themselves with that line and rethinking their plan to drop pigeon *caca* on my head. So I tell him about how a writer needs a catalyst to start the story, that a subplot—B-story—is super necessary. I totally get into the nuts and bolts, though I try hard *not* to get into the nuts and bolts. But the boy makes it difficult. He nods and asks questions, and seems genuinely interested, so my mouth starts running itself. I know this is making the ancestors shake their heads in dismay, especially when I go overboard in detailing the Save the Cat beat, and how vital it is when creating characters that readers will identify with.

But it's not my fault that I head into the weeds and seeds with the cat thing. May it please the court, as I offer into evidence, that when I tell him, "Plus, screenwriters always need to save the cat," his face goes all confused and he says, "But not every movie has a cat."

"No, not a literal cat. Credit for the term to Blake Snyder."

He grins. "I love how you do that. Give credit where it's due."

"Intellectual property is currency, right? Gotta keep the copyright karma gods happy."

"Copyright karma gods. I like it."

And boy oh boy, I like Tristan. I give myself a breath to cool my heart jets, then say, "What Snyder's talking about is that early on in the story, the main character has to save something—a person, an animal—"

"Oh, like your sweater!"

"M—my sweater?"

"Sure. I tried to save your sweater. That's like saving a cat, right?"

Mmmmaaaayyyybbbbeee? If I actually owned a sweater and lost it. In this case, because I've lied through my whitened teeth, it's more like I accidentally stepped on a cat's paw. Except it wasn't an accident. I fibbed to get close to a guy. My teeny, tiny shenanigan is now a normal-sized shenanigan. I should totally come clean about this. It's still a small, kind-of white lie, and if I do it right, then it's funny.

Tristan gives me an over-the-top eyebrow wiggle. "But the sweater belongs to someone else. So I guess that makes me a villain for taking it."

That makes me laugh. Tristan, as a villain. "Only in the worst screenplay ever."

"Ouch. That's not fair. What if it was a James Bond sweater and the buttons were bombs?"

Good morning, nurse, this is a new level of imagination from Tristan. I like this interesting character twist. And okay, I know I should tell him I've never possessed a pink sweater and that I don't like the color, but how can

I? He's totally adorable sitting there, coming up with different origin stories for the sweater. In other words, this is bonding us together, and I mean, it's a sweater. It can't go *that* wrong, as buried secrets go, can it?

"Maybe," I say, "or it's the cardigan version of *Sisterhood of the Traveling Pants*. Or maybe the object that starts a rom-com, like *Sleepless in Seattle* meets *The Lake House*."

We spend the rest of the ride trying to one-up each other on the magical properties of the sweater. By the time we arrive at the rec center, I'm sad to give up the sweater. If I thought Tristan would believe it, I'd pretend it really was my clothing. But, you know, it belongs to someone else; and also, I've already denied ownership. And also, pink.

Tristan drops the sweater in the lost-and-found bin behind the desk.

"What about your bag?" I reach in to take out the sweater and hand it back to him, but he stops me.

"I know it's silly, but I don't want the bag." He blushes pink and it's wildly adorable.

I rethink my negative opinion on the color.

"I'm sorry we didn't find your sweater," he says as we walk back to his truck. "What does it look like?"

"Bubble-gum pink, white pearl buttons, but fitted so it's less Grandma Moses and more hip chick from the city." *Okay. Whoa. Where did that description come from? And how did it rapid-fire from my mouth?* I'm trying to think of a way to backpedal, but I have no idea. How do you casually do an edit and say, "Hey, sorry. Was describing someone else's sweater. Mine is darker, more plum colored." I mean, seriously, there's no takeback on this. I'm really going to need heavy edits to cool the shenanigan arc on this.

"Kind of like the one from the lost and found?"

THAT'S WHERE I GOT THE DESCRIPTION. "Yeah," I say, "but different, and my mom bought me mine." Oh, *Invasion of the Body Snatchers*, who is controlling my mouth?

"Like my shirt from my grandpa; it's got sentimental value. Do you want to take a walk and look around the grounds?"

See? *Now* would be a good time to come clean. Dang, Tuna, just open your mouth and speak truth! Except, I've noticed a cluster of freckles under his right temple, and I need time to count if it's a dozen or two dozen.

And also, may I throw myself on the mercy of the shenanigan, rom-com court? He's turned a random sweater into a mythical symbol and a plot device. If I tell him what I've done, then I take the magic out of the air. "It's entirely possible I lost the sweater somewhere else," I say. Which is true. In a multi-verse world, there could be a version of me that lost a version of the sweater in a pool hall or school bus. "How about I get you that coffee?"

CHAPTER SEVEN

The Glow Is Off the Tristan Rose...Maybe

"**W**HERE TO?" TRISTAN HOLDS OPEN THE DOOR FOR me.

"There's a place down the street, and they make a mean macchiato."

"Cool, but you okay if I order an acute one instead? You know," he says when I give him a blank look, "'mean' is another word for average. It's a math term, and acute is also a math thing—" He scratches the back of his head and gives me a one-eyed squint. "—It was funnier in my head."

"I love math jokes," I tell him. "I just have to *factor* in the *permutations*."

"Nicely played." He squints, squints again, then does a jazz hand thing along his body. "My sunglasses. What did I do with—I had them at your house."

"I remember. You had a whole 'California Boy' aesthetic going. Maybe you left them in the bag?" I jerk my thumb back at the rec center's doors. "Want to go and check?"

"In the bag?"

"I can sanitize them for you."

"Ah, yeah, let's check. I love those sunglasses."

We head back. I play the role of shining knight by delving into the bag and rooting around for the glasses because Tristan's low-key freaking out over having to put his hands in the lost-and-found bin. No luck on his accessory. "Sorry. Maybe they're back at my house."

"Thanks for saving me and my heebie-jeebies," he says. "It's cowardly, I know—"

"Nah, you're good."

"The coffee's on me."

"No, no, I'll buy," I say. "It's the least I can do for your epic quest on behalf of the sweater."

"I hope you find it," he says and leads the way out the door. "I lost a Cubs jersey a couple of years ago, and it still hurts. My grandpa bought it for me."

"I didn't know you were a Cubs fan." I hold the door open for him.

"I'm not," he says. "It was just a joke. I love bears, and when I was little . . ." He turns left for the coffee shop. "I'll stop now. It's not that interesting."

"Keep talking," I say. "I like listening." I point to the right. "But it'll be faster if we go this way for the coffee, since that's where the café is."

He tells me about his grandfather, who worked as an actuary, and how he's the reason behind Tristan's love of numbers. "Pops would see these patterns," he says, his voice catching with excitement. "And he'd show them to me and it was like, boom, the world was unveiling its secrets."

I never realized, until now, that Tristan's a hand talker. The more excited he gets, the higher and faster his hands fly. It's totally adorable. And slightly dangerous. I have to do a couple of stop-starts, freezes, and ducks to avoid getting beaned or smacked.

Also, I kind of get why Fi gives me *that look* when I go overboard on my screenwriting stuff. Tristan's passionate, and I love it, but yeah, not feeling the connection to integers and fractions the way he does. Still, I love that he loves it.

"Man, Tuna, the patterns and answers to life are everywhere; we just have to look!"

"I totally get you. Caribbean culture is similar. We're brought up to watch the world because the answers are there." *Mmmmmaaybe.* For sure, Robby and I were brought up like that. Our grandmothers were big on watching the world and listening to the universe. Their teachings came from their mothers, women who had to secretly educate themselves. A couple of my great-grandmothers took on the world with grade-three reading and math skills, and smashed it. Like, middle-class lifestyle, great jobs, summer vacations, send kids to school—smashed it.

I figure—no disrespect to science or anything—these women knew what they were talking about. I'm happy to overlay my adherence to science and facts with their intuitive knowledge, and to follow in the footsteps they created. But I really miss the Robby who looked to the stars for answers. I shake off thoughts of my bro and ancestors and concentrate on Tristan.

"I didn't realize your culture was so math and science based," he says.

"Oh, no, we're not. It's more about looking for signs and omens—messages—from the ancestors."

He stumbles—literally—as he does a whiplash turn my way. "You guys think dead people talk to you?"

Something about the way he says it gets my ruff up. "What's wrong with that?"

"It's a little . . . 'out there.'" He smiles.

I don't know, maybe it's a smile. It feels like a smirk. A condescending, patronizing, frat-bro with tinges of colonialism-hypocrisy smirk.

Tristan lifts his hands. "I mean, talking to ghosts? It's Ouija board and Bloody Mary, isn't it? Don't most of us outgrow that by grade four? By grade eight, for sure."

"Don't say it like that," I tell him.

"Like what?"

"Like people who go by the old ways are a bunch of knuckle-dragging meatheads who think the ability to make fire means you're a witch and should be drowned."

"Tuna, you can't honestly live your life by adhering to superstitions."

"Tristan," I say, matching his patronizing tone, "you can't honestly live your life thinking that superstitions don't run through every culture."

"I'm Scottish," he says, "and for sure, we have some wild superstitions. But it's not as though I live my life based on ancient ways of viewing the world."

"I've heard you say 'bless you' when someone sneezes."

"So?"

"So, the whole point of saying 'bless you' is because the ancients thought when you sneezed, it gave the devil a chance to possess you. Saying 'bless you' was protection."

"Fine, but that's etiquette, not me worrying about demonic possession," he says. I can hear him losing his patience.

"It's good to honor the ways of those who came before you," I say, losing my patience, as well. "And if you're not aware of how your ancestors viewed life, then you lose your history and context. So many people think Christmas trees are about Christmas without even realizing it originated as a celebration of the Roman festival of Saturnalia." It's not the best argument, but I'm too mad to try to find a better one. "If you don't pay attention to your history, to any history, you lose all of your connection to your past, to your roots. If you do that, then you lose the thread to your future." The speed of my words picks up, the sharpness honed until I finish the last of my rant with breathless, contained anger.

Tristan's stuck in place, staring at me like I'm a victim of the *Body Snatchers*.

And I realize I might be vibing a killer aura à la Jason Voorhees in *Friday the 13th*.

"No, sorry," he says. "I didn't mean to question your beliefs. It just caught me off guard."

"Sorry back." The way I spit the apology screams how much I don't mean it. "I wasn't questioning your beliefs in science, either. I adhere to science," I say as a way to offer an olive branch, "but I appreciate the connection to my past, as well."

"No worries." After a second, he adds, "I can see your points."

"We each have unique ways of viewing the world."

"Right. How we make sense of the world and move in it is what matters."

"Double-right. As long as you're not hurting anyone or breaking any laws, then there should be freedom of thought and individuality."

We've both apologized, both smiled our apologies, but a cool, brittle awkwardness slips between us. It's a third, unwelcome interloper in the day. No matter how much I try to lighten the mood, or Tristan tries to cut math puns, the vibe from earlier is lost. I don't feel guilty about standing up for myself, but I do feel bad about being so ruthless about it. No amount of smiling can take back my words or my attitude. It's obvious from the dimming in his eyes that I've dropped levels with him, too. If there's a chance between us, it's threadbare and easily broken.

I buy him an iced coffee, get myself a blackberry iced tea. Both of us take our time sipping because if there's a paper straw in your mouth, you can't talk, right? Tristan drives me home, and we have a painfully shallow conversation about music. It's when the topic shifts to the weather that I fear we're done before we even started. Weather? Come on, that's what old people talk about in elevators. It's not what cool kids about to fall in love talk about while driving around on a summer's day.

We lapse into silence, which is good. It gives me time to think. Truth is, I don't really need Tristan to believe what I believe. I just need him to respect our difference of opinion. His apology says he does respect said difference. And also, I like that he's not perfection, personality-wise. He's got things I like and things I don't like, but also respect for differences. Me too. Together, we're a multidimensional couple.

It's like the fun and games section of a screenplay, where there are complications, ups and downs, but the story still delivers the promise of the premise. In my case, that Tristan and I end up together. Now, I just need to figure out a way to show him all of this, and do it fast, before the threadbare chance between us is blown away.

Tristan pulls into my driveway.

"Your sunglasses," I say, not quite accepting love's defeat as I climb out of the truck. "We should check."

"I might have left them in the bathroom when I was washing my hands."

Come on, Tuna. You can do this. You can save the day! I wrack my brain, scrolling through every rom-com I've ever seen, every disaster movie I've ever watched (because, let's be honest, this almost-date has been a total disaster). I even mentally flip through some documentaries, but I can't think of the twist that will rescue our relationship, and I can't come up with the emotional beat that makes us see each other with the golden glow again.

I head up the porch steps and stutter to a stop when he says, "Can I meet your dog?"

"My . . . dog?" I do a three-second count before I make eye contact, mostly so I can mask my incomprehension at the question.

"Yeah, the rope on your door." He gestures to it. "You said the shoe thing is about culture, but the rope, that's got to be a dog. My aunt has a dog. She was supposed to be a service helper—the dog, not my aunt. She knows all the skills, like using a rope to open or close a door, but she's her own dog. Kept doing it on her own schedule." He grins. "Going to my aunt's house is like hitting a dance club. Gemma—the dog—turns off and on the lights at her whim."

"She sounds awesome."

"You'll love her when you meet her. Gemma, I mean. But you'd like my aunt, too."

When, not *if*. That's a good sign. *Okay, Tuna. Think of something and reel this boy into your net.* Except I can't think of anything because, apparently, the fish pun has depleted all my brain power.

"So, can I meet your dog?" he asks.

"Oh, uh—"

"Tuna," Robby calls my name.

Nnnnnooo. Not Robby. Anyone but Robby. When it comes to me and Tristan, my brother's the world's worst plot twist. There's no way his appearance means good things. He's the iceberg to my *Titanic*, the fire to my *Hindenburg*, the casting of Russell Crowe to *Les Misérables*. "Hey. Tristan, this is my brother, Robby."

The guys shake hands.

Oh, dang. Robby's here. David's photos—they're all over the house. "Do Mom and Dad know you're coming over?"

"Yeah," he says. "I texted to let them know." He turns his focus to Tristan. "You guys heading out?" Robby asks. When Tristan's not looking, Robby gives me a smirk.

I really have to rethink sharing my crushes with my family.

"Heading in," I tell him. "Tristan was dropping me off. We're just going to check for his sunglasses in the house. Why are you here?"

"Mom's working late." He lifts the cloth bag in his hand. "I thought I'd make dinner. Sugar snap pea and carrot soba noodles."

"That sounds delicious," says Tristan.

"It does, until Robby makes it," I say. *WHAT IS WRONG WITH ME? Why do I keep inviting conversation when I should be STOPPING it?* Okay, okay, obviously the presence of my brother is having a negative impact on my ability to make rational, level-headed decisions.

"I'm going to put the groceries in the kitchen," says Robby. "Then I'm going to look up a recipe for your dessert, Little Fish. Humble pie. Where do you think you left the sunglasses, Tristan? I can take a look for you."

"Bathroom, maybe," he says. "Can I still meet your dog?"

"Dog?" Robby says the word as though he's testing each sound.

Tristan points at the rope. "I was telling Tuna about my aunt's dog and the rope she uses to open and close doors." His face drops. "Oh, no. Wait. Tell me your dog didn't die and I'm reopening the trauma."

Robby starts laughing as I babble that we don't have a dog.

"There's no dog," says Robby, "just my family's stupidstitions."

"Their...*what*?"

"We should get your sunglasses," I say, and push Tristan toward the door.

"No, wait, what's he talking about?" He turns to Robby. "What are you talking about?"

I try to telepathically tell Robby to not say anything.

"The rope. It's to keep away bad spirits, *jumbee*," says Robby.

Forget telepathy. "Thanks for the cultural lesson," I tell Robby. "We're good."

"No, wait." Tristan looks between us. "Ropes stop spirits?"

"It's myth," I say, glaring at Robby. "You leave your shoes toes out at the front door and the knotted ropes. If a *jumbee* follows you home, it gets distracted by the shoes and rope, and stays out of your house."

"You forgot to add that you enter the house backward to fool the spirit, too," says my ruin-my-love-life brother.

"Thanks," I say through clenched teeth.

Tristan looks gobsmacked. No, he looks more than gobsmacked. He looks like what gobsmacked looks like when it's gobsmacked. I can see his synaptic processors whirring and the flashing message coming up in capital letters: 404, PAGE NOT FOUND.

"Your sunglasses," I say. I let Tristan in the door. He does a forward-back shuffle, trying to decide how to enter the house. I catch him when he opts for going in backward and trips on the door lip. He walks—shoeless—to the bathroom. Tristan closes the door and I smack Robby. Hard. "How could you do that?"

"Do what?"

"Talk about our traditions like we're a bunch of loons that divine our futures by casting chicken bones and reading tea leaves." I have to whisper to make sure Tristan can't hear me, and it's a lot of effort to inject contained rage, but I'm making it work.

"Isn't he Tristan? *The* Tristan who you've been panting over since freshman year?"

"You don't need to bellow it like you don't know!" I give him another smack. "But, yes."

"I thought you guys were friends. How was I supposed to know he didn't know about your quirks?"

"Uh, how about the way I was vibing you to shut up?"

"Sorry, my vibe-o-meter must need a tune-up."

"You should be sorry," I say. "You shouldn't even be here!"

"Calm down, panic fish. These superstitions are core to you; he should know about them."

I hate it when he's logical. I hate that my anger at him is partially directed at myself. "You totally wrecked my chances with him!"

Robby's eyebrows go up. "You're the one who kept talking to me. Why didn't you just go in the house?"

"I'm supposed to ignore you? That would make a great impression with Tristan."

"Don't act like I did this. Face it, you're nervous about him and used me to deflect."

Did I mention how much I hate it when my brother tries to play psychoanalyst? In case I didn't, I HATE IT WHEN ROBBY TRIES TO PSYCHOANALYZE ME!!! "Go burn dinner," I say as Tristan comes out of the bathroom.

"I don't know how you think you'll have a relationship with him if you're not honest."

Seriously, how am I supposed to deal with this guy when he keeps spouting truth and logic? It's like he wants us to keep fighting. "I was never going to hide my beliefs, but that's kind of a third-date kind of thing." Judging from the wary stride of Tristan as he comes out of the bathroom and toward us, there won't be a third date or a second date. Technically, we're not on a date, so it's a moot point. And even more technically, the crash and burn isn't Robby's fault. The vibe was off already, but it feels like any chance for salvaging it was destroyed by my brother, and I'm struggling not to clobber him for it.

"Found them." Tristan holds up the sunglasses.

I walk with him to the door.

"I hope you find your sweater," he says.

"Thanks."

"You lost a sweater?" Robby asks.

"Shouldn't you be in the kitchen committing unspeakable culinary crimes against food?"

"Redundant, Tuna," he says. "By definition a culinary crime can only be committed against food."

Ah, verifying my vocabulary. Obviously, he's as ticked with me as I am with him.

"Remind me again, what's the definition of fratricide?" I say.

Panic skitters across Tristan's face. He does a quick check of his surroundings as though confirming he hasn't fallen into one of the *Saw* movies. "Her pink one," Tristan offers as he backpedals to the door. "She lost the pink sweater."

"Pink?" Robby's face goes slack.

I push Tristan out the door before my obtuse brother can reveal I don't like pink.

Tristan all but runs for his truck. He gives me a quick wave and peels into the street so fast, I'm sure he's left rubber marks on the driveway.

I head back to the house, fuming at my disastrous attempt at wooing Tristan. Most of all, I'm done with my brother, his being over all the time, and his magical ability to ruin my day. No more Mr. Nice Tuna. It's time for this story to break into two before my brother ruins my life.

CHAPTER EIGHT

Let the B-Story Begin

"**I**'D CALL YOU A WING NUT," FI'S VOICE COMES THROUGH in digital clarity, "but that would give a bad name to wing nuts. Who in their right mind talks about their life in beats and measures of a screenplay?"

"Fine, then let's take out the art influencing life's textures." I head to the bedroom window and adjust the offering of grapes for the screenwriting gods.

"If we could."

I ignore the Fi sarcasm in her tone. "He killed my opportunity with Tristan."

"To be clear," she says. "*You* put the opportunity on life support."

"But he tripped over the cord and pulled the plug."

"Oh, boy."

"Don't 'oh boy' me. We have to do something to kick this little bird out of the nest." I debate telling her more about my plan. There's an app called Eros and Agape in which people can create profiles and look for friends— Agape love—or a partner, Eros love. If I could get Robby some friends, it would give me room to breathe and have a life, without feeling guilty that I'm leaving him behind.

"Tuna—"

"You know what he needs? Someone to distract him."

"You want me to babysit him? He and I already text daily."

This, I know. My family has a way of adopting everyone's friends and turning them into surrogate children and siblings. The memories of David, Robby, and their friends, crowded in the kitchen while David concocted some new David-esque desserts, echo in our walls. Robby may have dropped all his friends, but Mom, Dad, and I are still in their group chains, and they still show up for dinner when their schedules allow. "I want him to find a friend."

"Oh, no, *Tuna!*"

"Not a *friend-friend*. But someone he can hang out with—someone who doesn't share his DNA."

There's dead silence and I know why. Fi's rolled her eyes so hard, they've fallen out of her head, and our conversation is on pause while she crawls on the floor, looking for them.

"Tuna." She draws out my name. "Do I really need to break down all they ways this idea is both impractical, insensitive, and ill-advised?"

"You said 'both.' Then you listed three things."

"Good," she says. "You can still count. You haven't totally lost all your marbles."

I stretch out on the bed and rub my calf. This morning's swim wasn't super great. It's hard to relax when you're carrying your brother and your crush in your head and heart. They add weight and drag in the water. "Are you going to help me?"

"Yes," she says. "I'm texting you a list of therapists who are taking on clients."

"Fi, be serious." I fluff my pillow and flop on the bed. The mattress bounces under my weight.

"I am being serious. In the best of times, forcing someone into a blind date is a bad idea—"

"That's the genius bit." I sit up. "He doesn't even have to know it's happening. We can be all low-key and sneak him into it."

"I know you think you're arguing your case, but you're not. No one wants to be ambushed by a blind date, let alone the guy who lost the only person he's loved since he was five. How do you not see this?"

"How do you not see how bad it is for him to stay stuck in his sadness?" I move to the window, hoping a butterfly will appear, and I can use a picture of it to prove my point. "It's not natural for him to be over here all the time."

"It's not natural for him to go to his family in his time of emotional need? Girl, do you ever listen to yourself?"

"All the time," I tell her. "It's a great way to learn how to write dialogue. I'm not saying it's wrong for him to come to us. The problem is that Robby's forsaken everything else. His friends haven't heard from him in months. *Months*, Fi, not days or weeks. He won't go to the movies or theater. All he does is come over, berate Mom and Dad over their food and health choices, and make fun of me for listening to the ancestors. Oh, and he runs. He's run around the city so many times, there's Robby-sized ruts in the pavement. Mom, Dad, and I can't be the only eggs in his basket."

"You're a cracked egg in the pan," she says. "With shells in the yolk."

"You're a yolk."

"He does have friends," she says. "He talks to me and Mom."

"You don't count," I say. "You're family. He needs friends." I glance at the collage of David. "Mom and Dad won't let me put up the photos of David anymore. Robby's over so much, they're worried he'll show up unexpectedly and be traumatized. How can they be so blind to how destructive his behavior is?"

"And how can a girl so obsessed with character and plot be so blind to her true motivation?" she says. "Don't you see how obsessing over your brother allows you to not focus on the thing that has an actual ticking clock?"

"Meaning?"

"Tristan, you fool. You have a few weeks before college starts and the two of you are on opposite sides of the country."

"You should really check your map and your geography. Georgia's—"

"See? You're deflecting. Just like you ignored all the times you could have asked him out during school. This summer is your last shot and you know it," she says. "And you're using Robby as a way to avoid doing the thing that scares you."

A minute later, she shuts down the call, and I'm left staring at a blank and black screen. Well, every heroine faced obstacles. If Fi won't help me, then it's time for this Main Character—me—to find other allies.

"God, no. Have you lost your mind?" Dad stares at me from over the rim of his glasses with a mix of disbelief and disappointment sketched on his features. "Setting Robby up on a date? Don't be ridiculous."

"Why does everyone think I'm trying to find him a new partner? I'm not. I'm trying to find him a friend."

"He has friends." Dad shoos me from my perch on the edge of his desk and rescues the papers underneath me.

"But he hasn't talked to them in months. Probably because they remind him of the times he was with David. He needs a new start, a clean slate, with people who don't reference him with a David lens."

Dad sighs and leans back in his chair. Rolling the sleeves of his sweater along his arms, he says, "You're right, but this isn't your call, Little Fish."

"One of us has to do something," I say. "You can't think what he's doing is healthy."

"I think he's my son and I'll support him the best I can. He's your brother, Tuna. Support him."

"Fine." I toss myself into a linen-covered chair. "But if we're talking about support—"

"Forget it. Your mother and I are not going away for a weekend just so you can have the house to yourself."

"But I'm eighteen and starting college—"

"I've heard this song before," says Dad. "Can you play the next track?"

"It would be great practice. What if I'm scared to be alone, and I decide I don't want to go to SCAD anymore?"

"The Ice Age could arrive and you'd snowmobile to SCAD, but nice try." He steeples his fingers. "What's this really about? More specifically, *who* is this about?"

"What? How can you say that?"

"Is this about Tristan?"

Yeah, I *really* need to stop oversharing my life with my family.

He rocks the chair upright and returns to his work. "Don't bother your mother about any of this—Robby or the weekend. She's got enough on her plate with this new picture book."

"Fine, but you'll regret not getting on board with me for either of them."

He's already turned back to his screen.

Of course, he's right about Mom and the stress of the new project. But he's not taking into account that she and I have a special bond from having shared the same body, or at least the same body parts. Okay, okay, so it's a little skeezy to use the womb as a negotiating tactic, but desperate times, right? Screenplay tip: when a character has a goal to accomplish, sometimes they have to go into the shadows to get things done. I head up the basement stairs and to Mom's office on the main floor.

"Don't even start with me," Mom says, not looking up from her screen. "And stop where you are. Don't break through the threshold of my door."

"What are you talking about?" I stand in the doorway, but let my toes push into the borders of her room.

"I'm talking about your weekend plans and your wildly inappropriate ideas for Robby."

"What—?"

She holds up her phone with her right hand, keeps drawing with her left. "Your father already texted me."

"How could he do this? He said I wasn't to talk to you about it." This is so frustrating. I know the second act of a story is all about the main character facing defeats and obstacles, but does my act really have to include my parents shutting me down with Robby?

"Yeah, and like any good father, he knows his kid's tricks." Blue light from the computer reflects in the lenses of her glasses.

"Well, he doesn't know me that well. I wasn't coming here to talk to you about any of it." I cross into the room, my stride full of betrayal and wounded loyalty.

"Uh-huh. And why are you here?"

Oh. Snap. I did not fully think this through. "I wanted to see if you wanted to watch a movie with me tonight." I lean over, hug her tight. "I know how stressful your drafts can be, and I thought it might be fun to have some mommy-daughter time."

Mom pinches her nose. "Oh, girl. The stuff you're shoveling is a mile deep and smells like a cow field."

"Mother! How can you say that? I'm wounded to my very core."

"Fantastic. All great artists need trauma to create." She slides her glasses up to her forehead. "Honey, I don't know if your head or heart are in the right place with Robby. For sure, I know where both your head and heart are with this ludicrous idea to get us out of the house for a weekend. Specifically, I know with whom your heart and head are—"

"Am I really that transparent?"

"Polished glass. But Robby." Mom reaches around to take my hand. "Little Fish, I know you've had both love and heartbreak, so you know what it's like to lose someone you love. But Robby and David were together for a long time. Regardless of what you think he needs, Robby has to decide what he needs."

"But what if he's slowly suffocating in the meantime?"

"Don't think your father and I don't worry about that." Her voice trembles. She coughs to clear her throat of tears. "But he's a grown man. It's not up to us to parent him like a child. And it's not up to you to move him around like a character on a storyboard. Do you hear me?"

"Yes, ma'am."

"Do you *hear* me?"

"Yes, ma'am!"

She digs into her drawer and pulls a wrinkled photo from the bottom. It's Robby and David on their first official "date," twelve years old, a movie and a shared bag of licorice. Robby still has the ticket stubs and the empty bag of licorice. Maybe. Maybe he tossed it out with everything else.

Mom smooths the photo and traces the outline of David's face. "I remember this date. His mom and I in the front of the theater, the boys in the back so we couldn't see them. Of course, we kept turning around." Her finger stills on David's hair, as though she could push it off his forehead. "I thought that boy would be with us forever, visiting your father and me in our senior care center, and arguing with me over the difference between turquoise and cyan." She wipes the tears from her cheeks. "God, he loved the color blue."

We hear the lock in the front door, and she rushes to hide the photo, catching her fingers in the jamb, and sending out a stream of curses.

"Anyone home?"

"The bigger question is: Why are you home?" I meet Robby as he's setting bags of takeout on the counter.

"It's a great noodle place I found. They've got amazing *pho*."

"Are you saying it's *pho*nomenal?"

He doesn't even crack a smile. Instead, he takes off his windbreaker. (And I'm sorry, but did the nineties file an injunction? Is there some kind of minimum retro style he has to wear or he faces fines and sanctions?)

"I'm glad you're here," I tell him. "You can join us for a movie."

"Yeah? What are we watching?"

"Something from Bollywood."

"I'm your brother and I love you. I would give you my kidney, my lung, my bone marrow, but I'm not giving up time to watch that movie."

"What's a couple hours of brother-sister bonding over some cultural entertainment?"

"What? No! Altuna Kashmir Rashad! I'm not watching that horrible movie!"

"What horrible movie? I haven't even told you which one we're watching." I take the containers from the bag. The scent of pepper, onions, and garlic rise up and make me happy I have taste buds. I'll need to put up a CAUTION: WET FLOOR sign with all the drooling I'm doing.

"Because it's the same one. We watch it all the time! That horrible, clichéd thing with the cardboard supporting cast and a magical dog who somehow saves the day and the main character? Tuna, no!"

"We don't watch it all the time!"

"We do!" He sets down the plates with more-than-necessary force. "All the time!"

"Yeah? Then what's the name of the movie?"

"What? I don't know—I can't remember."

"See? So it can't be all the time, or else you'd remember." I take out serving spoons for the fish dish and rice.

"The reason I can't remember is because my brain has repressed the title for the good of my mental health."

I snort. "There's an oxymoron, Robby's good mental health."

His face goes tight. "What's that supposed to mean?"

"It means we had plans and you just waltz in here and throw everything overboard. The world doesn't revolve around you."

"Well, it's not like the sun shoots beams out of your butt, either, sweet thing. I thought it would be nice to come over and bring dinner. Mom's working on that picture book, and you know she's stressed. Did you think about that? Did you think about her? No, because if you had, you would have made dinner."

"How do you know I wasn't thinking about her?"

"Because you don't think about anyone else, just yourself!"

Mom swoops in before I can fire the words burning in my mouth.

"Thank you, sweetheart." Mom kisses his cheek. "It's nice of you to think of us."

"Someone needs to," he mutters.

Mom works her Mom magic, which means Robby cools his jets and so do I. We end up watching my movie, which surprises me to no end. I figured Robby would have put up a fight and the folks would have sided with him, for his mental health.

"I still hate that cliché Bollywood movie," he says as he hugs me goodnight and heads to his car. "But I take it back. Dogs *are* magic."

Houston, we have a sign.

CHAPTER NINE

Dogs Aren't the Only Ones with Bark and Bite

THE DAY STARTS WITH THE USUAL WORKOUT AND ROU-
tine for swimming. I'm home for a few hours, then I head to work. I
park the car. The construction's still going loud and strong. Today,
it looks like they're replacing some of the glass. I wave at the construction
guys and head inside. Tristan's in the staff room, waiting for his shift.

We haven't talked since The Incident. Not that I haven't tried, but
sending cute photos of dogs and getting adorable videos of birds and cats in
return is . . . well, it's keeping the lines of communication open, but it's not
exactly putting us back on the bullet train to Lovesville, is it?

"Hey." I slide next to him, like it's no big deal. "How was the weekend?"

"Brutal. Did you know how easily grown adults turn into a mob when
you have an open house and offer cookies?"

"They mobbed for the house or the cookies?"

"Both," says Tristan.

"Maybe don't bake the cookies?"

"You have to bake the cookies," he says. "It's an old trick. You make chocolate chip cookies right before the open house. That way, the place smells like home sweet home. It helps put viewers in a buying mood."

Huh. I file that one away for some future project when I'm middle aged, questioning my life choices, and writing a character going through a divorce and trying to reclaim their place as the number one real estate agent. (Not that I will be divorced. At least, I hope not. But I could see me questioning my life choices. If I do it at eighteen, why would I stop at forty?) I'm not sure where to go with the cookie story, so I opt for, "Did the open house viewers erupt in a bidding frenzy for the house?"

"Not at first," he says. A slow smile spreads across his face. "Then, I went proactive. I started on about how big the backyard was, how much I would have loved having a tree house in it, and they bought it. The story, I mean. So, a family put in an offer, but then another couple heard, and they put in an offer." He nods, pleased with himself.

"Does that mean your folks have promoted you from unpaid intern to paid intern?"

"Kind of. The house ended up selling for an extra five thousand. I got a five percent commission on that amount, and they put it toward my college in the fall."

"That's—" My brain stutters from trying to rebuild the bridge between us and do mental math at the same time.

"Two hundred fifty dollars," says Tristan. "Enough for half of a textbook, but I'll take it."

We grin at the shared pain. College was expensive when Robby attended. Now it's uber expensive. Since I started working at fifteen, half my wages were put into an education fund that I can't touch. Still, if it wasn't for my job, my parents helping, and some academic scholarships I was awarded, I'd be pulling a Mitchell and pooping in the pool over the stress about tuition. As it is, if I go for my Masters or PhD, I'll be on my own. Mom and Dad's help will end with an undergrad degree.

The moment between Tristan and me fades out, and we're left with awkward silence. "I should go and check on the status of the pool." When I get into the reception area, there's a lady by the counter.

"Can you help me?"

I glance around for Penny. She's in her office with the construction foreman, and it looks intense. I catch her eye and point at the counter, and do a mime thing that amounts to *I'll take care of this lady, okay?*

Penny gives me a thumbs-up and a mime response of *Thanks, I'll be there soon!*

"I can try to help," I say and smile at the woman. "What are you looking for?"

"There's a grief support group that's starting in a couple of weeks," she says. "I—" she gulps a breath "—I want to sign up."

That last part comes out in a rush, and I figure it's taken all of her strength to get out of bed, shower, and put on makeup. The last of her energy is drained by her words. I want to tell her I know how it feels, that I know how something as simple as brushing your hair can feel like all of the twelve labors of Hercules combined into one. Instead, I say, "Sure thing. Let me pull up the information."

I'm having trouble getting the sign-up file to load. Enter Tristan, who helps me sort it. He stays by me as I take the woman's information.

"All done," I tell her. "I've emailed you the schedule. If you don't see it in your inbox, check your spam folder."

"Is that it?" she asks. "I don't have to tell you anything about—my loss? I don't have to give a reason for attending?"

"No," I say. "That's for you to share once you're with the group."

"Oh. It was my husband." Her face tightens and the words spill out: part confession, part trauma blood-letting. "He was in an accident and got hooked on opioids. It was a drug overdose."

"I'm sorry," I tell her, because I am, because I can feel the pain of the loss that rolls from her in fractured waves. It's all I can say, because her pain is touching mine. I'm all for Act Two introductions of new characters in my life, but not her, not now, when I have to teach in a few minutes, and I can't go to pieces before my shift.

She gives me a cold, empty smile. "You're lucky. It's obvious you've never lost anyone."

Her words slice through the paper-thin restraint I have. My calm facade isn't because I haven't lost anyone, I want to tell her. It's not even because I've lost someone and come through on the other side of therapy and healing. It's because the pain is so deep, I haven't touched bottom yet. I don't know what to do with my feelings, so I just push it down, punching and punching until my knuckles are cracked and bleeding.

I don't say any of it, because all of my confusion and pain pours out in a sudden, embarrassing, unstoppable torrent of tears. I spin from her, from Tristan, and rush to the safety of the staff room.

Behind me, I hear the woman.

"Oh, god! Oh, no!" she says. "I'm so sorry—I shouldn't have—I should go."

I don't hear the rest, but I wonder about the two-faced nature of grief, and how it can push people together or pull them apart. There's a box of tissues on the table. I grab a handful and swallow the tears, the grief. It's time for swimming and getting Littles excited about water and floating. It's showtime, and the show must go on.

Penny comes in. "I saw," she says and holds out her arms.

I take it, soak in the friendship and the comfort. "For a tiny woman, you pack a lot of strength into a hug." I pull away. "Sorry. She just caught me off guard."

"Grief and loss will do that," she says. "It's been twenty years since I lost my mom, and the smell of bread can still undo me." She gives me a once over. "You're good to teach? Are you sure?"

If the high and mighty ever ask us how the rec center managed to turn itself around, I'll be the first to stand up and give Penny credit. She genuinely cares for people and always chooses humanity as her priority. Is it any wonder that the employee turnover has dropped? That people sign up and come to the center for the chance to be part of anything she's in charge of? "I'm so good," I say, and head to the locker room.

Tristan's gone. No doubt, he's got to get the field and equipment ready. Still, I find myself wishing for a text as I put my stuff in the locker. I'm still wishing for the text an hour later when class is done and I've dispersed everyone. His silence isn't just a sign. It's an LED and flashing one telling me we'll never be a couple.

I clean up, head out, and find him waiting at my car. "Hey."

"I don't know what to say," he tells me. "Except, do you want a hug? An ear or a shoulder?"

And it's sweet, unexpected, and a perfect combination of beat, character revelation, and plot twist. And honestly, I need the emotional win. I find the tears rising.

"How about all three," he says softly, "with a side of garden burger from this food stand I know?"

"Only if I buy," I say. "In payment for the body parts offered."

"You don't have to buy," he says, a faint note of hurt in his voice. "You're my friend."

"Then you buy." I step close and he hugs me. "But I'm getting a large of everything, including a strawberry shake."

He laughs. "Extra-large because you had Mitchell today."

"I did." I step back and miss the warmth of him. "But there were no accidents today."

"Things are looking up," he says.

"Any day you don't have to fish kid poop out of a pool is a good day. Shall I drive?"

He nods and I unlock the doors.

As we're pulling out of the lot, he says, "For what it's worth, the grief group is open for anyone eighteen and older."

"Thanks," I say. "I'll look into it, but I don't know. I'm not sure about mixing all that emotion at a place I work."

"I get that," he says. "But if you ever want me to go with you, I will. It might not be a bad thing for me, anyway, because of Grandpa. And with the real estate stuff, too. At some point, I'll have to sell to someone who's just been divorced or lost their spouse. It would be good to have an idea of what people are going through."

I don't know if he's saying that because he's being logical about his loss and his job, or if he's saying it to make me feel okay in asking him to join me. Either way, the boy is feeding my heart, soul, and stomach. If that's not a sign, then what is?

"Why are you in my house?" Robby's bleary eyed, surveying me in his rumpled flannel bottoms and a gray t-shirt. His hair sticks out at sharp, unexpected angles.

"Doesn't feel so great when people just turn up at your house without warning, does it?"

"Tuna, it's—" he glances at the clock on the microwave "—ten in the morning. Ugh, why are you here so early?"

"It's not early; you've been off shift for hours. I've already been to the pool and everything."

"Aren't you working today?"

"That was yesterday. Come on, the day's starting, wake up!"

"The day hasn't started. It's the crack of dawn when you've pulled the night shift." He shuffles to the kitchen and roots around for his reusable coffee pod.

It's like watching a puppy try to tie its shoes. Not that a puppy would wear shoes. Or they might. Who am I to judge the fashion choices of the canine set? "Sit down before you hurt yourself." I steer him to the one chair at the kitchen table and brew him a mug. "I'm here to take you out."

He casts a wary gaze over the rim. "Don't think it's lost on me that there are two meanings to the phrase 'take you out.'"

"Don't be a baby," I tell him. "You think Mom and Dad would let me do anything to you? You're their firstborn."

"So was Zeus," he says. "Didn't matter much to Cronus."

"Only you would (1) reference yourself as a god and (2) say something so incoherent."

"It's three in the morning."

"That's Robby time. Here, in the real world, it's almost time for brunch."

The code word lights his eyes. "Brunch?"

Robby hasn't eaten brunch since David died.

"I'm talking pancakes with real whipped cream and strawberries." I can almost see drool puddling at his feet.

"Nah, that stuff's full of sugar and wasted calories."

I'm deeply impressed by his restraint.

"Thanks, though."

I shrug, like the offer was no big deal. "No worries. I'm going to head out to the place on Walnut, by the market. I remember how much you liked their strawberry stack. I thought I'd try it."

His eyes go dreamy at the mention of pancakes. "It's good." His strength is weakening, I can hear it in his voice. "You'll enjoy it. Tell me how you like it."

"I will, but I may not order the pancakes. I hear they've brought in chocolate honey from Quebec. Maybe I'll get something with that in it."

"Chocolate honey from Quebec?" His eyes glaze over. "Give me fifteen to get ready." He downs the coffee, then he's racing to his bedroom.

I pat myself on the back. My brother never stood a chance. He was tired from his shift, sleep deprived, and hungry. I couldn't have planned my ambush any better. "Don't worry, David," I tell the air and hope my bro-in-law-in-life-and-afterlife is listening. "I won't make it weird." And I swear, I can almost feel David hugging me in thanks.

Okay, okay. It's me and David, so I can almost feel the hard eye-roll and David saying, "Little Fish, you always make it weird." But at least David and I are talking, right?

I wonder what it's like for David and the ancestors, watching out for us. I imagine them in a theater-style room, viewing our successes and failures on a big-screen television, throwing popcorn at the screen when we choose the wrong path. Is it frustrating, being an onlooker and relying on us to catch their signs and messages, wishing we were more like the old-timers and less like the young techno-dependents? Before she died, one of the great-aunts had shaken her head sadly and said, "I can hardly hear the spirits anymore. The technology interferes." I was never sure if she meant frequency or our obsession with anything digital, but I think about it, a lot.

Ten minutes later, Robby's out and ready. Time to stop reading the signs and do something about them.

"Why are we here?" Robby squints at the sun and holds up his hand to block the light.

"Put your sunglasses on, genius." The car chirps that it's locked, and I put the fob in my shorts.

"Why are we here?"

"Because you ate both of our body weights in waffles and pancakes."

"They were delicious."

"Meanwhile, I'm going to have to sell a kidney to get the money to pay for your meal."

"Come on, it wasn't that bad."

I pinch his forearm. "You run so much, you have zero percent body fat. I'm surprised you haven't inhaled all of Ontario to keep your metabolism going."

"Do you want me to reimburse you for the bill? I can."

"I know that, Dr. Rashad. Geez. I was just kidding." I step through the chain-link gate and close it behind us.

Robby surveys the emerald grass and trees, lifting his face to the wind. "Why are we here?"

Is it terrible that I'm getting a perverse kick out of making him repeat the question? "Because I need to walk off my food. You can just breathe and burn your calories."

"Why here—?"

The rest of the question, if there was any, is cut short as a Great Dane gallops Robby's way and hip checks him. My brother holds his balance and takes the giant dog's eager greetings in stride.

"All good, champ." Robby dodges a French kiss from the Dane, then laughs as the dog gets in a sneaky lick.

The dog takes a run at me. I don't even bother putting up the pretense of dignity; I go to ground and give him butt and belly rubs until he's drooling, because, dog. He spots new people coming into the dog park and lumbers away. Wiping dog drool from my cheek, I say, "Dogs. That's why we're here."

"Is this because I was grouchy about the movie last night?"

"Were you? I couldn't tell."

"Really?" There's a hopeful lift in his voice.

"No, Robby! You complained about it the *entire* time. It was exhausting!"

He brushes leaves, grass, and faint dog prints from a bench and sits. The shade of the tree behind him sends rippling shadows of branches and leaves along his face. "I don't know how you can watch that movie. Stereotypical characters, forced plot beats to shove the story forward, horrible acting—and by the way, people don't break into spontaneous dance numbers."

"Like you've never been part of a dance mob."

"That was years ago." He brushes a blade of grass from the seat.

"It's comfortable," I tell him and perch on the edge of the bench. I'm glad of the dogs chasing after balls, grateful for the shy ones pressed against their guardian's legs, blessed by those on their back demanding tummy rubs. They distract both Robby and me, give us eye and heart candy that's somehow delightful, wholesome, and filling, all at once. "You're right about everything you said. If it's not the worst movie in existence, it comes really close. But the characters are happy, Robby. They go through rough times and come out the other side."

"Not all of them," he says. "Have you seen how often those movies off Indian mothers in childbirth? Also, grown men do not fall down cliffs or off buildings and survive."

"They do in Hollywood," I say. "Why not Bollywood?"

"The cracked ribs that have no negative impact on them or their ability to catch the bad guy." He laughs. "That's the worst place to be injured. You would feel like you're dying every time you breathe."

The sound of his laughter is pure bliss, and the light on his face warms me more than sunshine. It hits me, hard, how much I've missed this Robby. Can I even remember a time he's laughed? Like, really laughed?

"I'm saying, Tuna, life isn't the movies. It's not even close."

"*I'm* saying," I tell him, "that it's comfort food for my soul. It's predictability and a guaranteed happy ending. It doesn't matter how many stairs or hills the hero topples down or how dark the night gets, they find their way back."

"Of course, the night has to be dark," he says. "How else will they read the messages in the stars and find their way?"

I can't tell if he's being funny, sarcastic, or making fun of me, but I'm not taking it, especially from a guy who used to love looking at the stars for messages.

Before I can get in a comeback, he says, "I'm going for a walk. Try to work off the chocolate honey."

I take out my phone and see a text from Tristan.

Did you know there's a ninety-eight percent probability that if you're texting and walking, you'll step into the sand bucket your little cousin left by the pool, lose your balance, and do a header into said pool? With your phone?

I take a breath, then another. How to play this? Go all caring and nurturing and ask if he's okay? Do the Rebel Without a Clue and cut a joke? I have to play it right and get us back on to the main plot of love and happy ever afters. I decide to go somewhere in the middle, lean into the math, and subtly support his love of numbers.

98%, huh? That seems high but you know the math.

It was actually 97.677777, but I rounded up. 💪

Did you really fall in the pool?

Giant, awkward cannonball.

Geez. Was the phone okay?

😹 😿 😹 I appreciate your support of my injury. The phone was fine. Pro tip, rice is not the miracle cure for wet phones.

Who knew you couldn't believe everything you read online? 🥴

I'm fine, thanks.

>Of course you are. Math Man is indestructible.
>
>Wet, but indestructible.

I do a quick survey of the park and spot Robby. He's crouched over some kind of doodle mix, rubbing the dog's head. They both look like they're about to achieve nirvana.

Sorry if I made the other day weird.

>Ah . . . just cultural beliefs are hard to explain,
>sometimes. No worries. You didn't make it
>awkward. My annoying big brother did.

Nah, he was cool. Your beliefs are yours, so is
your culture, but I get they can be hard to explain.
My family eats haggis. Try explaining that to people.

I clock that he acknowledges my culture without saying he's got a spiritual bent.

>What's to explain? Sheep's heart, liver, and
>lungs cooked in the stomach lining. That's just
>good eats.

That hurts my vegetarian heart on so
many levels.

>I capture some video of the dogs at the park
>and text them to him. For your heart and
>your withdrawal.

You're awesome, thanks!

>*I'm a delight,* I want to tell him, *and you're going
>to love me.* Instead, I go with a casual no prob.

> A few of us are going to play frisbee at the park on the weekend. Wanna join?

> > I'm dynamite with a frisbee.

> Cool. Teammates!

Any clever response is waylaid by the rise of angry voices. Three guesses *For Whom the Bell Tolls*. So much for using the brunch and dog park as a way to get him to sign up for the grief group at the center. I hit Tristan with a **Send me the deets!**, then shut down my phone and sprint to my brother.

Who's having a fight with a super gorgeous dude, who happens to be holding an illegally adorable cockapoo-mix. "What's your problem, man?" says the guy. "I said I was sorry."

"No, you didn't," says Robby. "You said you didn't notice. That's not the same thing."

I look to the sky, hoping the aunties will send a bolt of lightning or torrential downpour. "What's going on?"

The blond guy turns my way. "He belong to you?"

"Yes, but he's all bark, no bite."

"Tell your boyfriend—"

"Ew, gross, no!"

Robby echoes my horror. "That's my sister! My younger sister!"

"Tell him" —the guy pivots my way— "that I was tying my shoe and I didn't notice my dog evacuating her bowels."

Okay, pause for both cute and awkward description. I scribe it in my mental notebook.

"I would've cleaned it up. I'm not an asshole."

"Your dog was on the other side of the park. What if she'd needed you? You can't take your eyes off them for a second!" says Robby.

"Yeah? You want to show me how it's done?" The man, still holding his dog, swings to Robby. "Where's your dog, then, big shot?"

"I don't have one!"

"So . . . what? You come to the park to give actual dog owners a hard time?"

If this was a rom-com, it would be a perfect setup for a meet-cute and fireworks of attraction. However, this is real life and they both look ready to clobber each other. Cut to younger sister stepping in to save the day. "I'm sorry," I tell the guy. "My brother's suffering sunstroke." I babble compliments about his dog and yank Robby away. "What is going on with you? That dude was cute."

"Attractiveness doesn't undo global responsibility."

Guess dog time's over. So much for bringing him here as a way to up his dopamine and serotonin levels. I hurry to keep pace.

"He should've been looking out for his dog. She should have been his priority. Dogs, Tuna. Anything that looks to you for love and protection should be watched over with extra care." He lifts his head.

He's still wearing the sunglasses, so I can't see his eyes. But I hear the whimper. Robby's crying.

CHAPTER TEN

The Ancestors Send Assistance

"OH, ROBBY." I PUT MY HAND BETWEEN HIS SHOUL-
der blades and rub his back. "It's okay." Maybe I should
try to tell him about the Eros and Agape website or maybe
about the grief group? If this was a screenplay, this would be one of those
character revelation and growth moments. I have to be sensitive and handle
Robby right.

"It's not okay. That guy shouldn't be allowed to have a dog."

"He was tying his shoes."

Another whimper.

I soften my voice. "People are allowed to tie their shoes. We're not gods
and demigods, here. We can't do a million things at the same time. For
sure, guys can't. There's loads of studies that say men can't multitask."

"You shouldn't take your eyes off your pet. The final data's still out on the link between gender and multitasking, so don't be sexist. Anyway, if you can't multitask, wear pull-ons."

Wait a second. For a guy who's crying, his voice is remarkably strong. I twist him around but see only myself in the reflection of his sunglasses. Time for directness over diplomacy. "Are you crying?"

"Over that nimrod? No way."

There's another high, sad sound.

I tap Robby on the shoulder and signal for him to be quiet.

He hooks his sunglasses on his t-shirt and cocks his head, trying to orient to the sound.

After a few moments, I give up. I must have imagined it.

Robby catches my gaze and shrugs. "Maybe it's the trees—"

The sound comes again.

This time we're prepared for it, and we both hone in on the location: a small bush with pink flowers. I'm smaller than Robby—not by much, but enough to get on my hands and knees and gently push aside the branches.

"Hey, buddy, you okay? Hello, sweetie?" I keep my voice soft and low, croon in a baby voice. Cue me hoping for a dog and not a rabid anything else. I'm up for anything that will bring me closer to Tristan, but a romance blooming over a hospital bed is too shades of *While You Were Sleeping*. Also, I'm not down with getting my heart-freak on while a doctor injects a rabies needle into my body.

I push aside more of the bush. There, in between tan branches, green leaves, and pink flowers, are the sweetest pair of brown eyes I've ever seen. They're nestled in a heart-melting teeny face with mostly white fur. Said face has ears with brown-sugar-colored fur, a pink tongue, and a sad expression that makes me want to right every wrong foisted upon it. "Oh, baby."

The dog—maybe puppy—makes a nervous sound and pulls forward.

That's when I realize why they're in the bush. Their collar is caught on one of the branches. "Oh, sweet face. Just hold on. Aunty Tuna's got you, baby." I push my hand close, slow and gentle, and get eager kisses on my fingers.

"Where's their owner?" Robby asks.

"I don't know," I tell him. "I'm a little busy right now." I manage to catch hold of the collar. "Get ready to catch them. Someone must be looking for this fur ball." I hear the swish of dirt and sneakers, then a grunt.

"Ready."

It takes a bit of push, pull, and a lot of crooning "it's okay, sweetie, I got you," and I lift the collar off the branch. I brace myself for a speedball of fur and fear.

Instead, the pup shakes their head, sits for a moment, then smiles at me.

What kind of dog smiles at a person? Okay, I mean, dogs smile. Of course they do. But this teeny-tiny's been caught in the bush. Now they're freed. Instead of running for the open, they're just sitting and smiling?

This has the shivery vibe of an omen and the excellent energy of an amazing plot twist. For sure it has the vibrations of the ancestors looking down. Also, can I give a shout out to the ancestors, because as far as new characters go, a dog is an excellent choice.

"What's going on?"

"I think they're catching their breath," I tell Robby. "Give them a minute." I turn my conversation to the dog. "Come on, sweetie. You must want some water, right?"

The dog stands, shakes their head, then the rest of their body. Bits of dirt, dust, and leaves spray from their body. Then the pup saunters—*saunters, as though they have NO cares in the world!*—and emerges from the bush.

And not just emerges. They give me a once over, a sniff, a couple of kisses, then head to Robby like he's a long-lost friend.

Cut, edit, and print, because this is the best character introduction I've seen in forever!

My brother scoops up the ball of fur and checks the collar. "No tag." He spins the collar. "It's a breakaway collar. It shouldn't have gotten caught." His face darkens. "Piece of crap collar. Now the poor dog's lost."

"Hold on," I tell him. "No need to write an operetta about it just yet. Give me a second. Maybe the tag fell off inside the bush."

"Did it?"

"Was that a second? 'Cause it felt like a millisecond. Maybe a half-second at most."

"Just find it, Tuna. She needs to get home."

"She's a she?"

"Concentrate, Tuna. Where's her tag?" As he's talking, his tone changes from irritated brother to lovestruck pet finder. It goes to baby-talk softness, and I try not to laugh as he says, "Do *you* know where it is? Are you going to tell us? Of course you are, because you're a very, very good girl."

I scrounge around and come away with scrapped knees and palms, but no collar. "She must have lost it earlier."

He doesn't answer because he's too busy kissing her noggin and getting kissed in return.

"Am I interrupting?"

"No," he says. "I can ignore you and pay attention to her at the same time. I'm excellent at multitasking."

"Oh, you're sssoooo funny I forgot to laugh." I dust off my knees. "Come on, let's see if anyone at the dog park recognizes her."

We spend another hour wandering around the park, asking if anyone knows the dog or her owner. Luckily, Mr. One-Two-Buckle-My-Shoe is gone, so there's no drama there.

Also, and I'm not complaining, but seriously, what is it with gender bias and lost dogs? Everyone goes to a puddle of goo with Robby "rescuing" the dog (never mind that *I* am the one who crawled around for her). When they think I'm the one who rescued her, they seem to be one degree short of callous disregard. Because apparently the myth of maternal instinct is still alive and well, and covers dogs, too.

"Don't pout," says Robby as we head back to the vehicle. "It's about the dog, not who gets the most compliments."

"Can I hold her?"

"No," he says and pulls her tighter. "She's comfortable with me."

"She'd be comfortable with me, too, if you'd let me hold her."

"You're driving."

Point made and taken. We climb into the car. Robby takes the backseat because "I don't like the idea of you getting into an accident and the air bag deploying into her."

I want to roll my eyes *so hard* and say something sarcastic. But this is the first time in a long time that I've seen Robby do anything other than be overbearing, so I'm not ruining the moment. "Give me a second. I'm going to check my phone for vets that are close by the park. She probably lives near here."

"Not necessarily," he says. "Dogs can travel anywhere from three to five miles per hour, depending on their size and whether they're excited or scared."

I keep scrolling, but inside, I'm a mix of Mentos meets Diet Coke, 'cause I'm a bubbling, fizzing explosion of happiness. It's Factoid Robby! He's back! Whoever says dogs aren't magic doesn't know what they're talking about.

"Look for the vet with the highest reviews," he says. "They'll be more likely to put in the effort to find her owner."

Luckily, that vet ends up being a ten-minute drive from the park. Unluckily, no one at the clinic recognizes the pup when we come in. A receptionist takes us to an empty room where they scan the dog for a microchip and check her ears for a tattoo.

"Nothing," says the receptionist.

"That doesn't make sense," says Robby. "She's good with people, has a collar, been well fed and cared for. She's obviously a much-loved dog. How can there not be a tattoo or chip?"

"All of the things you listed," says the receptionist, "aren't linked with vet visits. The family may not have had the money to pay for a chip."

The receptionist speaks it without judgment, but Robby blushes.

"There are lost pet sites and pages online," I say. "Maybe we'll start there."

"In the meantime," Robby says, "maybe we can get the dog checked out to make sure she's okay?"

An hour later, she's declared fit, well-hydrated, and about two years old.

"You're just a baby," Robby croons as he slides into the backseat and belts in. "Just a teeny-weeny-baby."

"She's grown," I say, seeing if I can prompt a transition to Factoid Robby.

"A dog takes twelve to eighteen months to grow, physically, but emotion-ally, she's just a bean."

I press my lips together to keep from chortling (yes, chortling, because that is my level of glee) and take us to the pet store. "We need enough for a few days at least." I pull free a cart. "In case it takes a bit to find her people."

We get to the cash register and I consider how differently people can define words. By a "few days," I meant a small bag of dog food, maybe a toy or two, and a leash.

Robby, meanwhile, must be using dog math to define the term, where one day is the equivalent of seven. He buys a couple of small bags of hard food and cans of soft (hypoallergenic varieties because "we don't know if she has allergies or prefers beef over lamb"), every toy in the store (okay, not *every* toy, but pretty close), a dog bed, a dog bed warmer, and a toy that rep-licates a heartbeat for "when she's sleeping in her bed" (which is WILDLY laughable because, Robby. As if he's going to let that dog sleep anywhere but next to him).

I pull curbside to his condo. "Interesting, isn't it," I say. "I heard her first. I dug her out of the bush. Yet, somehow, she's going home with you."

"You have a social life," he says. "Mom and Dad are too old to care for a young dog. Besides, you called yourself *Aunty Tuna* when you were freeing her. No takebacks."

I file away the elder reference for later retrieval, when I need to blackmail him for something.

"I'm perfect."

"With your long hours at the hospital?"

It's like he's just remembered he has a job because his face drops to Def-Con dejected levels. "Wait. Can you babysit? I'll give you my schedule." He doesn't wait for an answer. Robby, holding the dog close, climbs out of the car. "Get the stuff and bring it in."

Annnndddd nnnnnnooooo. I hold out my hands for the pup.

Reluctantly, he gives her to me, and I snuggle into her fur.

"She must be part terrier. Later tonight, I guess you'll also find out if she's part terror." I grin at my joke.

He doesn't answer, but we share blood. I know he's laughing on the inside.

"We need a name for her."

That makes him tense up. "No. She's someone else's family. Be logical, Tuna."

This from the man who's bought out half the pet store.

"I'm calling you Sweetie-Pie," I whisper in her ears.

"Do not call her that cutesy name. Geez, Tuna."

Should a grown man who adopts a baby voice when talking to a fluff of a dog *really* be schooling me on what's cutesy? "Okay, Butch."

"No."

"Baker?"

"Tuna."

"Candlestick maker."

His face goes soft. "She does bring a lot of light." Robby shakes off the joy. "No, stick with 'dog.'"

"Okay, *perra*."

"The *English* word for dog."

"Spoilsport." I stay by the car while he schleps the inventory to his condo. "What is your name?" I ask the dog and wait for someone to answer. "I think you're magic."

She makes a small sound and licks my nose.

"Okay," I whisper as Robby comes out the door. "Between you and me, you're Magic."

My brother takes Magic, gives me a fast hug, and leaves with, "I texted you my schedule."

"I charge minimum wage plus a base of twenty dollars."

He ignores me and keeps walking. Robby whispers in Magic's ear as he goes through the door.

"Magic, indeed," I tell myself. On so many levels. She's not the human distraction I was hoping for, but hopefully finding her people will remind Robby to find his center.

I climb into the car and head home. I have a group date with Tristan coming up, and Momma needs to get herself educated on the rules of Frisbee. I'm all for ups and downs for the middle act. But I am not okay with embarrassing myself in front of Tristan. (And okay, okay. I'm not a girl who can pull off "Momma" as a self-reference. Edit and delete.)

CHAPTER ELEVEN

A Frisbee, a Boomerang, and a Fumble

MOM DROPS ME AND MAGIC AT THE PARK ON Saturday, and I go to the meet-up spot for the gang. I'd say Tristan does a double take when I see him, but that would be inaccurate. It's more like a triple-take-whiplash maneuver that has me hoping he's got an amazing chiropractor.

He points at Magic. "That's a dog."

"Not just any dog." I pick her up and give her a cuddle. "She's the best dog in the world."

"Is—is she yours?"

I respect the low-key fear in his voice. I mean, a few days ago, we were talking about how my family had no dog. Now, I'm holding one. I can see the wheels turning. Did my family already have plans to get a dog? Did his mentioning how much he loves dogs make me get one? How powerful is he at this whole power of suggestion thing? It's endearing in that adorably obnoxious-eye-rolling way that only dudes can be.

I debate keeping him on the hook and saying he inspired me, but (1) that veers into shenanigan territory, (2) I don't know him well enough to know if he'd find that funny or creepy, and (3) I'm trying hard to be his love interest, not his antagonist.

"She was caught in a bush—actually, under it," I say. "Robby's holding on to her until we can find her people, but my folks and I get to dog-sit when he's at work."

"That's so sad." He takes her from me and holds her tight.

Lucky dog.

"Your brother's awesome for taking her in. Have you had any luck finding her owners?"

"Depends on how you look at it. No, if you mean have we found her family. Yes, if you mean she's turning my winter king of a brother into a real, live boy."

Magic covers his face in kisses.

Sigh. Really, lucky dog.

"It's going to be really hard for him to let her go," says Tristan.

"Not just him. Me too. I've found myself hoping Robby gets double shifts and emergency surgeries, just so I have a chance to be with her." I've also found myself trying hard not to think about finding the owner. Robby is so happy with Magic, it's going to kill him when he gives her back. Another heartbeat he's about to lose. Just like last time, he won't know when. Sometimes, I don't know what the ancestors are thinking.

The rest of the group trickles to our spot. My plan is to sit on the sidelines and watch, with Magic by my side. But I've underestimated the pull of the pup with my friends. There's a quick talk and hands go up (seriously, people are raising their hands like we're back in grade one) for those who want a chance to rub Magic's belly.

Which I totally get. That belly is very rubbable. White, soft, and she makes the *cutest* little moan-groans when you scratch her, and when you get to THE SPOT, her leg starts kicking like she's doing a hundred-meter dash. Fi texts to say she'll be late. One of the kids takes the Magic shift while I take to the field for some Frisbee.

By the time Fi arrives, the sun's hot and Tristan's even hotter. Despite him being super sweaty, I want to drink him like a glass of cool water. I jog over to Fi and take over Magic-watching duty as Tristan's friend heads to the field.

"Out of breath," she says as I collapse beside her. "Is that the Frisbee or the guy you're playing with?"

"I should ask him out."

"There's no time like the present." She nods his way. "Stop talking. Start doing."

"I'm going to do it. I was just waiting for the perfect moment, but now, with time counting down . . ."

"Waiting on a sign or waiting on the wizard to give you some courage?"

I'm glad she went with the Cowardly Lion reference and not the Scarecrow. I'd have had to punch her in the arm, and it's not good for Magic to see violence. She's too young for anything PG. "I think I got it," I say. "Him texting me to hang out today. It feels like a green light or, at least, proceed with caution." I nod at the group. "You going to head into that?"

She shakes her head. "My back's hurting too bad today." She takes Magic.

"You didn't feel forced to come out, did you? Everyone would have understood—"

"I was going to hurt today, no matter what. I can hurt and have some fun with my friends and this cute dog. Or I can hurt by myself. This way, I have a chance a certain BFF might buy me a sundae on the way home if I drive her."

"I'll buy you two."

Fi's phone bings and she checks her text.

"Oh, the scrumptious helper from the frozen-yogurt place?"

She gives me a coy smile and doesn't answer.

"Yeah, that's who it is."

"Riley," she says. "Their name is Riley."

"And? Date? Friendship?"

"Girl, hold your water. We just started texting. Acquaintances." She gives me a hard nudge to my ribs. "The game's stopping for a break. Now's your chance to ask him out."

I take a breath and rub Magic's noggin for good luck. For extra good luck, I also rub Fi's.

She punches me in the leg, but not hard, and says, "Go! Time's counting down and you're not getting younger."

Well, ouch.

"Good game," I tell Tristan.

He hits his palms with sanitizer, then takes a swig from his cup. "You too. That was some power catch. You get great height."

"All the kicking in the pool," I say. "It has to count for something."

"This was fun." He smiles. "Then again, maybe it was you that made it fun."

This is the moment. THIS IS THE MOMENT. There's a patch of heat on the back of my neck. It might be sunshine or a pocket of warm wind gusting by. Probably it's the ancestors, whispering for me to take the chance.

"Ha! More like Magic," I say and promptly ruin the moment. "She makes everything fun." The warmth is suddenly replaced by cold. Maybe it's a shadow. Probably it's the great-aunts sighing at their *nu-nu* of a grandniece. At least it's just sunshine and clouds, and not—"Ow!" I slap the back of my neck. "Sorry. A mosquito or a fly just bit me."

"So, what happened exactly with you and the dog?"

I tell him the full story of Magic and make him laugh with my over-the-top indignation at the attention Robby received versus what I got. Which makes me feel super relieved. I was worried talking to him about it would make me seem petty, but his reaction puts *my* reaction in the adorable, understandable, "let's not make a mountain out of a molehill" variety. In other words, the boy validates my feelings and then helps me put them in their proper priority.

And he loves dogs. I could eat him with a spoon, he's so delicious.

"If I'd been there, I would have given you all the props," he says.

Cue another GIANT sign that THIS IS THE MOMENT TO ASK HIM OUT. FOR CRYIN' OUT LOUD, TUNA, ASK THE BOY OUT!!!!!

"You're so nice," I say. "You'd give anyone credit." Argh! What is *wrong* with me?! What kind of story is this if I'm my own antagonist?! Why can't I do something as simple as ask out this guy? It's easy. Simple. Ask the question. It's a binary answer—yes or no. Man. Do I have to make a flowchart for myself? Add in color coding and— "Ow!"

"What happened?"

I rub my ankle. "I think an ant bit me."

"I don't see an anthill." He does a slow turn. "Oh," he says. "But there's a line of them. I wonder if it's our food that's bringing them out."

Of course, there's a line of them. That's probably the doings of Great-Aunt Cecile. That woman wasn't happy unless she was pinching me hard enough to leave red marks on my skin.

"Maybe it's you that's bringing them out," I say. "'Cause you're so sweet." That gets me a smile and a blush. Okay, okay, now is the time to do it. TAKE THE CHANCE! Except my mouth is drier than the set of *Dune* and my brain has suddenly forgotten every word in the English language. I hear a buzz and do a magnificent duck, cover, and dodge.

Tristan does a rapid eye blink. "You okay?"

"Thought I heard a bee. Maybe a wasp. Could've been a hornet." Great-Aunt Cecile would love the hornet. They're almost as mean as her.

He tilts his head to the sky.

My mouth goes—if possible—even drier. This time from the sexy lines of his throat, and the way his position draws my attention to his jawline.

"I don't see anything."

Meanwhile, I've seen enough to combust. I hear another drone of ancestor-sent bees. "Doyouwanttogooutforlikecoffeemaybe?"

His blink rate is so fast in both speed and frequency, he creates his own wind tunnel. "What?"

"Iced coffee. It's so hot. We're all sweating. What do you think about grabbing one after the game? The place by the rec center allows dogs, but I'm sure someplace by here would do the same."

"That's a great idea," he says. "It's wicked hot out."

"So . . . yes?" I need him to say yes. Not just for me, but for any ancestors who're listening and readying locusts or hordes of fire ants to send my way. Yeah, Cecile, I'm metaphorically looking at you.

"Yes," he says. "That would be great."

I glance over his shoulder, spot Fi low-key surveilling the situation, and give her a subtle thumbs-up. We'll scream like sugar-jacked toddlers when Tristan's not around to hear.

She gives me a home girl head nod that vibes her pride.

"Let me check with everyone else," Tristan says.

Wait, what? "What?" Is our date a group decision? Do I have to take my intentions to the council for a vote? I threw him an invite to a date. How did that boomerang into a group thing?

"The iced coffee. It's a good idea. I'm sure they'll be up for it," he says and jogs to the group.

The way he's talking tells me it's not a polite brush-off or a pitying way for him to tell me "no chance." Okay . . . maybe it is, I can't tell. I am, however, deeply confused. Did I not specify it was just me and him? Did I ask him in a way to suggest it was a group thing? If I thought it would help, I'd count out the date math on my fingers. I'm still grappling with how I messed up asking him out when he returns to say that everyone's on board for the iced coffee.

I see Fi over his shoulder, hands raised, miming "What's happening?"

"I'll tell you later," I say when I get to her, "when Tristan can't overhear my weeping, wailing, and gnashing of teeth."

She looks over at him, then at me. "Think it's a sign?"

"No," I say, but that's exactly what I'm worried about.

Magic's harness has a seatbelt attachment. I'm securing her in the backseat when some rando dude who's obviously of the old-folk generation but trying hard to dress like my generation, swoops at Fi.

He greets us with, "Girls," and my Boomer-generation antennae go up.

"You know you're parked in a handicapped spot?" He says it in that weird, passive-aggressive tone old people use. You know the one. They're trying to sound friendly and inclusive, but they're full of judgment and condescension.

Fi and I give each other a slow look.

"Yeah," she says. "We're not illiterate."

He smiles, slow and patronizing. And it's extra patronizing because he's a BIPOC, like us. "Parking in a handicapped spot. You look fine to me."

The nice thing with being built strong and being an athlete is knowing how to be physical without being physical. I step into him, fast enough to make him pedal back, but not so fast that he views it as a confrontation.

"Look." I point at the Jeep's plate. "It's got the decal."

"I know that," he says, as though he's impressed by my ability to form words. "But is it her decal or her parents'?" He smiles again, then leans in like we're in on a secret joke. "Come on, girls. You know you got to live at a higher level when you're a minority. Do better, for all of us."

His audacity is both breathtaking and so offensive, I don't know where to start. I'm sputtering for a response.

Fi, on the other hand, has it in stride. "Honey," she says to him, "it's like your ignorance. Just 'cause people can't see it, don't mean it ain't there."

His smile slides from his face and he does an angry walk away.

Fi doesn't move. She's clutching the side of the Jeep and doing the breathing the therapist taught her, the one for her anxiety. Fi catches my eyes and gives me a small, but shaky smile.

I reach in her bag and take her keys. "I'll drive. You need help into the seat?"

She shakes her head. "I'll go in the back, with Magic."

We're halfway to the café before my anger for Fi ebbs and the question of Tristan rises again. We get to the shop, and I walk inside, but I still can't get the answer I need. Was Tristan brushing me off when he pivoted my invite into a group date?

CHAPTER TWELVE

My Selling Robby to the Circus Is Delayed…for Now

THE COFFEE AFTER FRISBEE GOES WITHOUT A HITCH.

Okay, okay.

I'm a total liar-liar, pants on fire, but can you blame me? It wasn't so much that the event veered into shenanigan territory as much as it skidded into wildly embarrassing, let's-not-ever-talk-about-this-again territory.

First off, as long as Magic stayed on the patio, everything was cool. So, Fi and I pushed together some tables and set up the umbrellas. Everyone arrived and it was playtime.

Tristan bought me a milk with amaretto flavoring on ice and a puppuccino for Magic. Don't worry, it's not coffee, just a cup with a bit of whipped cream in it. And I only let her have five licks of it because, you know, whipped cream.

But the darn cup situation.

Cut to the scene with me, Fi, and Magic at the table, and Tristan (super adorable dude that he is) brings us our drinks. Side note (but important): he'd taken out his contacts and was wearing these black-framed glasses. Which made him look like a super-sexy Clark Kent. (Okay, okay, that's a total digression, but credit where cute credit is deserved, right?)

Everyone's talking and laughing, and Tristan has my heart—and creative juices—all atwitter when he says, "What if the buttons on the sweater were magic? One could take you to the past, one to the future, one to an alternate timeline."

And it takes me a second to realize he's doing a throwback to our conversation about my fictional pink sweater, when he was so generous about me drowning him in my nerdvana over screenplays.

Fi, on the other hand, looks at him as though he's having a stroke, and a very careful, very enunciated "What?" drops from her red lips.

Tristan runs his hand on the back of his head and explains the sweater screenplay to her.

"Right." Fi gives me the kind of stink eye that will terrorize her future children—should she decide she wants any. "The sweater."

I have an entire conversation with her via eye contact. *I know, I should tell him there's no sweater, but look how cute he is. Did you even realize he was so imaginative with ideas and the thinking?* (Okay, that sounds condescending and as though I don't think Tristan is clever. I do. It's just super hard to have telepathic eye conversations with your bestie in front of your crush, y'know?)

Fi stays quiet about the nonexistence said sweater and gives me a subtle thumbs-up when I invite Tristan over to try a collaboration on a pink sweater screenplay, and he agrees. Which has me thinking maybe I overreacted to his turning the coffee date into a group thing, and maybe—despite the philosophical differences between us—there's still a chance.

We're walking out of the shop and I'm juggling Magic's leash, my cup, and a cupcake. At the same time, I'm trying to take the lid off the cup so it can be put with the recycling. Tristan, gem of a man that he is, steps in and takes the cup, allowing me to toss the lid.

What I've neglected to tell him is that there's still milk at the bottom. What I've neglected to do is remember, due to my excitement that we actually seem to be vibing, that (1) there's milk in the bottom (I know, I'm repeating, but this is important) and (2) to take back the cup.

Which means that when he gets really excited because he figures there's a way to introduce space aliens into the screenplay, and gestures with his hand, his action creates a milk tsunami. The white wave crests high and strong, and splooshes on his face.

And. I. Am. Mortified.

Tristan, meanwhile, is pasteurized from the sheet of milk sliding down his face.

I babble an apology.

Fi grabs hold of Magic's leash so I can take the cup from Tristan.

"No worries," he says, then wipes the milk off with the hem of his t-shirt. Which, anyone can tell you, is a super bad idea. Now, he's got a smear of cloudy—soon to be sour—milk on his glasses.

"Can you see?" I ask. "Maybe I should drive you home?"

"It's okay," he says. "I have my contacts in the car. I just took them out because they were giving me a headache."

Bless my heart but put me in the stockades. The boy didn't want to miss our coffee, so he wore glasses. Way to go, Tuna. You're looking for signs to be with him. Meanwhile, you're tossing out neon flares that he should run far, far away.

"I have some wipes in my car," I say. "Maybe they'll help."

"Nah." He puts on the glasses and manages to look both adorable and goofy. "I'll be good."

"About our screenplay—"

"I'll text you when I can come over? We'll figure out a day?"

It's not a brush-off, but it's not exactly a brush-on, either. And I can't fight the feeling that I've royally messed this up. Again. "Uh, yeah, sure."

Fi climbs into the car, wincing as she sits.

I belt Magic in, then climb into the driver's seat and drop my head on the wheel. "That was a catastrophe."

Fi cackles. "Even worse. That was a full-on shenanigan."

"Don't say that! I'm not a shenanigan dater—"

"Your entire family are shenanigans. It'll be fine," says Fi. "The boy is goo-goo ga-ga for you."

"Fi, that's baby talk."

"He's got to drop to your level, doesn't he?"

"Get out of my car and walk home."

"It's my car, Tuna."

Fi, as usual, ends up being right about Tristan. By the time she drops me home, he's texted me with a bunch of dates. I sit for a minute and bask in the glow of romantic victory. Then I turn my sights on warfare. Namely, how to get my parents out of the house so I can have it to myself. Weirdly, it's my brother who lends a hand.

When I get inside, Mom's on her laptop, in the kitchen. The screen's on a travel website.

"Did you finally snap at the lady who licks her fingers and touches the vegetables at the grocery store?" I ask. "Are we being forced to flee the land?"

"The one who snapped is your father," she says. "Or your brother. Depends on who you ask."

"Ohhhhh, drama. Dish!" I grab a glass of cranberry juice and set out a dish of water for Magic.

Her fingers pause their keyboard dance. "It was the dementia test," she says. "Your father forgot where he put his keys. Robby's convinced it's more than a usual mental gap."

"Why was he here, anyway? I thought he had that double shift." I rub the top of Magic's head and glory in the feel of her bones under the fur. "Isn't that why we've got Magic for the night?"

"Are you ready for this?" She peers at me from over her half-rim glasses. "He forgot his ID card here."

My eyes go capital-D Drama wide. "And *he's* accusing Dad of dementia? Oh, *girl*, the fire must have burned bright and hot."

"There were a lot of choice words." She grins, but the smile's resigned, a woman caught in the middle of two fighting bulls. "Most of them were five or six syllables."

I'm glad I missed it. In my family, the men fight with vocabulary. It's like the dance fights in *West Side Story*, but with less grace and drabber clothing.

David and I used to laugh about it. Now there's no one to laugh with me. I'm alone, save the mortal resignation of knowing that I, too, possess the gene. "Sooooo?" I draw out the word into eight syllables and point at the screen.

"Your father's decided we should go away for the weekend."

Oh, snap-a-doodle-do! "You're going away for a couple of days?"

"*We're* going away for a couple of days." She does a circle with her index finger. "Where we go, you go."

"Come on, the doctor cut the umbilical cord almost eighteen years ago. Shouldn't you do the same?"

She glances up at me. "One of these days I want to meet the boy who sends my daughter into such a tizzy."

"Mother. I'm going to go away in a couple of months."

"I'd be happy if you go away right now. I'm trying to get some work done."

"Hardy-har-har. One night," I say. "Give me one night to be by myself."

She stops typing and stares at the screen.

I give her a minute to take in whatever prices she sees on the screen, and another minute to do the math on the trip. After a couple of those minutes, though, she still hasn't moved. I'm starting to wonder if she's the reincarnation of Galatea, except in reverse. Instead of a marble statue come to life, she's the live woman returned to sculpture.

"Mother? Mom? Mama? Mommy?" This is a plot twist beat, I feel it. I just wish I knew whether this was going to be success or defeat for my Tristan goals. Also, this might be a sub-subplot, but I'll figure it out later.

Her eyes flick my way.

And I have to say, it's both creepy as all get out to have a hundred-percent immobile woman with only moving eyes. It's also kind of a cool thing, and I log it for future reference in a screenplay. Maybe the one I'm brainstorming with Tristan about the pink sweater.

"I can talk to your dad about it," she says slowly. "But it would only be for one night."

I don't say anything, too afraid any uttered sound will undo her decision.

"Tuna, you know the rules of the house."

I nod.

"You know the values of your dad and me."

Another nod.

"We're going to trust you to make good decisions."

I nod again.

"We understand each other? No wild parties?"

"You won't tell Robby, will you?"

"And have him invite himself along on the trip?" She slaps her hand over her mouth. "I shouldn't have said that. I'm sorry, honey. I take it back. He's going through a hard time."

"And sharing the wealth while he's at it," I say.

She smiles. "We can all do with some time apart, I think. Even for a day."

I nod. "Leave your travel info, if I need you." I head for the fridge for Magic's food. "But if I get scared late at night, can Fi come over?"

"Fi can come over, even if you're not scared." Her fingers resume their clicking tap dance on the keyboard.

I don't want to hover, so after Magic's done eating, I head for my bedroom. Mom stops me and takes Magic for some cuddle time.

I take to the stairs. Once I'm in my room, I text Tristan and let him know I'll be confirming our date, soon. Okay, so the exact words are: **just waiting on my folks to confirm some stuff, then I'll let you know the day** . . . 'cause we haven't actually called it a date and I don't want to push the word when I'm not sure it is a date. . . . Then again, it's not *not* a date . . . but hopefully is a date.

CHAPTER THIRTEEN

Change of Heart: I'm Selling Robby to the Circus

AS IT TURNS OUT, MY PARENTS' TRUST IS ENORMOUS, or their frustration with Robby is gigantic, because they opt to go for two days. The first night starts off okay. I mean, freedom, right? But around ten o'clock, when I'd be heading for bed and they'd be around, it occurs to me that the house is bigger than I thought. And louder. There are a lot of groans and creaks, and were they always there or am I just imagining it?

I try to keep to my routine, but it's *cccrrreeeeppppppyyy* being alone. I wish Magic was here, but Robby thinks we're all gone for the weekend. At midnight, I decide I'm being silly. So I lock up, then do another few rounds of locking up—don't judge, it's my first time alone in the house. I realize I'm being silly, but it's weird how cavernous the house feels without my folks, and I wonder if this is how Robby feels in his condo without David in it.

It takes a bit to fall asleep, but I do. And it's a great sleep.

Until something on the main stairs wakes me up. A thump? A bump? A poltergeist, long quiet and haunting the house, rising from its concrete grave to exact revenge for its brutal murder? I'm all for upping a story's stakes, and mashing genres, but in the case of *my* story, I don't want to cross rom-com with horror, or have this beat cost me blood or broken bones.

Wait. Edit. The house was a custom build for Mom and Dad. As far as I know, there've been no brutal murders. Well, there was that time Mom had one too many peach coolers and tried to sing "Staying Alive," but I don't think it was bad enough for any of the Bee Gees to exact ghostly revenge. Not on me, anyway. So no *Amityville Horror* for me.

I slide out of bed, action-hero style—if said hero got her foot caught on the bed covers and hit the floor with a thump—then I belly crawl to the corner where I keep my baseball bat.

Only, it's not there.

Belatedly, I remember lending it to Fi a couple of weeks back. Even more belatedly, I realize my phone—which is now across the room on my night table—would have been a better thing to reach for.

Mom was right. I'm really not prepared to be on my own. I'm not willing to shift from Resourceful Main Character to Character Who's Too Inept to Live, so I feel around in the dark, looking for anything I can use as a weapon. My fingers come across my duffel bag from work. I reach in and pull out a travel size can of hair spray. It'll do.

I do another action-hero-worthy belly crawl to the door. The only problem is that whatever's on the other side is coming my way. I can hear its scuttling, creepy footsteps, the wet snuffling and snorting—

What kind of burglar snuffles and snorts? And side note: Why did the house alarm not go off?

I shove myself close to the door and try to see in shades of black and blue. The shadow on the other side gives a low grunt and scratches at the wood.

I jump to my feet, flip on the lights, and wrench open the door. "Robby! You delusional paramecium! What are you doing here?" I bend and scoop up Magic.

Obviously, Robby wasn't expecting anyone in the house. He's at the door of his old bedroom, and the sound of my voice sends him rocketing upward.

"Tuna! What are you doing here? You're supposed to be out of town!" He realizes he's yelling and does a terrified-little-kid swivel. "Are Mom and Dad here?" He whispers the question.

I don't blame him. A rhino with a headache and a hangover (Can rhinos drink? And if so, *should* they?) is less grumpy than Dad if he's awakened before his requisite eight hours of beauty sleep. "No, they're not, but I am. You're lucky I realized it was Magic at my door. I could have hurt you!"

He gives my tank and shorts a once-over. "The hair is frightening, I admit, but I'm not sure about painful."

"Leave my luscious locks out of this."

He points at the hair spray. "Were you trying to fix your hair?"

"No, nimrod. I was going to use it like pepper spray."

"Okay, Swat Team Six, but the nozzle's pointing in your direction."

I look at the trigger.

So does Magic.

We look at each other.

She yips and wriggles closer so she can lather kisses on my cheeks. Then she reenacts her own version of *Megashark* as she burrows around, hoping to find treats in my pajamas.

"Magic gets me," I say. "I owe you no apologies." I can't believe it. My brother breaking into the house is so predictable, it's downright cliché. I'm irritated I didn't think of it. What does that mean for my screenwriting endeavors? I'd hate to graduate SCAD, sell my script for billions, and be the writer behind some big box-office movie, only to have the audience guess every story beat.

"Don't call her that," he says irritably. "It's not her name." He glances over my shoulder and sees the frame with David's pictures. His face tightens and he turns away.

"Please don't tell me you're calling her 'dog,' still."

"No. We change out the names. I don't want her getting confused over a new name when her people come for her."

Ice water slides into my veins. "You found her people?"

"No, not yet. Tuna, why are you here and the parents aren't?"

"Why are *you* here?"

"Oh." He blushes. You can't see it in his skin—it's too brown for that—but it's in the way his jaw flexes and his eyes do a walkabout in his skull.

"I left something in my room."

"From the last ice age?"

"From last week. You still haven't told me why you're here."

"I live here."

Emotion flashes across his face—jealousy? Wistfulness?

Realization flashes my way. He was coming here to spend the night. It hits how lonely he must feel, how isolated the grief leaves him.

"I'm awake now." I grumble the words to hide the pity. "You want a hot chocolate or something?"

"Sure." He takes Magic from my arms. "Come on, Potato."

"What? Of all the transitional names, *Potato* is the one you pick?"

"She likes to cuddle, okay? She's a couch potato."

"You need a better name for her."

We head to the kitchen.

"Tristan," he says.

"That one's taken," I say, taking the milk pitcher from the fridge. "And also a hard 'no' on calling her that. Super weird having a guy"—

I almost call him *my* guy—"and the pup sharing the name. It creates too many conflicting feelings."

"Not the dog, numbnuts. He's the reason you're home alone." His eyes gleam. "You persuaded Mom and Dad to go away for the night so you can have the house to yourself with Tristan."

"I persuaded Mom and Dad to go away so I can practice being alone," I say. "It has nothing to do with Tristan."

He snorts. "So, how did it go?"

"How did what go?" The milk's now heating in the pan, and I can't pull my attention from it. Dad will kill me if I burn the pot. (Okay, he'll kill me if I burn *another* pot.)

"The date with Tristan."

Now it's my turn to blush. "It's not a date, and it hasn't happened yet."

What follows is a long, painful interrogation about how it's not a date. (Like, does my brother—THE SURGEON—not understand vocabulary? "Not a date." How hard is that to understand?)

Just at the point I'm wishing for death to free me from the torment, Robby switches topics, telling me he's going to be around for the not-date because no way Mom and Dad would let me and Tristan have a date/not-date at home, where there are beds and no adult supervision.

That's when I realize: I'm dead. Death has a twisted sense of humor, and I'm about to spend eternity arguing with Robby, and I'll never date/not-date.

"It's not a date," I tell him, irritated. The last of the chocolate's melted into the hot milk. I give the pan a final stir, pour us two mugs, and top them with whipped cream. "We're working on a screenplay."

"Is that what kids are calling it these days?"

"Keep going. I have a pot full of hot milk, and I'm not afraid to throw it. Mom and Dad know Tristan's coming over."

"So, if I text them, they'll be cool with it?" He raises his eyebrows in challenge.

I add whipped cream to the drinks. "Bet you ten dollars."

That makes him pause. "No. Still texting. You're bluffing."

"Double it and make it twenty."

He smirks. "Now I know you're bluffing." He texts.

I sip the hot chocolate. Which is heavenly delicious, even if I say so myself. "By the way, you realize it's past midnight, right? And you've just texted Mom and Dad. And they're going to wake up, see your name, and go panic-blind for a good thirty seconds. Then they're going to read the text, realize it could have waited until morning, and wipe the floor with you."

His smile fades.

"It's been about thirty seconds, hasn't it? No, wait. In five . . . four . . . three . . . two . . . one . . ."

The first bing comes in. Then the second. Third. Fourth. It's rapid fire, so many at once, it sounds like a long drone.

Robby refuses to look at the screen.

"Wuss." I take it from him. "Oh, dang. They're double-teaming you on this. Both of them." I lift my gaze. "You never really wanted to be in the will, did you?"

"Shut up." He wrenches away the phone, reads the text. With every new message, he hunches down, growing smaller and smaller until he looks like he's five years old again and just been given a time-out.

"I saw the text that was relevant to me. Twenty dollars, please."

"Girl, I'm a surgeon."

"What does that mean? You pay in gold bullion or diamonds?" I offer Magic a small lick of whipped cream.

"I have a giant amount of student debt. My money goes to paying my loans, not paying people who shark others over bets."

"This is why people don't like doctors. Also, you're a cheater, cheater, noodle eater."

"I'm not comfortable leaving you alone in the house tonight," he says, "especially if you're rhyming. I should stay."

"I'd like to point out that the people who contributed to my DNA and conceived me—"

"Gross."

"You're gross. No one's asking you to imagine it!" I have to take a second, 'cause now the image of my parents canoodling is forming in my head, and it may turn me off life and love, forever. "Anyway, they're fine with it. But I'm not going to argue, because I'm tired and I have to work tomorrow." *And I know you're here because your condo's an echoing cave of memories with David.* "I'll see you in the morning." I rinse out my cup, take Magic, and leave.

By the time I wake the next morning, he's already had breakfast and is in his sweats, lacing his shoes for work.

"We should talk," I say. "About last night."

He frowns, genuine confusion clouding his face.

"About you coming over."

He knows where I'm going with this, and his expression closes. "It's still my house."

"You know what I'm talking about." I want to go close to him, to hug him and remind him David wouldn't want him locked in this limbo, but I can feel his need for personal space like a neon light flashing above his head. "There are people you can talk to about how you feel."

"I feel like I'll give you two hours with Tristan," he says, "Then I want to come home. There's a game on. I want to drink beer, eat popcorn, and watch it."

Yeah, well, I want to put you in a headlock and drag you to therapy, but life's not about getting everything you want, is it? "Four hours."

"One hour."

Ugh, trust my brother to be the obstacle in my love life.

We negotiate a settlement of sorts. He'll go to work, but he'll do something after his shift for three hours so he won't be looming over Tristan and me like some kind of reincarnated chaperone from the 1800s.

I take the win, head to work, and plan what I'm going to wear for my date/not-date. What do you wear for a not-date? I send the message up to the ancestors and wait for their answers.

At a traffic light, my gaze goes to a billboard with a smiling woman holding a string of pearls. Underneath is the text PEARLS ARE THE NEW BLACK.

"Cool," I mutter, sure it's the great-aunts sending that one. Trust them to recommend something an oyster throws up. "But I can't just wear a string of pearls to a date/not-date." Okay, I could, but that would be wildly traumatic on a bunch of levels, not the least of which is that pearls will make me feel like a senior.

I walk into the rec center and spot Penny.

"Oh, Tuna," she sighs. "You're always such a vision in turquoise."

Houston, we have an answer. I send up a silent thanks to the ancestors for their help and beam another request their way. No more submarine encounters, please.

CHAPTER FOURTEEN

A Sweater, a Dog, and Some Licorice Walk into a Bar

AT FOUR O'CLOCK, TRISTAN SHOWS UP AT MY DOOR with a package of red licorice and a variety pack of handmade dog biscuits. "One's for you, one's for Magic," he says, grinning before adding, "I'll let you guess which is which." As soon as he says it, the smile disappears. "Not that I'm implying that you're a dog." His mouth puckers as though it can't believe the words coming from it. "Or maybe I should."

My eyebrows go up, but he doesn't notice. He's too busy doing a hysterical "that's not what I meant" soliloquy on my doorstep. Let me just say, it's worthy of Shakespeare.

Or Valium.

I'm waiting for him to finish before I make the final call. In the meantime, he's talking faster and faster, and his voice keeps pitching up, and

I'm timing how long it takes before he sounds like a chipmunk on cocaine. (Not that chipmunks would ever take cocaine. They're far too sensible for the likes of that white powder. Donut powder on the other hand . . .)

"I was trying to make a joke, I wasn't trying to insult you," says Tristan. "Dogs are kind and friendly. They're totally loyal and protective. I've never seen a dog that wasn't beautiful. Plus, they're smart and excellent stress reducers. Did you know some hospitals use dogs to sniff out prostate cancer because their sense of smell is so sharp?"

Okay, look, I'm all for the cute guy losing his composure and going full throttle on the babble-o-meter. Especially when he's in shorts and a striped shirt that hugs all the angles and planes of his delightful body, AND he's called me beautiful. But the boy needs a save. So do I, because talking about sniffing out prostate cancer doesn't feel like not-date material.

"You should come inside before the neighbors start to talk." I step aside and open the front door.

He takes off his shoes—trust me, I clock that decision—and moves backward into the air-conditioned house.

"I wasn't sure if Magic was with—" The misery on his face gives way to divine pleasure as she launches herself into his arms.

"Let's try this again." He rises from petting Magic. "Hey, Tuna, thanks for having me over. I wasn't sure if Magic was going to be here, so I brought her some cookies. Here is some licorice for you." He says it with the pained, overenunciation of a kid reading lines for an audition.

"Hello, Tristan, I am pleased with your gifts." I take it from his hands. He bows.

Magic does a Swat Team Six dive-roll for the cookies.

"That's our cue," I tell him. "I have banana bread in the kitchen. Interested?"

For the next while, it's divine decadence. Tristan doesn't have a clue about screenwriting, so I get to play teacher. (Ha! Now, I'm wishing it was our third not-date and I could be saucier and do some role-play. I look excellent in white button-ups and pencil skirts.) I break down one of my favorite movies, *Sleepless in Seattle*, as an example of great screenwriting. We're just about to start act one, page one, scene one, when Robby comes banging into the house.

"Hold on a second." I smile my apology at Tristan, then book it to the front door. "What the what, dude? You said you were going to walk the streets or cure the common cold, or something, and give me some time."

Robby looks at me as though I've taken leave of my senses. "Tuna. My shift ended at four. It's almost eight."

I check my watch, just in case Robby's messing with me, but he's right. Now I know how Cinderella felt. I can't believe we spent four hours together. The bell's tolling midnight (well, symbolically, anyway), and there's Robby, the ultimate pumpkin.

"What have you guys been doing?" Robby's gone all Victorian maiden aunt chaperone suspicious.

"Figuring out the formatting for the screenplay."

His eyes go wide. "For four hours!"

"It's interesting stuff."

"Good grief, Tuna, it's grounds for cruel and unusual punishment." Robby's in the kitchen, with me trailing behind him. "Dude," he says to Tristan. "You okay?"

"Oh, yeah, all good." His gaze shifts between us and a wary light creeps into his eyes. No doubt, he's imagining what new cultural horror we're going to visit on him.

"Tuna says she's had you here for four hours, and all you've talked about is formatting a screenplay."

"Well, there's a lot of technical aspects to it," says Tristan. "And if you want agents and producers to take you seriously, your screenplay's gotta look the part."

Robby puts his hands over my ears and says to Tristan, "If you're being held against your will, blink twice."

He laughs.

Magic barks.

"Did you feed the spud?" Robby asks.

"Of course I did." I huff and puff the words. Mostly because Magic loves food and I love Magic, so the risk isn't that I'll forget to feed her. The risk is that I'll turn her from a spud to a sausage.

"And did you feed your guest?"

My gaze goes to the empty baking dish, then to Tristan. Dang. When was the last time we ate? I can't remember—I've been too busy feasting on Tristan's decadent form. "I have some excellent handmade dog cookies. May I offer you one?"

I phone for pizza and salad from a vegan place that Tristan loves. Robby pays, though Tristan argues for paying for half, if not all. (Doesn't it make you want to coat him in chocolate syrup and eat him up because he's just so flipping considerate?!)

We watch the game while we wait for the delivery. I thought it was something, you know, current, but it's some football—soccer—replay from a hundred years ago.

We settle in to watch Uruguay play Ghana. I'd rather watch women's soccer, but that's motivated by gender bias. Mia Hamm, Marta Vieira da Silva, Sun Wen, Christine Sinclair, Briana Scurry. Okay, okay, I'll stop. I'll also admit there may be a girl-crush thing going because I love watching them play and pretending I could be one of them.

Pizza arrives and I figure we'll take our slices and go to our respective corners. Robby, cave-dwelling brother, will descend to the bowels of our walk-out basement and watch from the theater room. Tristan and I will resume our screenplay writing, which is really just a front for what's really going on, the blossoming of young love.

Oh, gross, what a yuck image! EDIT AND DELETE. I think I'm channeling the great-aunties.

Imagine my pique when Tristan grabs his food and urges us to hurry back, because we're "missing the game." Now imagine my pique turning to feminine rage at my brother when he doesn't even blink at his intrusion into my plans.

Point of fact, that lumbering nimrod TAKES OVER MY DATE! One minute Tristan and I are debating if the pink sweater needs a prologue or origin story, the next minute I'm the lone person on the recliner while ROBBY AND TRISTAN SHARE THE LOVE SEAT, patting each other's shoulders and giving each other high-fives over each score.

My budding romance has just been hijacked and turned into a bromance.

The game ends, but then we spend a bunch of time debating the different ref calls, and it's painfully fun. Like, Old Time Robby fun, where he laughed, made jokes, and rattled off the stats of the players with machine-like efficiency.

He heads to the living room when the hospital calls his cell, and Tristan and I start cleaning up. (Side note: get you a crush that will help you clean a kitchen. Double side note: Tristan's hygiene-germ thing means the kitchen's going to be sanitized within an inch of its life.)

Tristan keeps telling me how lucky I am to have a sibling, which makes me realize I never knew he didn't have siblings.

"I'm not as lucky as you think," I say. "He can be a giant pain in the rear end."

"Everyone can be a pain," says Tristan. "You just have to roll with the pains that aren't that big and defend your lines on the ones that are big . . . What?"

"I always wondered how you can have as many friends as you do," I say. "Now, I get it."

His eyes take on a wary light. "Yeah?"

"Yeah. You're one of the most accepting people I know. It's cool you give space for people to be themselves. But so you know, Robby isn't people. He's annoying."

Tristan laughs. "Maybe, but I would have loved to have had an older sibling. The closest I ever got was Grandpa," he says. "He was always up for pranks or doing nonsense things—stuff a sibling would do." Memory lights his face. Sadness fades it to black. "You're lucky to have Robby. I'd have killed to have a brother like him."

He says it like Robby as a brother is what you find at the end of the rainbow. I want to tell him that he's not wrong, but Robby hasn't been that brother for a long time. I want to tell him that I keep trying to be that sister, but it's like putting my hand into a freezer. My arm is cold and my fingers are numb, and I'm starting to think I should close the door. Only, I'm afraid if I close it, it'll lock, and I'll never get it open again.

"I'll think about it," Robby says into his phone, coming back into the kitchen.

"Think about what?" I ask as he disconnects. I want to make a sarcastic joke about him getting a life, but on the heels of Only Child Tristan, it feels like an insensitive thing to do.

"Oh, one of the doctors at the hospital is doing one of those dinner fundraisers," he says. "Where they host a meal. Instead of bringing flowers or wine, you make a donation to a charity."

"You should go," I say. "It sounds like fun."

He makes a face. "I don't know. I have a lot of reading—"

"Robby, you can read anytime," I say. "Go to this!"

"Tuna, I can't read anytime, and wasting a night hanging out with coworkers—"

"But it's not hanging out," I say. "It's fundraising." I don't know how to talk to him about the other reason I think he's hesitating. Food. David was an amazing chef. To him, food was love and life. It was joy and connection. Every time I ate something he made, it was like eating love. Since his death, I've seen Robby restrict his diet. He's practically cut out butter and sugar and carbs, not because he's trying to eat clean but because he can't bear to delight in food without David beside him.

"What's the charity?" Tristan asks.

"We're raising money for the maternity ward," says Robby. He taps his phone against his leg. "I guess I can go for a minute. Stop by and at least make a donation."

"I'll go with you," I say. "Take me as your plus one." That way, I can make sure he stays. And eats.

"Yeah?"

Robby smiles and I want to run to the toolbox, grab some super glue, and paste the smile onto his face forever. I miss happy Robby. I miss smiling Robby. I miss my brother, Robby.

"I can bring as many people as I like," he says. "Mom and Dad should come. She loves talking anatomy, and there's a lecture on Ignaz Semmelweis. Dad will love it."

"Your dad's a doctor, too?" asks Tristan.

"No," I say. "Financial advisor, but he's totally into medical stuff. That's what got Robby's interest in being a doctor."

Tristan's eyes go unfocused, and I realize for a kid from a real estate background and one who's hyperaware of germs, my family would be nerd-vana for him.

"Man, a lecture on Ignaz Semmelweis," says Tristan. "Tuna, we'll have to meet up after. Promise you'll tell me everything."

I have a moment of silent, laughing surprise. Thanks to Robby, I'm getting another almost-date with Tristan. Who saw that plot twist coming?

"You know about Ignaz Semmelweis?" Robby asks him.

"Are you kidding? The guy pioneered handwashing as a way to reduce deaths in the maternity wards. No wonder he's the lecture topic. He was a hero before his time," says Tristan. "No one in his day thought handwashing could do anything. They made fun of him."

And he's genuinely upset that people mocked this long-dead doctor, that no one gave him space for his thoughts or ideas. Honestly, how can I not fall for a guy with that level of emotional intelligence?

"You and your folks want to come along?" Robby offers Tristan. "There are a few doctors in the market for new homes. You guys are in real estate, right? It might be good networking."

The guys exchange the information so Tristan can tell his folks. I watch from the sidelines, unsure of how I feel. It's trademark for my family to turn everyone into family, so Tristan and his folks meeting up with my folks before we've even dated might be odd, but it's not Rashad family odd.

But I'm worried. I'm worried about Robby. I wanted him to make friends, actual friends. I didn't want him borrowing mine. But all of this feels possessive and makes me worry I'm being a bad little sister to a grief-stricken brother. So I do what I've been doing for the past year and a half. I push down my feelings and pretend everything's okay.

"Was it really that bad?" Mom asks sympathetically the next day when they return. "And it's good your brother's getting out and meeting people."

I treat her to a full-on rage performance.

"He's not getting out! He's horning in and kidnapping my person."
I throw myself across her bed in full Victorian heroine mode, overwrought
by the obstacles. "It's upsetting to my delicate constitution."

"Delicate constitution? Is that the new Top Forty boy band?"

"Don't fret me, Mother. Honestly, if you were any kind of mother,
you'd fetch me tisane instead of vexing me. Maybe some smelling salts for
my nerves."

"What in the world is tisane?"

"I have no idea, but they always give it to overwrought Victorian ladies."

"Tuna Fish, underwrought yourself and find a way through this."

"That's easy for you to say. Your not-date didn't end up getting swept
off his feet by your obnoxious and obtuse brother. And your not-date
didn't have a better time with your sibling, who has the annoying habit of
being really fun when he wants to be. Tristan's one bro moment away from
adopting Robby as his big brother."

"That's my fault," says Mom. "Robby can't help how charming he is.
Both of you kids inherited the ability to light up a room from me. Your
father, bless his heart, has to work at it. You'll figure it out."

I peer at her, vaguely certain she's mocking me, but her face is full
of innocence.

I sit up. "How am I supposed to do that?"

"Light up a room? Oh, honey, you just throw your hair back—"

"*Mother. Please.* Have some respect for my delicate nerves at this time.
Did you know Robby and Tristan made plans to head to some amateur
match the week after? And FYI, I wasn't invited!" I fling myself back on
the bed.

"My brother's scored a second date with my crush, and I haven't even
had a first real date yet."

"But he won't get to second base," Mom says mildly, then frowns.
"What is second base these days? Anyway, no one's dating your Tristan.

We're all going to the fundraising event—don't you think that's brownie points with his parents? Getting them networking opportunities?"

"*Mooooottttttthhhhheeerrrr.*"

"Little Fish, your brother is struggling. We all know that. He needs some time and space."

Great, except I'm on a ticking clock with Tristan. If I can't get a date with him before college starts, it's never going to happen. I'm going to be at SCAD, and let's be honest, I'm too much of a delight to stay single on the campus for long. (Okay, okay, that conviction may have less to do with how lively a girlfriend I can be, and more to do with knowing Tristan will be snapped up by some girl. He's kind, funny, and generous in spirit. They'll be fighting over him like he's the last bottle of wine in the liquor store— er, not that I ever engage in underage drinking.)

"I think it's nice that Tristan and Robby get along," Mom says, her face soft. "I can't remember the last time he's hung out with someone that's not one of us."

"Yes, but why does it have to be *my* someone?"

Mom drops a kiss on my forehead. "Robby had to learn how to share when you came along. Now, it's your turn."

"Have you lost your mind? Robby's fifteen years older than me. We didn't share anything."

"What about me and your dad? You shared us."

"I should have sold him to the circus when I had the chance."

Mom laughs. "It's not like he's a piece of furniture you can list." She splays her hand. "Free to a good home, one gently used Robby."

The humor goes out of her face, and I know she's thinking the same thing I am. Life has been a hard taskmaster for Robby.

I know I should be understanding, and I know I should be empathetic, but I can't help the rising sense that Robby's holding us hostage with his grief. After I give Mom a kiss for listening, I head back to my room.

But I can't shake the thought that niggles at my brain and grows with every step.

Is Robby doing this consciously or unconsciously? Mom's right. Since David died, all Robby's done is hang out with us. There's a measure of comfort with seeing Mom and Dad together. They're like the sky and ground, always there, a forever touchstone.

But me? I'm different. I haven't really dated anyone in the past year. I had a boyfriend when David died. But the grief of losing my brother from another mother proved too much emotional weight for him to bear, and we broke up. (By which I mean, I was sobbing on the porch on the day David died, while he told me that having to deal with my sadness was "too much emotionally," especially with us going into grade twelve, but "we could still be friends." For the record, we are not still friends. When I'm rich and famous, I'll make a slimy, wimpy character and name him "Scott McCormick" after my ex-boyfriend.) All of this means I've always been free to hang out with Robby. But now there's Tristan and my chance to ask him out, last night.

But then Robby showed up, and the chance was ruined. Is Robby trying to keep me single so he'll always have someone to hang with, another body in the room so he can deceive himself into believing he's neither alone nor lonely?

I try to push the thought from my mind, but it's anchored in place. Did Robby befriend Tristan to sabotage my chance at love?

CHAPTER FIFTEEN

Run, Robby, Run!

"YOU'RE A LUNATIC," SAYS FI.

"Don't be insensitive and ableist," I tell her. "That's a terrible word to use."

"Don't be delusional," she says, wincing and stretching out on my bed. "Is that better word usage? Perhaps I should try for an entire sentence, like, *Come back from your break with reality. Move toward the light of reason and common sense.*"

"That's two sentences. And anyway, I'm not doing anything that breaks with reality."

Fi's eyes go funhouse wide. "Are you kidding? You're in full shenanigan territory." She points at my laptop. "You're setting up profiles for your brother on Eros and Agape's dating site. Without his permission. There are a lot of words to describe that, and baby girl, none of them are good out-loud words."

"It's not without his permission," I say. "It's without his knowledge."

"What's the difference?"

"He can't stop me if he doesn't know what I'm doing."

She's giving me that look, that insufferable "I know better than you and this will end badly" look, which is obnoxious. Mostly because that look is correct 99.9% of the time. But still, STILL, there's a 0.1% chance that I can FINALLY BE RIGHT THIS TIME. Think of how sweet and delicious that victory will taste. Especially as I watch Robby ride off into the sunset with a friend that's not me. Or Tristan.

Fi snaps her fingers in front of my face.

I slap away her hand.

"Do you have any idea how badly it's going to go, not just for Robby, but for those guys you're catfishing?"

"I am not catfishing." Finally, at least on this term, I have the upper hand. Okay, okay, I have the certainty of a dictionary definition. "Catfishing is about creating a fake internet persona so you can steal their money or identity. I'm not doing that."

"No," Fi says soberly. "You're stealing their hearts and their hope for a future."

"No, I'm not. You can set your profile to either partner love or friendship love. See? I put Robby as looking for friends." I swing the computer around so she can see the screen. "Double-see? It's Robby's picture, and not even all of it. Just the lower half of his face. You can't even tell that it's him."

"He does have an excellent jawline and smile," she concedes.

"I'm writing up the profile. It's in my point of view, as his sister. I'm not pretending to be him. Look at it. It's painfully obvious that he's not part of it, and that anyone who signs on will know he has no idea what's happening."

"Rewind and run that back," says Fi. "Slower, so your Swiss-cheese brain can hear what you said. What kind of guy would go for such a weird romantic or friendship setup?" She takes the laptop and reads. "'Gently used brother is at end of sibling lease. Fully vaccinated, comes with high-end education, culinary skills, and a love of animals. One sister who needs him to get a life and get out of hers. Take him for dinner, or a walk. Just take him. Priced to move. All reasonable offers considered.'" Her mouth quirks.

"See? It's good."

"No, it's walking the line with selling human beings. There's got to be a better way."

"You're right." I hate to admit it. "The jab about weird romantic setup hit hard."

"Good." She pushes the laptop back at me.

I erase the bio and start typing.

"Are you deleting?"

"Editing."

Her eyes do a hard roll. She takes the laptop back and reads my edits. "'Remember *Sleepless in Seattle*? This is my brother "Sam," and I'm "Jonah." He needs to find friends again. Help me out with some casual, platonic meet-cutes.'" There's a giant pause. "I don't know what to say."

"Because they're equally good, right? I can't decide, either. Maybe I'll share the bios around on two profiles and see which one gets more traction."

She opens her mouth, and judging by the look on her face, I'm going to get Full Fi, All Throttle, No Brakes.

Miraculously—or not, 'cause, you know, ancestors looking out for me—there's a knock at my door. Even more miraculously, Tristan walks in. Thank you, ancestors.

"Am I interrupting?" He smiles at each of us.

"Yes, you're interrupting her general lack of common sense," says Fi. "Come in and continue."

"What's going on?" His smile turns unsure.

I heave an inward sigh. At some point in time, I really hope Tristan stops looking at me with the wary caution of a guy trying to figure out if the grenade he's holding is live or a dud.

Not that I'm a dud. I'm just saying, I'm not about to blow up in his face. Even though I did that one time. Okay, you know what? Forget it. I can live with him being warily cautious of me. It'll add mystery and intrigue to our relationship.

"What are you doing here?" I ask.

"Robby said to meet him here. We're going to grab some food, then head to the game with our dads," says Tristan.

Fi looks confused.

"The fundraiser," I remind her. "It's a whole family bromance thing now. Tristan's dad's buying my dad and Robby dinner and the game by way of thanks for hooking him and his wife up with potential clients."

"You're not going to the game?"

I make a face. "I was invited, but it's a poker tournament. I'm good."

Tristan grins. "My mom's taking Tuna and her mom to a monster truck rally later in the summer."

Fi's mouth falls open and she shoots me a side-eye.

"Do you think your mom would mind if Fi came along?" I ask. "We'll pay for her ticket."

"I can pay for my ticket," says Fi.

"Mom will pay for your ticket," says Tristan. "But I never saw you as a monster truck fan."

"Are you kidding?" says Fi. "Horsepower and rumbling engines, all of it coupled with destruction and fire? I'm so there."

I wave Tristan into the room.

He glances at the collage of David and Robby as he takes a spot on the bed.

"What are we talking about?" he asks.

"*Sleepless in Seattle* and its real-life applications," I say.

"The movie with Tom Hanks and Meg Ryan?" He frowns adorably.

I'm not kidding. It's illegally adorable how cute that frown is. "You know the movie?"

"You mentioned it when we were first talking about the pink sweater," he says.

He remembered! I can't believe he remembered—I barely remember! Ladies and gentlemen and nonbinary persons, I give you the future Mr. Altuna Kashmir Rashad.

"What's the real-life application?" he asks. "Can there be one?"

"In the movie, Jonah tries to get his widowed-dad to meet a woman who Jonah thinks will be good for him," I say.

Tristan leans against a pillow. "You trying to set up a meeting? For who?"

"Shouldn't that be 'For whom'?" Fi asks.

Bless her heart and put the therapist on speed dial. The poor girl's spent so much time with the family, she's been indoctrinated into arguing about vocabulary and grammar.

"My brother is whom I'm talking about," I say. "He needs to find friends."

"Because of David?" says Tristan.

That stops both Fi and me in our metaphorical tracks. We stare at him as though he's grown another head. He stares back as though we're both live grenades.

"David." Tristan finds his voice. "His husband. Robby told me about him."

"He did?" says Fi.

"Yeah, at the fundraiser. It was undetected heart valve disease. The valve burst."

I swallow my tears. Trust David to die from something heart related. Maybe it was a burst valve. Maybe it was that David loved so hard and completely that his heart lived two hundred years in the span of thirty-one.

The frown's back on Tristan's face. "Should he not have said anything?"

"No," I say slowly. "I mean, yes, he should have told you what he wanted to tell you. We're just surprised. Robby doesn't talk about David. Like, at all." There's a small, sharp part of me that's jealous because Robby will talk to Tristan about David, but not to me. I tuck away the envy and remind it that we need all the help we can get for Robby. It quietens but doesn't go silent.

"He must feel really comfortable with you," says Fi.

A bloom of pleasure brings a slow smile to Tristan's face. The younger sibling being the confidant for the older one.

I know that feeling, and I gotta say, it's a cool feeling. "I can see that," I say. "You have a way about you."

The smile turns to an embarrassed but pleased grin.

"Anyway," I say, trying to keep my brain focused on the matters at hand, and not how I'd like to take Tristan in hand and kiss him breathless, both because he's helping my brother and because, well, Tristan. "I'd like to find a way to get Robby back in touch with old friends, maybe meet some new ones. A platonic reimagining of *Sleepless in Seattle*."

"That's sweet of you," says Tristan.

Pleasure rises inside me, delicious as condensed milk and just as rich.

"Tristan?" Robby's voice sounds from downstairs. "You here, buddy? Tuna! The potato wedge is home!"

Ack! Robby still refuses to call Magic, "Magic," and double ack on calling this her home. I mean, it is. But wondering if it's her "forever home" or just a vacation getaway keeps me up at night. Where, in the name of the ancestors, are her family?!

"That's my cue," says Tristan. He moves to the stairs, then turns back. "If you want any help with this, I'm here. Robby's a good guy. I like hanging out with him. He deserves to be happy."

Oh, Tristan, if only you knew how much I adore you. If only you knew how every time you open your mouth, I crush on you. Even if you think I'm off the grid because I listen to the ancestors.

"It's a sign," I say, before Fi can hit me with irrelevant, trivial things like logic and reason. "He wants to help Robby, and in helping Robby—"

"You get a chance for a healthy helping of Tristan," Fi says drily.

"He is kind of a go-back-for-seconds kind of guy."

Mom appears in the doorway with a bowl of popcorn. "The fuzz is gone. Anyone for popcorn, candy, and some frothy film that will not add to our intellect, but, in fact, take away from it?"

"I'm in," I say. "What's on the menu?"

"Some B-horror. Maybe even D or F," she says. "I like Tristan. Good pick, Little Fish. I wish you'd picked him instead of that grubby Scott McCormick."

"Right?" I say.

"Did you know Robby's been talking to him about David?" asks Fi.

Mom's body goes slack; so much so, I think she's going to drop the popcorn. "Are you serious?" She takes a handful of the salty snack and chews. "Tuna, Tristan's delightful, but this adds to my opinion of him." She moves to the stairs, muttering to herself.

Fi punches my arm. "Pay attention to *all* the signs," she says. "Robby's talking to Tristan. This is good. It's monumental. Don't blow whatever inroads your brother's making by making the profile live."

"Fine," I say. I may be obtuse sometimes, but I know enough to throttle back from shenanigan territory. "I'll let Tristan work his charm."

"Girls! Come on!" Mom yells from the bottom of the stairs. "Before Magic takes the good spot on the couch!"

"As if Magic would take the good spot on the couch," Fi says and climbs off the bed. "Anywhere she is, *is* the good spot on the couch."

I linger in the room for a second, viewing the profile, putting back the original description, and pondering what Fi's said. I think the app is a good idea. Anything that helps Robby (okay, okay, and gets me back in the running as Tristan's #1 Rashad) is a good idea, but I can't argue Fi's track record with knowing when I'm about to step wrong. I shut down the browser, close the computer, and run to meet up with the girls.

"Thanks for inviting me for the run," says Robby as he does some heel stretches. "But I'm surprised you asked."

"Because . . . ?"

"You hate running."

"Clarification," I say. "I hate running outside. There are only so many times you can swallow bugs before you start questioning your life choices."

He laughs and moves into quad lunges.

I put my elbow behind my head, ease into a stretch, and scan the sky-line of palm trees. The mountains rise in the background, and I wonder if Robby even remembers to look at them.

"Are you searching for someone?"

"The running group," I say, opting for a super casual vibe. Which, because it's me, probably has all the subtlety of shattering glass. "Didn't I tell you? We're running with a group."

His blue eyes narrow. "No, you didn't. Why are we running with people?"

"Because running with butterflies will be pointless." His scowl prompts me to keep going. "Come on, Robby. I'm going to be in college soon. You need to have buddies to hang with."

"You're ending your sentence on a preposition."

"Maybe, but consider my *proposition-position*." My clever wordplay nets me zero cred, but I like it, and shove it in my mental drawer for future, screenwriting use. Maybe the main character in my screenplay will say it. Maybe I'll just say it to Tristan the next time I see him, and he'll kiss me speechless for my wild and wonderful vocabulary. And I'll kiss him back for suggesting the running group as a way to get Robby out and about.

For the record, I didn't ask Tristan to partner with me on the whole get-Robby-a-life thing. It's too muddying the waters between Tristan and me, because I'm not sure where we stand as friends or more. Also, between the fundraiser, the poker tournament, and the football game, I feel like there's a conflict of interest (and loyalty). Aaaannnnnd, I'm not exactly sure where I stand—moral compass-wise—on any of this. So the fewer people helping, the better. However, Tristan texted the idea, and a good idea is a good idea. "Fi's going away for college, so am I. You need human interaction."

"You seem to forget that I work at a hospital."

"As a surgeon. Your entire shift is bossing people around or pulling them from death's door. You need to have relationships where you don't have the power of life and death over someone."

"You make me sound like a god."

He means to sound humble, but I see the braggadocio way his shoulders pull back.

"Spoken like a narcissist," I say. "Rein it in, faux demigod. I thought Tristan would have mentioned it when you guys were at the game over the weekend." I *don't* add how wildly bitter I am that Dad and Robby invited Tristan and his dad to the soccer game on a day I had to work.

"The guys were at the game," says Robby. "Tristan and I didn't get a chance to talk."

"Of course guys were at the game," I say irritably. "It'd be weird if only cats showed up." Okay, weird, but how wildly cool?

"Not guys, *the guys*. You know. Nicholas, Tomas, and Cody."

Hot dang. *Hot dang.* "The guys? Your guys? As in your friends from med school?"

"Yeah." Now it's his turn to sound irritable. "What's the big deal?"

I affect nonchalance because now isn't the time to point out Robby let all his friendships drop after David died. "Nothing. You haven't hung with them in a while."

He shrugs, like it's no big deal. "Tristan and I were talking about soccer, and it reminded me I hadn't seen the guys in a while. So I invited them. It's no big deal."

I bend into a stretch and hide the tears, certain Tristan had an agenda for their talk. Does Tristan even understand what a wildly amazing, life-saving thing he did for my brother? I doubt it. I bet he did it just because he's Tristan, and he was just being himself. I send up a silent request for the ancestors to smooth his paths wherever he may go. Friendship or not, dating or not, I will be forever grateful for Tristan doing this, not just for Robby, who needs his friends, but for Nicholas, Tomas, and Cody, who need Robby. "How are they?"

He shrugs, but I see the pleasure that lights his face. "Good. We're going to do the Trivial Pursuit Game Night at the pub next week." The smile dims. "Tuna, I don't want to run with anyone," he whines like an overtired toddler. "Why can't it just be us?"

I bite back my frustration and refrain from pointing out that had I known he was getting his life back in order, I wouldn't have arranged this. "I get Mom and Dad are all about coddling and holding your hand, and letting you decide your fate, but I'm not your mommy or daddy. Stop whining about the run. This is going to be fun!"

"Thank goodness you're not my parent," he says. "You would have fed me uncut grapes."

My self-righteous I'm-doing-this-for-your-own-good rant momentarily falters with his unexpected sentence. "What about uncut grapes?"

"They're a choking hazard. Geez, Tuna, how do you not know this? You work with children."

"As a swim coach, nimbus. I don't know if you know this, but we tend to frown on people bringing food into pools. You're stuck in a rut, Robby, and you need to make some big changes before you are so immobile that people start mistaking you for a statue."

Robby stares off into the distance while the wind finger-combs his hair.

"Admit it," I say softly. "You had fun the last few weeks, right? The fundraiser, the poker tournament, the game. There was laughing and good food and no serious discussions about anything."

"Yeah." He drags out the word but smiles. "It was good."

"Now, think of continuing to do that with people who don't share your DNA. Wouldn't it be nice to do more than work and sleep? Wouldn't it be nice for you to eat for more than sustenance, but pleasure as well? You remember condiments, don't you?" I put my hand on his shoulder. "Ketchup would love to catsup with you. Think of how much mustard would relish seeing you."

His lips quirk. "That is painfully bad."

"Bad? Do you mayonnaise good?"

He nods as a group of people starts gathering.

"That's the meeting point," I tell him. "Come on, let's go."

"I've had a couple of interesting job offers," he says. "I wasn't really considering them, but—"

"Consider them," I say, acting nonchalant at this breaking revelation. "You should do something adventurous and new. Step out of your comfort zone."

He nods and says, "I'll think about it."

Little do I realize he'll think about it through the run, and when his answer comes back, I'm going to regret everything I told him about breaking out of his comfort zone and doing anything new.

"I say this with all the love in my heart, but have you lost your mind? Are you in some kind of hypoglycemic shock?" We're back after the run. I thought the afternoon would involve carbs and sweets. Instead, I'm staring at my brother, feeling like Alice being pulled down the rabbit hole. My brain's whirring, trying to incorporate where this would fit into a screenplay, but it's just so horrible and shocking—no one would ever believe this twist.

"No," says Robby. "I'm listening to what you said and taking your advice."

"No, you're not. I told you get *a* life. I didn't tell you to get *my* life." I wave at some of the people in the running group as they go by, give them a big smile so they don't know I'm plotting fratricide.

"It's not your life," he says, immeasurably calm, which just makes me want to fratricide him again. Fratricide him until he's dead.

(Okay, I realize fratricide is the murder of a sibling and it's redundant to talk about fratriciding until he's dead, but the man is pulling a weird adaptation of "Person or Persons Unknown" on me, and I can't let him. Side note: if you haven't seen that episode of the *Twilight Zone*, for real, watch it.)

Robby takes our duffel bags from the backseat.

I pull out my towel and wipe the sweat off my face and neck. I'd really like to drain the sweat pool that's collecting under my bra, but there are too many people around to be able to do it discreetly.

"I'm not off my rocker," he says.

"You're off your rocker, off the rails, you've lost the hotel reservation."

He blinks, trying to sort the hotel reference.

I meet his gaze, as though it's painfully obvious what I meant. Meanwhile, I don't have a clue. I've just run five miles, and I'm coming off an emotional high—not just because of the run, but because I saw a few people exchange numbers with Robby—only to be pitched off the cliff by my brother's decision.

"It makes sense, Little Fish. You can go to school, I'll work at the hospital, and we can rent an apartment."

"Georgia was supposed to be my thing." I can hear the desperation in my voice and I'm trying to think of which *Twilight Zone* alternate world I've fallen into that makes my brother think his "idea" is brilliant.

"The Southwest Memorial Hospital offered me a spot," he says. "I didn't take it—"

"Suddenly, a hospital in Savannah offers you this position?"

"No, it was a few months after—" The skin on his face tightens as he realizes he's said too much.

"After David died," I say quietly.

"The timing wasn't right," says Robby. "But they said if I ever wanted a change of pace, I should look them up. They'd be happy to have me."

Of course they would. Not only is my brother a brilliant surgeon, he's got the kind of bedside manner people only think exists in Hallmark movies. Plus, let's face it, he's also got a double-diversity and the kind of McDreamy aesthetic that would make him an excellent poster boy for all their fundraising endeavors.

"It's a good idea," says Robby. "You won't be alone in a new state, or alone in the apartment. Mom will love that."

Of course she will. I made the mistake of telling her how I felt when they were gone, when the house was quiet but creaking, and I thought a burglar was breaking in. I could almost see her wishing she could cover me in bubble wrap and put me behind an electric fence.

"Dad will love it," he says. "Because I'll split the rent, utilities, and groceries."

"Do not tell Dad. Do *not* tell Dad! I've seen him drink from a juice box two years past its expiry date because he wasn't going to let the money he spent go to waste." Seventy-five cents. The man rolled the dice on his health for seventy-five cents.

A flying bug lands on Robby's shoulder, and his face lights with delight. "See? Even the ancestors approve."

It's an omission of the tongue. David's the one who sends butterflies, but now's not the time to confront Robby. "Firstly, just because a butterfly lands on you doesn't mean it's been sent by the ancestors. Second, that's a moth. Third, it's wildly convenient that you're suddenly back on board with signs just because it suits you. Listening to the ancestors isn't something you do when it's convenient. You do it always. And fourth, that's a moth."

"It's a butterfly!"

"It's sitting on your shoulder, so you can't even get a proper sense of it, and it's a moth."

The insect takes to the sky and Robby follows its trajectory. "That was a butterfly. The ancestors approve of me moving to Georgia."

"It was a moth, and it's a sign the ancestors approve of your openness to moving, but not the location."

"How do you know?"

"Because I know how to read their signs and wonders."

He scowls my way. "I find it convenient that they only talk to you."

"That's because I never stopped listening."

"No, you don't. This isn't about omens. It's about you not supporting me."

That stings.

"What's your problem, anyway?" Robby asks. "We had fun over the weekend. You don't want to live with me?"

The hurt on his face is so explicit and vivid, I can almost hear the cracking and tinkling as his heart shatters.

"That's not it, bro." I take hold of his arm. "I'm worried about you."

"Me? Why?"

"Robby, you're over all the time. More than I think is healthy."

"Should the girl I caught eating condensed milk straight from the can be the one who lectures me about healthy choices?"

I hear Fi's voice in my head, along with Dad's and Mom's, and along with my doubts, it's a barbershop quartet, doo-wopping about restraint. But Robby's five seconds away from going down a path, and I'm terrified it's a one-way street that dead ends. I miss my brother—the one who used to laugh and have a life. It's like he crawled into the crematorium with David, and I'm left with two deaths, not one.

"I think you hang out with us because it's safe," I tell him. "But safe isn't always good. Now you want to move to Georgia with me. Don't you see? It's not about a new change or getting out of a rut. It's just the same life you're living here, except it's a lighter version. Home Sweet Home, version two-point-oh."

"This life? The one where my sister is horrified by the thought of being part of my life?"

"What! Robby, no, you know that's not what I meant!"

"'You hang around the house too much. You can't move to the same state as me.'" He says it with that super annoying, high-pitched, whiny voice he uses when he's imitating me. To add extra insult, he adds a Valley Girl spin on the words, complete with hair toss and hip thrust.

"I didn't say that, and for sure I didn't say that in that voice. Or that hair toss." I point to my head, where the hairstyle's two Dutch braids wrapped in a bun. "See? I can't even toss my hair."

"If I'm such a burden to be around, why did you invite me for the run? Oh, yeah." He slaps his forehead. "I forgot. You're trying to pass me off on new people."

"That's not true!" I'm starting to lose control of my temper, especially when he stalks away and heads down the street. "But you do need new people in your life. You can't keep borrowing my people."

He dead stops. "My god. This is about Tristan. You're jealous because Dad and I hung out with him a couple of times."

"It's not about jealousy." Okay, fair point, it might be a little about jealousy, but now's not the time to give him fight points. "It's about getting your own friends."

"For the record, *your honor*, you're always invited. You just choose not to come along. Tristan's an only child. I'm nice to him because he's a nice guy, and oh, yeah, my sister's got a wicked crush on him. I'm doing what I can for your cause, Tuna. I'd think you'd be grateful for it!"

"Having you around makes it harder to ask out Tristan—"

"No, it doesn't. You just say, *Tristan do you want to go out with me?* It's not that hard."

"Of course it's hard! It's dating!"

"Not the way you do it," he says. "You're looking for the perfect time, the perfect sign, and we both know there's no such thing. If you're waiting for the music montage, or the rain to pour on the downtown streets, you'll be waiting your whole life."

"I'm not looking for a Hollywood scene. Relationships have arcs and beats, just like stories—"

He does a hard eye-roll. "Did it ever occur to you—" he swings back to glare at me "—that what happened last year has made me appreciate my family more? That the reason I'm around all the time is because I understand how precious life is and that our time together can end just like that!" He snaps his fingers.

I speed up to get around him. "I know that's part of it, but it's not all of it, and screaming at me isn't going to change my worry over you."

"Whatever." He bumps me out of the way. His gaze goes over my shoulder and his face blanches. "Oh my god, Tuna. It's the potato cake."

"What?" I swing around, looking for Mom or Dad, and Magic on the leash.

"No, on the lamppost."

For a second, I think he's having some kind of aphasic episode, because it doesn't make sense. Then I see the lamppost, the paper that's taped to it, the words glaring down at me, MISSING! LOST DOG! MUCH LOVED! And the sweet, sweet face of Magic underneath.

I thought fighting with Robby was the worst thing that was going to happen to me today, but it looks like we've just entered the Dark Night of the Soul story beat.

CHAPTER SIXTEEN

Will the Shenanigans Never End?

ROBBY LOOKS LIKE HE'S FIGHTING NOT TO THROW UP.

Me too.

"That's her face, isn't it?"

I hear the unshed tears in his voice and feel them in my throat. "Yeah, I think so." It comes out thick and husky.

We move to the poster in slow motion and all the memories of Magic are crashing into my brain, overloading my system. I'm angry at these people. Why didn't they look harder for her? Why didn't they scour the heavens and the earth, rip open the underworld, and wage war to bring her back? I've only known her for a few weeks, and I would do all that and more to protect and keep her safe.

"I should call," he says.

I nod, because what else am I going to do? "Put it on speakerphone."

He takes out his cell and his hands are shaking. It takes him a couple of tries to get the number keyed in. Then it's ringing, ringing, ringing.

I hope they never pick up. I pray to the ancestors to let an automated voice answer and say the phone number's no longer in service.

"Hello?" A woman's voice. She's got a deep, rich voice, and a Nigerian accent that makes me think of glorious sunsets and women whose strength is shown in their quiet words.

I vibe a blistering, foul-mouthed message to the ancestors for not giving me what I need.

"I'm looking for Ali," says Robby.

"I am Ali," she says.

I want to yell and scream at her, to demand she defend herself against the negligence she showed Magic, but all my strength's being used in keeping my tears at bay.

"I think—my sister and I think we found your dog," says Robby, and he's trying not to cry.

"That is very kind of you to call," she says, "but you are wrong. You do not have my dog."

He blinks.

I do too. Twice.

"Ma'am? I'm certain—"

In the background, we hear a bark. Ali ignores us to say something to the dog. "*Wannan yarinyar nan mai dadi ce? Zan kasance a cikin minti daya.*" The love in her voice washes over me. She returns to our conversation, and that love infuses her words. "As you can hear, our daughter has returned."

"Oh, yes." Relief floods Robby's voice.

It makes me light-headed. In a minute, I'll deal with the rising guilt that Magic still hasn't found her people, and what it says about me as a human being, after that.

"Our dogs, eh?" she says. "When I arrived in America, I thought, so silly, this American love of animals. I tell you, I would turn over the grave for her."

Robby swallows. "Yes, I understand."

"Would you do me a favor and take down the poster? I thought I got them all."

"Sure, no problem."

I'm already ripping it off the post.

"Listen—do you, do you remember where you got your dog?" The pain's back in Robby's voice. A thin sheen of sweat covers his face. "I ask because we found one that looks just like yours. Maybe they came from the same place."

"I cannot answer that for you," she says. "I got her from my coworker last year. My colleague moved to France. I do not know how to reach her."

"Okay, thanks, I appreciate it." Robby ends the call.

We stumble to a bench and sit.

I bend over, put my head between my knees, and catch my breath. "I'm a horrible person. When she said Magic wasn't hers, I was so happy." I tell my secret to the pavement. "I don't want to give her up." I lift my head. "Somewhere out there is a family who's probably going through the worst moments of their lives because they can't find their dog. Meanwhile, I'm celebrating because I get her for one more day."

"It's complicated," says Robby. "You find someone who needs help and you think, no big deal. Then you fall in love, and—" he swallows "—and the love grows, even though you know you may have to give them back." His eyes mist but he forces the tears away. Robby's fingers clench into fists.

I want to cry, with relief for having Magic one more day, with guilt because she's not ours and the search must continue, and for David. For all we had with him, for all we lost. But Robby won't give space for his grief, and it makes me feel like I have to contain mine. I shove down all of the feelings, stretch the pain into my fingers and toes, and say, "Let's go."

Robby may be rusty when it comes to listening to the ancestors, but I'm not. As soon as I get home, I text Tristan and ask if he wants to go for coffee. Okay, so I may have gotten back, showered, applied a hydrating mask on my hair, exfoliated the heck out of my pores, and done a host of other things, including applying perfume and dressing up, before I sent the text. But you know, dress for the role you want, not the role you got. And visualize your dreams. And call them into reality.

However you name it, it works, because Tristan's totally up for it. We pick a time and I volunteer to pick him up. Our usual place is closed so the owners can go on vacation, so we opt for a chain coffee store. I download the app.

I heard Tristan say once that he loves espresso, so I take the chance. While I'm in his driveway, I place an order for one espresso for him and a mint iced capp for me. This way, it'll be ready and waiting for us. I'm hoping he'll see the move as "Tuna takes initiative," or maybe "Tuna guessed my favorite summer drink," and not "Tuna is overbearing by ordering for me without asking what I want," or "How could Tuna possibly think this was the drink I wanted?"

He answers the door, and the tips of his hair are still damp.

Is it weird that I'm wildly delighted by the fact he showered for me? (I'm guessing it's me being weird. Anything else on the emotional scale—being delighted by a guy who showers, period—feels like a bar so low, even snakes have to look down to see it.)

He's wearing jeans and a red-checkered shirt, and that smile that makes me want to cover him in chocolate sauce. "Right on time."

"Always. Are you ready?"

He nods, steps outside, and slides into his sneakers.

I observe this with silent glee but say nothing. I mean, it's conceivable that he always takes his shoes off, or that there was something on the bottom of them. I don't care. I'm calling this cultural influence. I, Altuna Kashmir Rashad, am an influencer.

"The place by my house is crazy busy on the weekend," says Tristan. "You up for going to the one a few miles down?"

"Totally good."

"Can I help with gas?"

"You cannot."

We get to the car. I either lose my mind or I'm trying to delight him, but I find myself unlocking the car and then bowing as I open his door.

"Thank you, milady." He covers his mouth with his fingers, as though he's overstepped the bounds of propriety, then pretends to lift the hem of a floor-length dress as he climbs in.

I pretend to gather it from the door frame so it doesn't get caught when I close the door.

This is a sign that either we are meant for each other, or meant for years of long-term, intensive therapy. I'm rooting for the former.

"How's Robby doing?" he asks as I back down his driveway.

"Not great." I don't tell him about the meltdown after the run. Not that I don't think he'd understand, or that he wouldn't empathize, but the pain is right at the surface and raw. I'm terrified that if I say anything, I'll start crying and never stop. Also, I'm not wearing waterproof mascara. He and I are not at the raccoon eyes portion of our relationship. That's an intimacy months in the making.

I tell him about the run, but I skirt the whole "my brother wants to move in with me," because it sounds shenanigany, and like the start of a cliché d B-plot movie that involves overflowing toilets and exploding blenders.

"On the bright side, at least he knows you're trying to find him friends," he says.

"You'd think that would be a positive, but to hear Robby tell it, I'm one step shy of putting him on a melting iceberg with only a moldy sandwich to eat."

"Aren't there some molds that are good for you?" he says. "He's lucky to have a sister who looks out for him."

I can't tell if he's being serious or funny, so I opt with, "I should hire you to be my PR guy."

"As an added bonus, as a realtor in training, I can get you a great deal on office space."

"Well, aren't you a multidimensional treat?"

He gives me a grin that almost sends me off the road. "Did I tell you Dr. Armstrong bought the house on West Phillips Boulevard?"

I do a double take. "Dr. Armstrong? The guy who once argued with a thirteen-year-old fast food cashier over an expired coupon that would have saved him fifty cents?"

"The same one."

"Hold on." I make a show of looking out the windshield and windows. "I'm checking for the riders of the apocalypse or flying pigs."

"Maybe flying pigs of the apocalypse?" His eyes light up. "Tuna! That's the name of the screenplay!"

Oh boy, this boy delights my heart. I wish I could just suck it up, find the courage, and ask him out. "Done—but back to Dr. Armstrong. How did you get him to spend money?"

"The original owners did a ton of environmental upgrades. I pointed out that while the initial outlay in cost is more, over time the house pays for itself."

"Genius," I tell him. "Dr. Armstrong is all about people and inanimate objects paying for themselves. Did you get a commission?"

"Two-fifty," he says. "Now I can afford the other half of the textbook."

He gives me that heart-stopping grin again, and I spend the rest of the drive trying not to crash the car. We pull into the café, and Tristan was right. The coffee shop parking lot has a ton of open spaces, and once we get inside, the place is mercifully empty.

"What can I order for you?" he asks as we take a spot by the window.

The cold of the wooden seat seeps through my peasant skirt. "I already ordered."

His head tilts, and it reminds me of Magic when she's trying to figure out what I'm saying. (I'm not comparing him to a dog, I'm just saying, two sentient creatures remind me of each other. Even if I were comparing them, it's okay because (1) Tristan started it by comparing me to a dog, and (2) it's Magic. He should be so lucky to be compared to her.)

"Mobile app," I say, suddenly feeling as though every sweat pore in my body has unleashed its reserves. "I got you a *corazon de paloma* and a *crème de menthe* iced capp for me."

"Oh." He sits. "Okay, cool."

"Is it?" I say, too worried about upsetting him to do anything but give into my insecurities. "I was trying to show you that I pay attention to what you order and like." My back hurts from the tight way I'm holding myself. "But now I'm worried it might be overbearing."

He does the head tilt again and doesn't say a word. Not because he's dragging out his answer, but because he's genuinely considering his response.

And even though I'm 99.9% sure I've soaked my clothes in Tuna perspiration, I kind of love that he takes his time and doesn't go with a knee-jerk, placating answer.

"I suppose I can see how it would come across as you treating me like a 1950s housewife," he says slowly, "but—" his cheeks go pink "—I think at this point, we're . . . our relationship—I think it was okay. I'm good with it."

"Oh." The tension drains out of me, leaving me feeling light-headed, weightless, and warm. "Okay, good." I smile at him.

He smiles back.

I grin.

So does he.

I need to think of something to say before we're locked in a good-natured version of a rictus grin. I want to say, *We should date.* Instead, I go with, "How is the real estate training going otherwise?"

His face lights with surprised pleasure at the question. Then he laughs. "Terrible. Pro tip, never volunteer to be an unpaid intern for your mother."

"I'm brown," I tell him. "We come out of the womb as unpaid interns. What happened to the parental gratitude for the cookies and buying frenzy, and the fundraiser?"

"Like my parents have any long-term memory for that," he says, then regales me with the working life of a real estate mogul in the making.

I lean forward and listen, and try to keep everything in the mental notebook for character creation. To be honest, I was imagining glamorous doings, rushing to show a multimillion-dollar home to a celebrity disguised in sunglasses and silk headscarf. Instead, it's a lot of filing, paperwork, and glaring at clients so they'll be honest about floods or rotting roofs.

His real estate life is out of my wheelhouse, both in understanding and interest. But I love listening to him talk about it. His face lights up and he's hand-talking. Real estate may not be his dream, but it's obviously a passion, and I love, love, love watching Passionate Tristan and sitting in the warm glow of his energy.

Also, it's good research for characters, so I'm doing my best to find my professional interest and ask relevant questions. And just at the moment I think the realization will come, another realization hits. "Where are our drinks?" I've interrupted him and I put out my hand in apology. "Sorry, it just occurred to me that we've been sitting here for a while and no one's put our drinks at the pickup counter."

"How long ago did you order it?"

"When I got to your house." I take out my phone to show the clerk and maybe get a refund. That's when the second realization hits, as cold and clear as ice water. In my desire to win him over, I've jumped into another shenanigan. "I ordered from the wrong location." Turning the phone, I show him the screen. "I used the one by your house."

His mouth forms an *O*. "That's my fault," he says. "I told you to come here."

"No, it's my fault. Brain blip about it being close to you."

He swings his thumb to the cashier. "I can get us something, or do you want to go and pick it up?" He smiles. "For sure, it's got to be ready by now."

We head to the original location, but by the time I get the drinks, they're a disgusting mess of melted ice, congealed whipped cream, and cold beverage.

"I'm really sorry," I say. We're standing just outside the door. The sun's beating down like a baleful eye, a glaring spotlight to my overeager need to impress. I can almost hear the great-aunts sighing and shaking their heads. Belatedly, it occurs to me that this might be punishment for the not nice psychic message I'd beamed at them earlier today, when I thought we had to give up Magic.

"Maybe it's a sign," Tristan says, staring at his drink. He tries to swirl it around, but there's no saving it.

"A sign?" That we can't be friends—or more? That I'm a shenanigan in the making and breaking?

The sunlight catches the glint in his eyes. "A sign that we should do this again. This time, at the right location with the drinks."

I try to form words, but my brain's cotton candy, full of sweet floss. "Again?"

He nods.

It takes me a second to process whether he's making fun of me. The slight twist of his lip is smirk territory, but good-natured smirk. Like, he'll tease me for signs and omens, and I'll make fun of him for math and germs.

My heart starts crashing through my chest, because—his teasing aside—this *is* a sign, an omen, a neon strip of handwriting flashing GO FOR IT! I can hear my ancestors in the spectator box raising the cheer and screaming me on. A butterfly flits around us, gossamer wings sending heaven's and David's blessings. "Let's do this again."

"I'm good with it."

"But different."

There's the frown and head tilt. "A different café?"

"No." I swallow and ponder if I should ask him to get 9-1-1 on standby with a defibrillator. "I mean 'different' as in: a date. Let's go on an official date. I'm asking you out on a date. Will you go on a date with me?" I stop because I'm sure I've just said "date" a billion times.

There's hesitation in his eyes. Before I can process why it's there, he smiles, slow and broad. "A date with you would be epic. It needs to be epic."

"Is that a yes?"

"No."

Cue breaking heart and me trying hard not to cry in front of him. (And also, whoever's writing his character arc really needs to go back to their storyboard and review things like consistency and personality logic, because none of this is making sense.)

"Before we go on a date," he says, "we should plan for it."

Okay, pause. I think this is his logic, rational, and science part of his personality wheelhouse, but still. "What?"

He grins. "We should meet and plan for the date. Then we can consider the date." Insecurity pulls the confidence from his eyes. He does a quick, one-shoulder shrug. "You know, like how we're planning the screenplay before we write it. Like that."

All I can do is grin and smile and grin some more. I still have no idea what's happening, but I do know it's positive and happening with him. "Okay. Cool. What will the planning meeting look like?"

"Leave it to me," he says. "It's going to knock your socks off."

Okay, who even says that anymore? He's so breathtakingly weird, I just want to stick a bow on his head, because his existence is the best gift in the world.

"I shall make sure their elasticity isn't in question." Obviously, I am also breathtakingly weird. If we're not a matched set, I don't know what is.

"I'll let you know the time and—" He stops. His forehead wrinkles. "It's not a date, but it'll be a . . . meet-up? A not-date?"

"Sure. Good."

He grins. "Good. Yes."

He said yes. Shenanigans beware, Tuna Kashmir Rashad's going on a date, and you better stay out of her way!

CHAPTER SEVENTEEN

When Life Gives You Lemons, Eat a Sundae

THE DOORBELL RINGS AND I CHECK MY WATCH. TRISTAN'S fifteen minutes early for our not-date. It would be easy to say he's over-eager, but I'm the girl that's been ready and waiting for the last hour. I open the door and my smile fades.

"You! Go away!"

Robby pushes past me and Magic follows. "That's what I said when you were born. It didn't work then, it's not working now."

"What are you doing here?" I rescue Magic from the ground because, you know, the floor is lava, and cuddle the heck out of her.

"Mom said Tristan and you were going on your first date." He smirks and holds up his phone. "I came to mark the occasion."

"It's not a date—" The flash goes off and momentarily blinds me.

Robby cackles.

I blink away the multicolored spots dotting my vision and grope for his phone. The photo is epically awful. He's caught me in mid-grimace, half-scowl, my mouth open to yell at him, and of course my eyes are closed.

"This is perfect. I'm keeping it for your wedding."

"Who says I'm getting married?"

Robby's laugh sobers. "Tuna, really? I always thought you were the marrying kind."

"Maybe I'm not."

The smirk is back. "Then I should send it to him now." He snatches the phone from my grasp.

"Don't you dare! Don't you dare!"

Dad comes into the foyer, glasses in one hand, newspaper in the other. In his maroon cardigan and gray slacks, he looks like an old-fashioned father about to bestow some firm but kindly discipline on his children. Of course, he's *our* father, so he's more likely to fling his slippers at our heads.

"Daddy, help me." I opt for helpless little girl who needs her heroic father to step in. "Robby took a terrible photo of me," I tell him, adding enough sugar to coat our daddy-daughter bond. "Make him give it back."

Dad gives me an indulgent smile. "Oh, Tuna Fish, you can't possibly take a bad photo." He takes the phone from Robby and peers at the screen through his glasses. His mouth does a rapid-fire pucker-unpucker as he tries not to laugh.

"Father! Defend my honor!"

Dad clears his throat. "I'm sure your brother will do the right thing."

"You mean posting it online?" I swing back to my brother. "Why are you here?"

"I heard a great podcast for seniors looking for supplementary income and the tax implications," he says. "I thought it would be good for Mom and Dad to hear."

Dad's face goes slack. "What did I do to you to deserve such punishment? I fed you, clothed you, loved you. Why are you forcing me to listen to a lecture on filing taxes?"

"There are some great ideas to supplement your income," says Robby.

"I'm not even retired!"

"Right," says Robby. "It's never too early to start planning for retirement."

"I know what I'll do," Dad says darkly. "I'm going to build a moat."

"A water feature, maybe," Robby says, not listening as usual, "but a pool isn't environmentally friendly."

Dad takes a long, slow breath and exhales it to the ceiling. "Little Fish, what are your plans with Tristan?" He takes Magic from me and buries his fingers in her fur.

"There's a late showing at one of the indie theaters of *Sleepless in Seattle*," I say. "We're doing dinner, then the movie." As not-dates and planning for real dates go, it's dang epic. My sockless feet attest to this.

"*Sleepless in Seattle*?" Dad says. "Nothing as a new release?"

"This has sentimental meaning," I say.

Mom, who's obviously been listening to the conversation from her office, comes out to say, "Oh, you know what you should do? Wait for one of the really good songs, then kiss him in the theater. It'll be wildly romantic. Dark. And with the ushers patrolling, just the right touch of danger."

"Gross. Please don't give me romantic advice, especially about kissing."

"Please." She adjusts the lapels on my dress. "Like you haven't been thinking about it since you saw him in freshman year."

I really have to stop oversharing. "I'm going to wait for Tristan outside." I take in my family's faces, including the special glint that says they're planning torment and teasing as soon as Tristan arrives. "In fact, I'm going to wait for him down the block. Maybe at the next block."

"Don't be like that, Tuna Fish," says Dad. "We won't make it weird." He follows it with an eyebrow wiggle that defies both his promise and the laws of physics.

I slide into my sexy sandals, throw open the door, and almost smack into Tristan. He's standing on the other side, one shoe off, one shoe on, diddle, diddle, dumpling, my son John. (Okay, I don't know if it's nerves at the date or irritation with The Tyrant that has me channeling Mother Goose, but for the record, Tristan is half-shod. He's also full-on gorgeous, but tell the world something it doesn't know, right?)

"Uh, hey." The color rises from his neck to his forehead as though we've caught him in some kind of criminal act. "I was taking off my sneakers in case I was going to be inside." He stops, no doubt realizing that there can't be any other explanation for the shoe removal. His blush deepens.

"Come on in," says Dad. "You're halfway there anyhow."

I squint at him. His invitation has less to do with welcoming Tristan than with delaying Robby and the world's most painfully boring podcast. "That's fine," I tell Tristan. "You're also halfway out the door. Let's go."

Dad reaches past me, grabs hold of Tristan, and yoinks him into the house.

I can't tell if Tristan kicks off the other shoe as he comes through the door, or if the terminal velocity at which he's being pulled has blasted it off his foot.

"I'm sorry," I tell him. "They're using you to avoid listening to a podcast on taxes."

"Is it about home offices? Because if you have questions with how things like home offices or even garage space can be claimed on your tax income, I'd be happy to connect you with someone from my office."

It's so wildly not the expected reply, and yet so much like something Tristan would say, that there's a temporary moment of silence where we're all dumbfounded and staring at him.

He's such a nerdlinger, and I want to kiss him. Badly. I mean, I want to kiss *badly* as a measure of my desire, not kiss him *badly* as a measure of my ability. (Just clarifying.)

"It's about retirement income," Robby says, finding his voice. "Mom and Dad should start thinking about what they're going to do after retirement."

"I'm not watching any podcast!" Dad heads to the kitchen.

"You don't watch podcasts," Robby yells back at Dad. "You listen to them."

"Let's go," I say to Tristan, "before all your biology knowledge about inherited traits and Mendel's pea plants come back to you, and you start wondering how much of their nonsense has been inherited by me."

"Listen to me." Dad comes out from the kitchen. "I want no part of it! Go do something else! Anything else!"

"Like what?" Robby's frustration is a tangible thing.

"How about coming to the movie with us?" Tristan asks.

A vacuum of silence descends. Even Robby's shocked out of his self-involved cocoon. "That's . . . nice of you." His eyes flick my way in silent apology for creating the entire scene. "But I'm good, thanks."

"What are you going to do?"

Bless Tristan's heart. He's got a whole mother hen vibe going. And I feel a little guilty—not at the sibling glare and the telepathic message promising death that I'm beaming at Robby. I'm on a high and stable horse of moral high ground.

The guilt is for Tristan. He's being sucked into Robby's vortex of grief, just like the rest of us. And just like the rest of us, Tristan's ready to jump on a white horse and ride in for my brother.

"We'll watch the lecture." Robby catches himself. "I mean, listen. We'll listen to the podcast."

Dad and Mom exchange a long, pained look.

I touch Tristan's hand. "We should go."

There's an awkward goodbye.

Tristan lets me guide him outside, but once we're on the step, he doesn't move to his shoes.

"Tristan?"

"We should take him with us."

I don't know what to say. Okay, I do know what to say, but none of those words are exactly sweet and melodious to the ears. "Our not-date." It's all I can think of to say, because I don't know how to find the other words. Does he not care about it as much as I do? Am I a heartless person for wanting a moment of unfettered delight among the shards of grief and control that my brother strews?

"Let's call it a rescue instead." His smile lights up his face. "We're rescuing your parents from a fate worse than death."

"My brother?"

He laughs. "A night of tax information." He grabs my hand. "It's like a plot twist in a movie or an unexpected detour. What did you call it? Fun and games."

"But those tie back to the grand theme and central story," I say. "How does this have anything to do with our date?"

The glimmer in his eyes brightens. "I don't know," he says. "Let's find out."

"Are you sure we just can't drug him with sleeping pills and wake him after the next ice age?"

"We can have an epic planning date next time."

I'm momentarily rendered speechless by his use of "next time." I can't believe Robby's ruining my night with Tristan. "Why? Why do you want to do this?"

His face squinches. "It feels like the right thing to do."

There's a lie in those words, or at least a lack of full disclosure. He's hiding something. He's too eager to end the not-date before it begins. What I don't know is the "why" behind his words and actions. I want to ask, to call him out on the things he's hiding, but I can't find the words or the courage. And even admitting this makes me feel weak and small.

"Tuna? What do you want to do?"

The date is ruined anyway. If I force us to go, it'll wreck the night and any good feelings between us. Robby's shadow will follow. The big, wet blanket that is my brother may as well join us in the physical.

"Sure, let's bring him along." I turn the knob, remember it's my family, close the door, ring the bell, then give it a three second count. "They're probably fighting," I say to Tristan's unasked question. "No need for you to hear it."

We step inside just as Mom comes from the kitchen. Her stride stutters to a stop. "Tuna?"

"We'll take Robby," I say.

Robby looks like he wants to die, have the ground resurrect him, just so he can die all over again.

"No. You kids go out. We can watch something else," says Dad. "I'm sure there's something painfully educational that Robby will find for us." He claps his son on the shoulder. "This kid's like a homing pigeon when it comes to boring garbage. We'll be fine."

"Are you sure?" Tristan asks.

If a guy who'd give you the shirt off his back means someone who would go the distance, sacrifice their comfort to care for someone else, then Tristan's the level that's above it. He's hiding something from me, but he's also genuinely concerned for Robby and my folks.

I don't know if that's an amber flag, that he's a guy who will violate his own self-care in favor for someone else, or if it's a for-sure green flag, that if this ever becomes super serious, this is the guy who will love my family to his dying breath.

It's a flash of ice-cold to hot when I realize there was another guy who was just like that. Who stepped in and stepped up, and who loved us to his dying breath. I'll never see him again, save his gravestone and the butterflies he sends. And the tears are a flash flood, rising so hard and fast, I barely have time to gasp, "I need to use the bathroom." I get inside and shut the door just as they hit, and I turn on the water so no one knows I'm sobbing over David.

I can't believe this night. This night that should have been so brilliant and wonderful, that devolved because of Robby, that got hijacked by the memory of David. All of it's wrapped in the soft, fuzzy gauze of Tristan, but I can't tell if he's gossamer blend meant to keep me warm or a thin, easily ripped confection that will irritate my skin.

When I come out, it has been decided. The parents and Robby will go off and do their own thing. Robby looks miserable. Mom and Dad, too. Tristan . . . I can't tell. I walk him outside to his sneakers. "So."

"So." His laugh is awkward and unsure. "I think in trying to help, I ruined everything, didn't I?"

"No, you did really good. My brother—" I stop because a first date isn't the time to go all banshee-rant about my sibling. Plus, there's a level of hero worship that Tristan has for Robby. It's not my place to ruin that image. We all need our heroes, even when they disappoint us, even when their grief turns them more villainous than heroic. "—my brother has just vexed me of late."

Tristan's mouth quirks. "Did you know you channel a Victorian lady whenever you get really mad?" He takes his shoes to the steps and sits. "Robby must be giving you a lot of chances to channel your inner Victorian. I like your brother. He's a good guy going through a brutal time."

"I know." I push down the tears. "Sometimes, it's hard to tell where care ends and enabling begins."

"Do you know where the line is?" He pulls on a shoe. His hands hover over the laces as though my answer is too important for him to do anything but wait for it.

I shake my head and sit beside him. "No." I mean it to come out as a word, but it comes out as a sigh and ends on a shaky resolve not to start crying.

Tristan ties his shoes, then stands. "We really have memorable hangs, don't we?"

"That's one way to put it. I'm sorry the night didn't go the way we planned."

"Me too." He holds out his hand. "Where do you want to go?"

I blink. "What?"

"Just 'cause we're not on a not-date doesn't mean we can't hang. What do you feel like?"

"A triple sundae with hot fudge, nuts, and enough whipped cream to drown a grown man."

He jiggles his keys. "Let's go."

I run inside to let my folks know, then I'm back out, taking his hand and climbing into his truck.

It's not Hollywood. There's no music montage while we drive for the sundaes, no adorable misunderstandings when it comes to the ordering. We don't dance in the rain.

We end up sitting in his truck, eating sundaes and trading stories. He talks about his grandparents. I tell him everything I remember about David. Our time together is funny and depressing and confusing. This isn't how dates or not-dates are supposed to go, and this isn't how you're supposed to impress the guy you like. But there's something special and magical in the air between us.

When he drops me at home, he walks me to the door, but he doesn't try to kiss me. Instead, he gives me a long, slow hug that's full of our growing friendship and more, and I think if this had been our first date, even if it wasn't Hollywood, it would have been perfect.

It would have been epic.

CHAPTER EIGHTEEN

Sometimes a Sister's Got to Do What a Sister's Got to Do

WHEN I GET INSIDE, THE HOUSE IS DARK. MAGIC'S sleeping on my bed. I'd like to think it's because she loves me best, but I'm positive it's because Robby snores. I change into my pajamas, cuddle into her, and tell her everything about the night until she falls asleep. Then I text Fi and regale her with every detail of the night, and she updates me on Riley. She assures me that they're still in friendship phase, but I know Fi. Love's around the corner. When we've texted our brains out, I shut down the chain and wish her good night.

I drift to sleep with Magic in my arms. It's been an exhausting time, which is why I'm surprised to wake in the middle of the night. The dark is unsettling because something's pulled me out of my sleep, but I haven't figured out what it is yet.

Leaving Magic to the warmth of the pillows and blankets, I creep out into the hallway, my ears straining for the sound. Nothing. But I'm sure there was something. I tiptoe to Robby's room, press my ear against the door. I'm not certain if he stayed the night or if he's still at work, but I don't hear anything at his door.

That leaves Mom and Dad's room, but all's quiet on the parental front. I head for the stairs, stopping when I hear a soft whisper behind me, like leaves on pavement. It's Magic, padding along, her small figure a shadowed blob.

We head downstairs and the noise is louder, but weirdly still faint enough to be unidentifiable. It's coming from Mom's office. I grab an umbrella from the bucket. It's not a great weapon, but what could someone want to steal from a children's author? I figure an umbrella and a loud shout will deter any possible burglars.

But as I get closer, I realize it's a heaving, wrenching sound. Panic bolts through me. It's Mom, probably working late, and throwing up? Having some kind of respiratory incident? How is her heart? When's the last time she had a full medical?

The questions race through me. Magic's running for the door, the umbrella's clattering to the ground, and I'm sprinting for the office. I'm through the door and flipping on the light, expecting to find Mom convulsing or throwing up into the wastebasket.

Instead, she's hunched in the corner by the bookshelves, tears wetting her face and turning her hair into soaked tracks that cling to her cheeks. She sees me, says nothing, but waves me off.

I ignore the dismissal. "Mom? What's wrong?" I whisper the words and drop beside her. "Do I need to get Dad?"

She shakes her head, yanks a tissue from the box beside her, and wipes her face. "I'm fine."

"We have vastly different definitions to that word."

She blows her nose and tosses the used tissue into the garbage.

"Why are you crying?"

"Your brother stayed over tonight."

"Yeah, that would make me sob, too."

She laughs through her tears. "No, I didn't want to him to hear me crying."

"Worried he'd find some weird elder condition that involves crying and relegate you to a battery of tests?"

"Something like that."

I shift closer to her and wrap my arms around her shoulders. "Why are you crying?"

She doesn't answer at first. Not because she doesn't want to, I think, but because the power of the emotions she's feeling overwhelms her. Mom's fingers clench around mine, and it takes a few moments of deep breathing before she can find the words.

"Tonight, with Tristan and Robby." She stops. More breaths. "Little Fish, when Tristan offered to take Robby—"

"It was something David would have done," I say.

Her eyes fill with tears and she nods.

"It was such a David thing," I say. "He was always the peacemaker and the glue. He could stop Robby in the middle of a self-important, self-involved rant like no one else."

Mom can't talk. Her pain's so great, she doesn't make a sound as she cries. She squeezes my knee, rolls to the bookshelf, then pulls a set of books off the lower shelf. Mom wriggles forward, then pulls something from the back and hands it to me.

"A photo album?"

"After David died, I didn't know what else to do." She sits next to me and opens the cover.

A David Retrospective. "Where did you even find photo paper? I didn't think you could even print images anymore."

"There's always a way for an elder with a will."

I trace the lines of David from grade one. Chipmunk cheeks, giant teeth, mischief in his eyes.

"That was the first day of grade one," Mom says. "I had to fight with the principal to get them into the same class."

I know this story, and I used to roll my eyes every time she'd talk about it. Now, it's like water on parched earth, and I'm drinking in every syllable and breath. She tells me about Robby getting her up at five in the morning because he had to look perfect, about the drive to school where Robby talked nonstop about him and David being in the same class, then the shock and broken heart when they got to school and a last-minute shift meant they were in different classes.

It's a mundane topic as far as story fodder goes. But it's comforting and familiar, and Mom only halts once, when she thinks she hears a door open upstairs.

She freezes, her fingers ready to slam shut the book and shove it back into its hiding spot. When no one comes down the stairs, she resumes the story. And so it goes. Every picture is another recounting. Their junior grad, high school grad. The celebration when they went to college.

I listen, and with every passing moment I find myself raging at my brother. For forcing us to bury any mention of David in a dark void, for forcing us to hide any memento of him.

I love my brother, but I *despise* him for this. Especially when Mom's voice breaks in her recounting of the disastrous haircut–hair dyeing incident that left David looking like a plucked rooster for weeks. She bends in half, hunching over as the grief washes over her and pulls her into the deep.

I hold my mom, crying with her, crying for her, and promise myself I'm going to stop this. Mom shifts, spilling the photo album from her lap. One-handed, I set it to its side before the pages bend or break. The album falls open to a photo of David at the Butterfly Sanctuary. His chin is tilted skyward, his hands are raised, joy lights his face as dozens of butterflies—monarchs, common blues, morphos, green hairstreaks, eastern tiger swallowtails—swirl around him.

I put my hand over his, acknowledge the message he sends, and send one back. *I promise, I promise, I will pull Robby from his grief, whether he wants me to or not.*

"Don't look at me like that." I keep my focus on the profile of Robby on the dating site. "I'm not changing my mind."

Magic nudges my hand.

"No, you had treats. You had lots of treats." I point to the screen. "You've been sent as an emissary from the ancestors. What am I supposed to do? Make the profile live or not?"

She nudges my hand again. I know she's not pushing me toward either the RETURN key or the DELETE button. She's simply trying to get my arm out of the way so she can shove her snoot into my pajama's pocket and help herself to a dog cookie.

"You are the definition of incorrigible," I tell her as I surrender and give her a treat.

Then I prove I'm the second definition as I reach over to the nightstand and help myself to a human cookie. I bite into it, crunching through walnuts and letting the chocolate chips melt on my tongue. "Do I do this? Do I make the profile live? Because that might find him emotional space? I mean, I can set it up like the run. Casual, low-key. Maybe it'll find him some friends." And maybe that will mean I won't find my mom hunched in a ball late at night, weeping over someone whose name she can no longer say out loud.

I play around with the profile, changing out the picture to the one from Halloween two years ago. I rearrange the photo so all viewers see is the bottom half of his face—from the lips down. But I like the contrast, the flowing white of his pirate's shirt, the red kerchief around his neck, and the fake, bright-green parrot with a cracker in its mouth. Then I play around with the font and ponder if I should add more photos to his profile. For kicks, I put one in of Magic's tail, because who doesn't love a guy with a dog? Okay, lots of people, but this is a good way to have them self-exit. No point in them meeting Robby, then walking away because of Magic.

(And yeah, I know I'm talking about Magic as though she's ours, but it's been billions of seconds—okay, millions—and there's still no one claiming her. If she's not meant for us . . . I don't know, then the sun doesn't shine and the birds don't sing.) I don't know what to do about putting the profile to live, and Magic is listening to her stomach, not the ancestors. So I opt for a text to Fi.

Are you awake?

A few seconds later, she's video dialing me. As soon as I connect the call, she says, "Don't do it. It's your worst idea ever, and you will regret it as long as you live."

I stare at her in wonder. "That's amazing. How did you know what I was calling about?"

Her head tilts, but not in the cute way Tristan's does. Fi's head tilt is less "I'm trying to understand you," and more "If I could reach through the screen and rap you on the head to knock some sense into you, I would."

"Tuna, it's one in the morning. There's no way your being awake means anything good. Therefore, whatever you're calling me about is a bad idea. Don't do it."

I'm affronted. Deeply wounded by her prejudgment. "How do you know I wasn't texting about something college related and I needed your sage and thoughtful advice?"

"Because we've been best friends for a long time. Those things, you text. Your shenanigans, you always want to video chat."

"But I didn't ask you to video chat." My offense is growing. Less because of any true sense of a violation of my honor. More because she's totally called me on the shenanigan, and I can't stand being that transparent. It hurts my belief that I can be spontaneous. Who wants to be the person that someone else can predict like a story beat?

"Subtext," she says. "That text is a plea for me to call."

She's got me there, and she knows it.

Fi sits back with smug self-satisfaction.

"You look very awake for someone being roused from their sleep for a shenanigan." It's all I can manage as a comeback.

"Mom had her church group over," she says. "There's no sleeping when you got a bunch of middle-aged folk in your basement hollering for Jesus." She settles onto her pillows and rearranges her lavender tank. "What's going on?"

"Remember that thing you said I shouldn't do because it was ill-advised, reckless, and possibly thoughtless?"

"Which thing? You have so many."

"The thing with Robby and the dating—"

Fi bolts upright. "Altuna Kashmir Rashad. If I have to explain one more time how wildly inappropriate this is—"

"He needs a life!"

"You're not the one to get it for him. Especially a love life!"

"He wants to move to Georgia with me, where we'll live in the same apartment. Fi, not only is he going to cramp my style, it's not a move. It's not a change like he thinks it is. He's just repeating the same lifestyle he has here, but with peaches."

"Georgia does have great peaches."

"They're my peaches, Fi, not his."

Magic, realizing there are no more treats to be had, settles beside me and closes her eyes.

"Tuna, I get you don't want him living with you. I wouldn't want that, either. I love Robby, but he'd be buried in the backyard if he and I tried to live together."

"Preach it," I tell her. "You're singing my pain."

"But forcing him into a relationship, even a platonic one, is wrong and you know it."

"I need him off my back. I need space." I ponder my options. "What about sending him to a nonprofit that helps struggling countries with medicine and healthcare? Do you think I can persuade him to leave the States?"

Her eyes go wide. "You want to send your brother from the comfort of America to the harsh realities of a developing country?"

"He's a big boy; he can survive it."

"I'm not thinking of him," she says. "I'm thinking of the people of that country. Life is hard enough without your loving but wildly overbearing brother."

She's got a point. "What about Canada?"

Fi leans into the screen like she's misheard me. "You want to send your brother to Canada? A country with universal health care? They probably have a doctor for every person. What's your brother going to do there?"

"I don't know," I say. "There's got to be a need for surgeons. Plus, Canadians are super polite. He can drive them crazy and they'll be too nice to say anything."

"That's true," she says. "Plus, they've got some great wineries."

"Didn't you know he stopped drinking?"

She closes her eyes. "That boy's sure taking the 'fun' out of dysfunctional."

"There's more," I say, and tell her about Mom. By the time I'm done, there's tears in Fi's eyes.

"I get it," she says, "and if I could figure out a way to bring Robby back from this bleak landscape he's living in, I would. But some things, you can't do for other people. Some things, they have to do for themselves."

She's right and there's no arguing that. We sign off, but I still have no answers, which can't be right. There's always an answer, isn't there? I look toward the window and ask the question to the ancestors, "Now what am I supposed to do?"

My laptop bings.

Okay, even for me, that's spooky. But when I check the screen, it's not a message from the Great Beyond. It's a message from Tristan, and that's beyond great.

> **I checked the showtimes for Sleepless.**
>
> **There are no more showings.** 😞
>
> **Any ideas for planning the epic not-date?**

I suppress my squeal of delight and channel my glee into an assertive hug and tummy rub for Magic.

She has no idea why I'm happy or why she's suddenly getting love, but she kicks and rolls to her feet, tail wagging.

Aren't dogs great? Doesn't matter what's going on, they're always ready to party. "He texted me," I tell her. "He's up to get down!"

She doesn't have a clue what I'm saying, and how would she? That's slang from the sixties and she's only two. But she catches the excitement. Unfortunately, that means she does a hop, skip, bounce onto my keyboard, and I manage to grab the top and bottom of the laptop before she can do any damage.

I give her a cookie because, let's face it, that's what she was looking for, and return to the texts. Magic's dance minimized a bunch of the windows and she may have scheduled an update to the OS, but Tristan's text is there, in all its shining glory.

> I take a breath and text, **Are we sure we just don't want to cast our fate to the wind and go on a date?**

> Our first date will be epic. There must be talks
> about how epic, then a meeting to talk about
> planning, then planning.

Bless his organizational heart and ten dollars that when we meet, he'll have a flowchart. I count up the number of meetings he thinks we should have and feel my heart zip around my chest. He wants to meet up three times before we even date. I love this not-dating dating.

> Your point is well-reasoned and well-made, sir. I
> doff my cap to you.

At least, I think I doff my cap. I'm hoping this isn't about him hedging his bets about us going out.

And I doff my chapeau to you.

> Shall we meet on the morrow? Perchance you
> are free at the noon bell?

I shall endeavor to be free, my lady.
Shall I pick you up in my carriage?
I shall have the stable hand arrange the horses.

> Ah, we're such nerds. I love it. Forsooth, I doth
> have an engagement at the Center of Rec for the
> swimmers of the early morn. I shall rendezvous
> with you at the café by your house (??).

It is agreed upon, I swear it. (The one right by my
house, right? Not the one we went to instead?)

> I shall see you tomorrow. (Yeah, that one—
> where I accidentally ordered our drinks.)

I sign off, hug Magic, and feel lighter in spirit than I have in a long time. I know, in every story, that when the main character says *Things are finally looking up*, that's usually the point where it all goes wrong. But really, really, things are looking up. (Okay, so it's pinging around my brain that this might be a moment of False Victory, but I'm feeling victorious. Now's not the time to question myself with logic and reason.)

Fi's right about not stepping in for Robby, but I can't keep letting his grief mess with my life. I'm going to step back and start creating some boundaries with Robby. I can't save him. I shouldn't, anyway. He needs to save himself (but I'll be here to help).

In the meantime, I'm going to create some space between us. No moving with me to Georgia. No more weird, tasteless food, and no more drab, boring movies. Boundaries. (Because I'll say it, loud, proud, and without fear of challenging the universe: THINGS ARE LOOKING UP!)

CHAPTER NINETEEN

Character Edit: I, Tuna Rashad, Love Pink Sweaters

THE DAY IS CLOUDY AND OVERCAST. I OPT FOR JEANS AND knee-high boots (in case it rains) and a thin, oatmeal-colored sweater for my not-date with Tristan. Then I spend the morning in the pool, smiling at the seniors. Most of them. I have to chastise an octogenarian for trying to start a water fight in the pool (he was trying to impress Mrs. Lancaster, a flirt of adorable proportions).

My admonishment to practice water safety gets a finger salute from her suitor, plus an "I've been swimming since before you were born, Missy. I know how to conduct myself in a pool," for my efforts. The fact that half an hour later I have to save his sorry state from the deep end is lost on him. He insists he was just fine, gives me another finger salute, then shuffles to the men's changing area. Mrs. Lancaster, proving that with age does not come wisdom, is smitten by his rebellious act of fighting the power.

I tuck the story in the back pocket of my mind for Tristan. As soon as the shift's over, I'm in the shower, scrubbing off chemicals and chlorine, then dodging the construction cones and heading to the café as fast as the speed limits will allow.

"Hey." Tristan greets me outside the entrance with a strong, warm hug.

"I love your outfit."

His cheeks flush with pleasure. "Really?"

"Dare I hope it's an homage to our screenplay?"

His smile broadens. "You noticed."

First of all, how do you *not* notice a hearty helping of man-hunk like Tristan? And also, how can I not be aware of the cable-knit pink sweater? It's got two square pockets on the front and the cuffs are edged in storm-grey yarn. He's wearing a navy-blue checkered shirt underneath (the boy is obviously partial to checks; I'm okay with this) and dark jeans. "If I'd known, I would have put more thought into my outfit." Yeah, right. Like I didn't spend all last night mentally going through my closet.

"I'm sorry we haven't found your actual sweater."

"I'm okay with it living on in our screenplay." You know, since it doesn't exist, it's only fitting it shows up in a work of fiction.

"Speaking of which," he says as he holds open the door. "We should get on it if we're going to finish it before school starts up. Three weeks, then it's back to the grind."

Not that I need to say this, but I really hate the idea of college separating us just as we're getting to know each other. "Maybe you can come over later?" There's another set of doors. This time, I hold it for him. "In the meantime, how's the internship? What happened to that country property?"

"Oh." His shoulders deflate. "No celebrity sighting. Just an old couple who got in with computers and tech back in the eighties."

"I'm sorry."

"Me too," he says. "It would have been fun to have some bragging rights when I headed to class." He makes a face. "Actually, no. I wouldn't have said anything. Client confidentiality and all." He bumps my shoulder. "Except you. I would have told you."

"You better have, or else no more iced coffees for you."

"My turn to buy. Grab us a seat?"

I do a quick scan of the interior and opt for a table by a set of couches. Tristan heads to the line while I spend most of my time waiting for him with a goofy smile on my face, until the conversation at the next table pulls my attention.

For the record, I'm not an eavesdropper. Okay, okay, so I'm totally an eavesdropper, BUT listening in on people is a great way to learn dialog. Also, in this case, I actually wasn't actively listening, so I have some self-righteous honor on my side.

"I think it's cute," says the girl with red hair.

"It's gross," says her friend, who has a line of small, gold hoops that run from their earlobe all the way to the cartilage at the top of their ear. "What a horrible sibling."

"Loving," the friend corrects. "I can understand why they'd do it."

Gold Hoops snorts.

I pretend to text, but the conversation has me hooked. They're obviously on polar ends of this debate, but what's the controversy?

"They're totally doing it with the hope of going viral," says Gold Hoops. "Isn't it obvious?"

No, I think. *Tell me more.*

"I don't think so," says Red Hair. "I think they genuinely want to do something nice for their sibling."

"By posting them to Eros and Agape and whoring them out like the daily special? Who does that, anyway?"

"Lots of cultures have arranged marriages." Red Hair takes a sip of her iced mocha.

"It's barbaric," says Gold Hoops. "People shouldn't be matched together like a cardigan set. What's even worse is how the OP is trying to spin it like it's something cute and adorable. Gently used brother. What kind of person—"

I miss the rest of Gold Hoops's rant because of the sudden roar in my ears. "Gently used brother"? That was what I had in the profile for Robby, but it can't be live on the site. I never set it to live. Maybe someone else used that term. It's not that original, is it?

"Excuse me, sorry, I don't mean to butt into the conversation," I say, doing precisely that. "But I couldn't help but overhear—*gently used brother*?"

"Right?" says Gold Hoops, mistaking my horror at a possible live posting of the profile for commiseration with their position. "It's insulting, right? Someone posted on one of the dating websites, saying they're trying to give away their brother to a good home."

"That's not what it said," their friend interjects.

"Like the brother is a commodity to be given away. Not only is it in bad taste, it's got shades of human trafficking. And I bet they think they're being so funny and cute, instead of recognizing the tone-deaf post smacks of privilege and elitism."

"Poli-Sci major," Red Hair says good-naturedly, pointing at their mate. "Also, only child. Meanwhile, I have three siblings and I'd pay someone to take them away."

Gold Hoops glares at her.

"What? You try sharing a bathroom with Morgan."

The signs are all there. I've somehow made Robby's profile live. But like any numbnuts character in a horror movie, oblivious to the serial killer on the other side of the window, I cling to the small, infinitesimal chance that the noise I hear is just the furnace in the basement and not the murderer about to hack me to pieces. I mean, the couple at the table may not be talking about my profile, right? "Where can I find it?"

"The website is down," says Red Hair, oblivious to the destruction every word they speak creates. "But here, you can see the screenshot and thread." She turns her phone my way.

There's the picture of Robby from Halloween. My vision goes panic blurry, and I can't read the profile. *Please*, I pray to the ancestors, *I did not put in any identifying information.*

Just then, Tristan comes to the table with our drinks and a slice of banana bread. "In case you're hungry," he says.

I take it with what I hope is a smile, but I'm sick to the core over the profile. It was never a real idea. Okay, so it *was* a real idea until Mom and Fi pointed out how it could hurt Robby and whichever guy is clicking on his profile. And it was a real idea until it went from theory to reality, and I'm sitting here with the horror of what it means to have outed my brother's private grief to the world.

The people viewing the profile won't know what my motivation is, but Robby would know. I send up a silent, screaming plea to the ancestors that Robby NEVER find out what I've done.

"So, about work." Tristan grins and launches into what would be a hilarious story involving a snotty middle-class couple, a mixed-up address, and an unfortunate party for swingers, and I'm trying to listen to him.

Sadly, I'm also trying to listen to the people at the next table, and I'm trying to figure out how the profile went live.

"Maybe we should go."

Tristan's words yank me back to reality. "Huh?"

He points at my untouched coffee and the half of the pastry that's waiting for me. "Maybe you're not into this today," he says, but I hear the subtext, *Maybe you're not into me.*

And I want to cry because I'm super into him, and I want to cry because I can't believe, once again, our not-date has been shenaniganed. And I want to cry because why is he vibing disappointment but also vibing hesitancy about us? I don't want to tell him about what's happened, but I can see from his face that if I don't fess up, he's going to walk away thinking I don't care about him.

Once again, Robby's shadow sabotages my time with Tristan.

Okay, okay, I realize and acknowledge I'm the one who created the profile, but if it wasn't for Robby, I wouldn't have done it in the first place.

"We should talk," I tell him. "Outside."

"Yeah, sure." He rises slowly, like he knows what's about to come.

"I did something bad, only I don't know how I did this bad thing," I say when we get to his truck.

"Bad, like illegal?"

"Bad, like morally ambiguous."

The possibilities of what I mean flit across his face. Mixed in is the shade of possibility that he's absolutely chosen the wrong girl to crush out on, and he's regretting ever having darkened my doorstep.

Before he can say anything, I remind him about the day he saw Fi and me, and my plan to get Robby some friends.

"Yeah, right," he says. "I remember, which reminds me, have you thought about grief groups? He'd meet people, but also have a chance to talk about what's going on with him. I meant to tell him when our moms took us to the b-ball tournament at the park on the weekend, but I forgot."

I file away all of the information and resist the urge to snap that now is not the time to talk about his ideas. Because, you know, selfish, unnecessary, and inappropriate behavior on my part. Also, because it's wildly generous of him to think of my brother's emotional health. I recalibrate and tell him about wanting to post the dating profile.

"Tuna," he says, "a dating profile isn't the same as a group meet-up or friendship circles. You're playing with people's emotions and future plans."

I file that one away, too, and remind myself that when it comes to confessions of deep, dark wrongs, Tristan has a habit of telling me the blatantly obvious. Another recalibration and I get him up to speed on last night with Mom, my fiddling around on the computer, and calling Fi to get her opinion. I give him every trivial, boring, painful detail about the night, even about Magic and her treats. My saga ends with my confession about eavesdropping and today's subsequent horror show of finding out the profile is both live and viral.

"I don't know how it happened," I tell him, not that it matters. What matters is that it *did* happen, and now there are terrible consequences and a very angry Robby, if he finds out.

"Probably when Magic jumped on the keyboard," he says.

That stutters my brain, because now I have to consider if it was an accident or ancestral meddling. It takes a millisecond to decide on accident. The ancestors may not understand technology, but no way would they be up for Robby being traipsed around like a piece of meat, available to the highest bidder.

"Maybe," I say. "I feel sick. I just made up the profile to blow off steam. It wasn't supposed to be live. I can't believe it's viral. What is wrong with people? This, they signal boost. But the stuff that matters? That gets one or two likes online."

"Tuna, it's okay. You just have to go to your profile and delete it."

"I would, but the people at the café said the website's down."

"The website maybe," he says, "but what about the app?"

I hadn't thought of that.

"Come on." He unlocks his truck and opens the door. "Climb in; we'll fix this."

I still want to cry, but for a billion different reasons. I love him for saying "we." "Thank you." I give him a watery smile.

He squeezes my hand. "It's okay, we'll solve this, I promise."

I could kiss him for that. But later. Right now, I have to fix this mistake. Trust the app store to be down. Neither one of us can download anything.

"I'll go home," I tell him. "Download it on another device. Or maybe the site will be up again, and I can just use my laptop."

He walks me to my car and gives me a hug and a "good luck."

Anxiety eats my stomach. But Tristan's close proximity has me eating my heart out. Is it super weird that in the midst of the worst moment, I kind of totally want to kiss him? Is that hormones? Crushing out over how kind, cool, and helpful Tristan is? Asking for a friend. Okay, asking for me.

It must be all over my face, because Tristan does this soft intake of breath and steps closer. It's a question, a request.

It's a sign.

I close the distance between us.

He leans toward me, and then he's kissing me.

Oh, my signs and omens, *Tristan Dangerfield is kissing me*.

When we come up for air, he says, "I'm sorry. It's bad timing. But you looked like I really needed that."

My brain and heart are too busy processing this AWESOME EMOTIONAL MOMENT and the feel of his body and lips close to mine. It takes me a second to sort what he's saying. Then, "Don't you mean, I looked like I needed that?"

"No. You looked kissable, and I really needed that. I've been wanting to kiss you since freshman year."

For a guy who's gotten what he wanted, he looks pained. Which has me wondering if I'm a bad kisser.

"I really am sorry," he says. "That was really bad timing."

True. If this was me writing it, I wouldn't have put the kiss in here. Sure, it's main plot stuff, but Robby's B-story is priority right now. Then again, this is my life, so I am writing it, aren't I?

"I wish you hadn't sprung it on me," I say. "If I'd known, I would have prepared."

"How?"

Good question. "Pre-pucker? Flavored gloss?"

He laughs. "It's not a real kiss," he says, "it's a warm-up for the first date." He gives me an insecure smile. "And it takes pressure off when we actually do the date, because technically we've already kissed. Right?"

I'll take it because I'm too flummoxed to concentrate on what happened. And since this is my story and I'm the heroine, I kiss him again, because, what, I'm not taking the opportunity? Besides, if Mom and Dad find out about the profile, I may never see the light of day— or Tristan—again.

I climb into my car. Then, once again, I'm heading to a destination as fast as the speed limits will allow. When I get home, Mom's office stuff is scattered in the foyer. I find her, on her hands and knees, slotting her desktop's cables into a power cord tidy upper.

"Oh, Little Fish, good. I realized that if I rearranged my office setup, I could do this." She groans as she rises and flips back her hair.

"Do what?"

She drags me around to look at the screen. "Ta-da!"

"Uh—" I glance at the black screen. "I love you, but was Robby right? Are you slowly losing your mental faculties?"

"What? No." She glances at the screen, grunts, and hip checks me out of the way. A few seconds of typing, then, "Ta-da!"

The screensaver scrolls along the monitor. Images and images of us, which is no big deal, but also images of David, which is the biggest deal in the world. "Oh, *Mom*."

"Isn't it great? I've set it up so no one coming through the door can see the screen. See? You can't even see the reflection in the window."

She's so proud of herself, and my heart is breaking all over again. "You shouldn't have to hide—"

"I know." She dismisses the words and excuses Robby with a wave of her hand. "But this is the best of both worlds. I can see my little David, and Robby's not . . . hindered."

Maybe he should be, I want to say. Maybe he should come over and find pictures of David hanging from every spot on the walls, dangling from the ceiling, floating on strings from the bannister. Or maybe I shouldn't do anything about the profile on the Eros and Agape site. Just go with the flow, let the requests come, book meet-ups, quietly push Robby into group meetings and let friendship take its course.

The stirrings of a headache creeping into the back of my eyeballs and temples is a sign that allowing the profile to stay live is a bad idea (not that I needed my body to offer its opinion). This is Robby, I remind myself, the kid who wants to move with me to Georgia. My brother might look like a human male, but inside he's a glacier. Cold and frozen, and moving at an iceberg's pace. I can't be the global warming trend that melts his world and floods his lands.

Sighing, I take myself upstairs. I boot up my laptop, then try logging into the website, with no luck. More than no luck, worst luck, because I can't get a Wi-Fi signal. "Mom! Plug in the router!"

"Just a second. I'm almost done."

No, I'm the one who'll be done if Robby finds outs. "Mom! Mmmooomm!! Mother! I require your assistance! PERCHANCE TO PLUG IN THE ROUTER AND THUS VANQUISH THE FOES THAT DARKEN MY DOOR!"

"Vanquish your own foes!" she yells up. "I have to finish organizing the office."

A brain wave hits: I can plug the laptop into the router. I rush downstairs, then stumble to an ignominious stop on the stairs. "Where is the router, woman?"

Mom comes out of the office and surveys the pile of objects, knickknacks, and bric-a-brac cluttering the floor. "Huh. I put it . . ." She trails off.

I don't have time for an elder version of memory. Stepping around the boxes, books, and assorted stuff—and making a mental note to myself to have a serious talk with Mom about clutter (*Gah! Who would believe I'd side with Robby on this?!*)—I search for the elusive router. Which, after a few minutes of panic searching, remains elusive and bounces up a level to invisible.

With no choice left, I dash back upstairs, and phone Fi.

"No text, no video call?" She doesn't bother with "hello." "Calling on the phone like the reincarnation of Alexander Graham Bell? What kind of a psycho are you?"

"A psycho who's in so much trouble." As fast I can I give her the backstory on why I need her help, and I finish with, "So I need you to log in—"

"You did *what*? After I expressly told you *not* to mess around with dating apps?"

"Lecture me later, Fi. I need your help. His profile going live is an act of ancestor or act of dog—"

"Or act of Tuna the Loon."

"Please." I'm almost crying. "I can't let Robby or my parents find out about what I accidentally did. Please log in and save me."

There's a small pause. "Save yourself."

For one sick second, I'm terrified she's about to hang up.

"I always wondered why you're such a fan of screenwriting and movies. Now I get it. It's because you're totally useless in a real-life crisis."

There's an echo of laughter in her voice, which I take to mean she still loves me and won't leave me hanging on this. "Fi, come on! Help me! I'm trying to avoid an 'All Is Lost' story beat!"

"See? Who talks screenwriting when they're about to get an ass-kicking from their brother?"

"FI! HELP ME! This can't end with me being vanquished!"

"Use your personal hotspot and log in."

Oh. "Why didn't I think of that?"

"Because you're useless in a real-life crisis. Let me know how it goes?"

"Promise."

"And we're going to talk about what you did, right? No blaming pooches or ghosts."

"It was an accident."

"Freud said there are no accidents."

"Who listens to Freud?" I say. "He's dead."

"On that note of blinding irony," says Fi, "I'm hanging up."

I open my phone settings, activate the hotspot, and log in with my laptop. The website is still down. So I try downloading the app, with no luck. Then I make the colossal mistake of looking up how the profile is trending on social media and immediately regret reading the comments.

I take a break and keep trying to log in or download the app, but both options are getting me nowhere. And my body, somehow thinking I am open to its opinion, has an acid roller coaster going in my stomach, and the shakes attack me.

I do a quick pace around the bedroom, but I don't look at the photos of David. I can't bear to see the disappointment in his eyes. Instead, I go to the window and jab my finger at the sky. "This is your doing," I tell the ancestors. "Whether by hook, crook, or Act of Dog, this profile is live and it's going to be the end of me."

All I get is the leaves of the trees rustling in the wind.

"If Robby finds out, he's going to murder me until I'm dead," I tell them. "And then you know what will happen? I'm going to spend eternity with you. And you know what else?" I point at the sky. "I'm coming for you, Great-Aunt Cecile. I'm going to sit beside you until kingdom come, our work be done, and I'm going to talk nonstop about screenwriting. Opening images, theme stated—I'm going to go so hard into the weeds, I'll spit seeds." I have no idea what that means, but I hope it gets the ancestors off their couches.

The wind picks up, and the branches of the tree begin to move. A sliver of sunlight breaks through the clouds and the leaves and lands on the laptop. It might be the ancestors directing me, it might be the solar cycle and the winds doing what the cycles do. I don't care. I take the sign and go to the bed.

I opt for the website and, bless the ancestors' hearts, I can log in! Silently, I beam a thank-you to them, then go to the message center. And holy, holy smokes, there are four thousand messages for Robby. Well, for Robby via me. I head to the settings and delete the account.

Can you believe the website has the audacity to ask me if I'm sure?!

"Yes, yes," I mutter and rapidly click the ENTER button. "I'm sure."

It processes the change, then tells me I can reactivate in thirty days if I choose.

I log out, then go to the main page of Eros and Agape and try to find my profile. The error message saying there's no account is the most beautiful thing I've ever seen. Gritting my teeth, I head to social media, click the links, and find the same error message. Thank you, ancestors, thank you. My heinie, flat as it is, has been saved.

CHAPTER TWENTY

Cheesecake Is Not a Projectile Weapon

"**T**UNA, YOUR BROTHER WILL BE HERE IN FIVE MIN-utes," Dad calls up from the bottom of the stairs.

"Got it!" I turn back to the video chat I'm having with Fi and Tristan.

"Stop looking like you know where Jimmy Hoffa's buried," Fi commands. "You screwed up with the profile, but you deleted it. Robby doesn't know, your parents don't know. There's no need for anyone to know. *Tu comprendes?*"

"I understand," I say, irritable, because Fi always pulls out the French when she thinks I'm being extra useless.

Fi shakes her head. Her gaze goes to Tristan. "She doesn't understand. She's going to confess, and something that should go with her to the grave will end up creating some huge family rift because she and her family love being dramatic."

"We do not love being dramatic."

A black eyebrow goes up. "Your brother is taking everyone to some fancy restaurant to make some giant announcement."

"That's totally normal." I'm weirdly moved to defend his honor because it defends mine, as well. "Lots of people do a fancy dinner to announce something big."

The other eyebrow rises to join the first. "When the announcement is that he's moving with you to Georgia? Doesn't everyone already know that?"

"Maybe the announcement is that he's *not* moving to Georgia," I grumble. "That would be big news."

She laughs. "You're not that lucky." Her gaze returns to Tristan. "You don't have a clue what the announcement is?"

He shakes his head.

"But you guys hang out," I say. "He must have said something."

Tristan laughs. "We tag along when our parents hang out. How else can either of us afford to watch a basketball game from courtside?"

Fi rolls her eyes. "But it's not like you and Robby are babies. Surely, your folks leave you unsupervised and you talk."

Tristan goes pink. Either he's blushing or he's put a dream filter on the call. "Sort of, but we're still circling each other."

"What does that mean?" I ask.

"It means I like your brother, but—" The pink deepens to red. "—you're always between us, so there are some things he wouldn't tell me, because I'd tell you."

"Would you really?" I'm flattered. "Doesn't that break some kind of bro code?"

"The only code between us is *don't hurt Tuna*."

Now it's my turn to wince. Even at his obnoxious best, my brother tries to protect me. I can't believe how much I regret playing around on the dating site.

Pink infuses his cheeks again.

Man, that boy can really make me like that color.

"Also, there are things I wouldn't tell you if he told me," says Tristan. "You guys are family, but I want to keep our friendships separate."

"I get that," says Fi. "It's the same for me." She turns her focus to me. "Tuna, do *not* do this, okay? Don't confess or come clean with anything. You got away with something, take the win! Maybe it was your ancestors, maybe it was the technology gods, who cares? What matters is that no one knows you set Robby up for auction like some well-fed cow."

"Wouldn't that be a bull?" Tristan says.

"Really?" says Fi. "We're trying to stop Tuna from being grounded for life and potentially ruining her relationship with Robby—"

"He'll understand. It's not as if Tuna meant to find him a partner or was trying to be disrespectful of what Robby lost with David—"

"—and you want to dissect vocabulary right now?" Fi doesn't acknowledge anything he says. She shakes her head, and I can almost see the thought bubble forming in her head. *He must be a Rashad in the making.*

Meanwhile, I feel every sharp edge he didn't intend. Robby will think I was being disrespectful about David. So will Mom and Dad. And no matter how much I try to explain what my intentions were, the doubt over my motivations will niggle at them. That hurts worst of all, because I would never do anything to harm David's memory. Just like in life, I'd never have done anything to harm David, period.

"I can't believe you're doing this." Fi scowls at me. "I can see it in your face. You interrupt my life with this emergency call. You don't say hello, you don't even say my name. You just come into my room and ask for advice."

I'm not sure if she's adapting a quote from *The Godfather* or just impersonating Marlon Brando, but that's my Fi. Speaking French, referencing blockbuster movies, channeling Italian mob bosses, and doing it all with a Haitian attitude. She's a multicultural wonder.

"Why did you even bother videoing us if your mind's made up?"

"Because it's not made up," I say.

"Don't lie," says Fi. "You didn't call to get us to weigh in on what you should do. You called so we'd tell you that you're doing the moral thing by confessing, but you're not. You're doing the easy thing. Robby doesn't need to know what you did. It's going to hurt him to think you were trying to pawn him off, and it won't matter how much you tell him that it's a joke. And the whole thing went viral. It's Robby; he'll read the comments. He's going to wonder every time he sees someone if they were on his side or yours with those comments. It's going to color every relationship he has." Fi sits back and takes a breath.

I glance at Tristan.

"She's right," he says quietly. "Robby can be obnoxious and a know-it-all, but at the end of the day, he loves his family and his friends. Having anyone, even strangers, think that he did something wrong as your brother will hurt him."

"Maybe he won't read the comments," I say.

Fi snorts. "Robby would read instructions on how to toast bread if you gave it to him."

Tristan lifts his hands. It's not a surrender, it's a plea for me to be okay when he says, "If you tell your family, you'll take the guilt away from you, but you'll hurt them. They don't deserve that. You can't be selfish. You screwed up, Tuna. You have to live with it."

It hurts, but he's right. And I'm mad at him for not siding with me, but weirdly happy with him for siding with his integrity and morals.

Robby arrives a couple of minutes later, and I shut down the call. Then I go to meet up with my family and hope they won't pick up on the guilt that seems to follow behind me like a dust cloud from *Dante's Peak*.

"Why are you so jumpy tonight?" Robby's eyes lift from the menu to meet mine.

"You have news," I say. "And you're stringing us along by taking us out to dinner and not sharing what it is." I set down the menu and cast my gaze around the restaurant. I'm not interested in people-watching; I'm just trying not to make eye contact with anyone who shares my DNA.

The only problem is the other patrons. Every time I see them check their phones, then look our way, I'm convinced they've somehow deduced it's Robby on the profile. They're going to come over and tell everyone what I've done. Even when the patrons don't look over, I'm convinced every glance at their devices is a glance at my Eros and Agape profile. Why, oh why, must everything online be forever?

I pull my gaze from the patrons, not that there are many of them. It's a Wednesday, so the bistro is quiet, but it's a trademark Robby choice. Dark wood tables and wine-red cushions on the booths. Strategically placed pot lights and chandeliers offset the heaviness of the décor. I'm having heart palpitations from the anxiety of being with everyone; but on the other side, Robby taking us to a restaurant with actual food harkens back to his old self. It's a sign that he's slowly returning to the world.

"It's good news," he says.

"For whom?" I ask.

"Tuna," says Mom with an anxious smile. "It's Robby's news. He can tell us when he's ready."

"If it's that he's moving home," I say, "I'm out."

"He's not moving home," says Mom, the anxiety showing itself in her eyes.

I cover my laugh. I'd bet money that if Robby moves home, Mom's moving out. She's only just rearranged the office, and seeing David has been a saving grace for her. There's a quietness, a calm around her now. It's as though she gets to relive the memories in the photos, and in reliving them, she brings David back from the grave.

"Of course you're out," Robby says to me. "You're going to Georgia."

"Oh." I relax into my chair. "That's right. Fine. You can move home."

"I'm not moving home," he says.

Mom steers the conversation to other, mundane matters, and I take the opportunity to mentally check out. Keeping my mouth shut is proving harder than I thought. And this overwhelming need to confess my sins doesn't make sense.

After all, I didn't make Robby's profile live on purpose. And also, there's nothing identifying about him on it. No one would know who he is. Really, it was a good-natured venting exercise that inadvertently went public.

And viral.

And with the right kind of troll, identifiable.

"Tuna, honey, you look sick."

"All good," I say. I wish I didn't agree with Fi and Tristan. I wish I could just do what I want—confess—because it would make me feel better. The realization that I will never be able to say anything to them is heavy. The fact that my actions landed me here and that I'll always feel like I betrayed them, no matter whether they know or not, is the proverbial hard pill that's stuck in my throat. "Just wondering when dinner's coming."

I'd say dinner plods along, but that suggests a breakneck speed that doesn't match how painfully slow the meal is. I'm half-convinced I've slipped into an alternate world where time runs backward. Mercifully,

Robby takes the break between dinner and dessert (I'm eagerly awaiting a cookie-dough cheesecake) to tell us his news.

"I was telling Tuna that I've been offered a job in Georgia," says Robby.

My breath stops. "But you didn't take it, did you?" The question comes out reedy and thin.

"I'm thinking about it," says Robby.

"No, no you're not!" I catch myself and lower my voice. "Are you kidding right now? I told you, I don't want you there!"

"You don't own the state, Little Fish," Mom says, her tone mild. "Where is the hospital?"

"Savannah," says Robby.

Dad chokes on his red wine.

Even Mom coughs.

"Savannah, where I'll be." I shoot Mom a hard stare as though she may have forgotten that's where SCAD is located.

"Right, but we won't be living together or anything," says Robby. "So there's no need in getting hysterical."

"Why not?" Dad asks.

I'm not sure if the question is about living together or me getting hysterical.

"It would save Tuna money," Dad says.

"Tuna doesn't want to save money," I say through tight lips. "Tuna wants to have an existence where she doesn't live with her family."

"Oh." Dad blinks as though my familial independence has just occurred to him. "Right."

"You're doing this on purpose." I swing around to face Robby. "You've put it in his head, and now it's not going to let go until it gives you and me matching house keys and reduces the rent."

"Hey," Dad says. "I'm right here and nothing's in my head."

"Please. Didn't you try to get a discount wedding cake when you married Mom?"

"That bride and groom weren't getting married, and who was going to notice the names on the cake once it was cut?"

"I was," says Mom. "Honestly, who buys someone else's wedding cake? It's bad juju."

"It's not like they were dead," Dad says reasonably. "They didn't need it anymore. You and I were still in school; budgeting was a good idea."

"They may not have been dead, but their marriage certainly was!" Mom says. "And you wanted to bring their cake to our wedding." She sucks her teeth and glares at him.

Dad shoots me a dark look for bringing up what is obviously an unresolved marital spat. "Let's get back to the matter at hand. Robby, you're moving to Georgia."

"Maybe," he says. "I want your input."

"You have my input," I say.

"And you know where you can put it," he says.

The waiter comes with the desserts, and now I'm emotionally eating. I can't believe I was sitting here feeling bad for him and guilty for my accidental accident, when the whole time he's been plotting this ambush. I hate that Robby's my antagonist, hate that I'm hoping for his failure in this beat because I need to win. He's my brother. He's Robby. Why can't he go back to being *my* Robby? The restaurant blurs and I blink away the tears.

"I suppose it will be nice to have you kids together," Mom says. "I would worry less about Tuna, and Little Fish, Magic would be with you."

"Can you even do that?" I ask Robby. "Take Magic out of the state?"

He looks at me like I'm unhinged. "She's not a child, and I'm not sharing joint custody with an ex. Besides, it's been weeks. No one is coming for her. She's mine." He pauses. "Well, she'll be mine after I take down the notices. Which I'll do in a couple of weeks—just in case her owners are out of the country or something."

We watch his mental chess game in silence.

"What?" he says. "If she has a family, then she needs to go home. Someone is missing her. Someone needs her back."

Dad's eyes mist, so do Mom's. We know he's thinking of David.

And okay, keeping Magic is a momentary bright, beautiful light in an otherwise super crappy moment. "Who's taking care of her when I'm at school and you're at work?"

"Doggy daycare," says Robby.

I realize I'm already talking about us living together as a done deal, and it depresses me to no end. "Robby, you can't take this job," I say. "You didn't even care about Georgia—" I stop, take a breath. "—We talked about this, and I'm not repeating anything. It's wrong for you to come."

"It's my job and a chance for promotion," he says. "I can't believe you're being so selfish."

I restrain myself from smashing the cheesecake into his face, and that's because it's unbelievably good cheesecake. Why waste it on his face? "I'm not the one being selfish. If you're all about promotions and moving, then go volunteer with Doctors Without Borders. I'm sure they'll take you."

"Tuna, this makes sense for both of us."

I hate it when Robby tries to be logical and reasonable, especially on stuff that has nothing to do with either of those things. He's my Bad Guy closing in, throwing me and my plans into peril. "It's not about sense. It's about life. *Separate* lives."

"You can have a drop in the rent, there's someone to look out for you—"

"I knew it," I say bitterly. "I knew you wanted us to live together."

"It's your first year alone and in a new state—you're lucky to have someone watching over you."

I feel the bitterness growing until it's a tangle of thorns, rising from putrid soil. "It's not my year alone, because you're going to be there. And this isn't about me. Stop trying to act like you're doing me some kind of favor! This is about you being a cold coward Robby Hosea Rashad. You know you need to move on—"

His face tightens.

"—but you can't or you won't. This move is just another way for you to stay in your toxic rut and never change, but delude yourself into thinking you've done the brave thing."

The table goes painfully silent.

"I'm doing my best," he says quietly. "Moving on as fast as I can. Maybe it's not fast enough for you, Tuna, but it's as fast as I can go. I thought, as my sister, you'd be happy for me. That you'd support me."

"What do you think I've been doing for the last year and a half?" I say.

Dad rises, takes his wallet from his jacket and walks toward the hostess table.

"All I've done is support you. It's what we've all done. What about us?" I look to Mom, to get her to back me up, but she stares at the white table-cloth and stays quiet.

"I didn't realize I was such a burden." Robby wipes his mouth with a napkin. "Thanks for the reality check." He tosses the cloth and stands. "I'm going home."

"Honey, wait." Mom stretches out her hand. "We can drive you home."

"No need," he says. "Obviously, I don't have a home with you anymore."

"Thanks a lot," I say to Mom as he walks away. "You couldn't have stepped in and stood up for me?"

"Tuna," she says my name slowly. "Honey—"

"Don't 'honey' me. You know I'm right."

"It doesn't matter," she says. "He lost his husband and his best friend in one swoop. You need to be more understanding." She stands as Dad returns, tucking his payment receipt into his wallet. "I expect you to apologize to him by tomorrow."

I follow them out the door and realize there's a twisted bright side to the fight. I don't feel guilty about the app anymore. If anything, I find myself wishing I'd left the profile live and let the pieces fall. It's not fair. Robby demands handling with gentle voices and soft touches because he's so overwrought. But in reality, he's the ultimate bull in the China shop, and I'm tired of him breaking my wares. I'll apologize, by text, when I get home. But I'm not sorry about anything I did or said.

CHAPTER TWENTY-ONE

Will the Fun and Games Never End?

THOUGHT THE BLACK MOMENT WAS THE FIGHT AT THE
restaurant, but I guess that's the difference between screenplays and
real life. In fiction, it's a moment, then the story moves on. In reality,
it's been eons.

If there's a silver lining to the ongoing fight with Robby—other than
the fact that he's still so ticked, he refuses to come over when I'm home
(except to drop off Magic)—it's that I'm done playing shy and coy. I've
been waiting for Tristan to tell me how he feels about me, waiting for him
to come clean about his hesitation and the push-pull (which, now living it,
I can say is highly overrated as a rom-com trope), and I'm done. I'm all for
not-dates, but I need a win. I need an actual date and an explicit "I really
like you, Tuna," from Tristan.

And kisses. For sure, Momma needs more kisses. (Yuck. I thought I'd try the "Momma" self-reference again and see how it feels. It feels gross. Permanent delete.)

Which is why, before my shift at the rec center, I ambush him at home. And I know it's not the smartest or most logical thing I've ever done (and if I ever doubted it, Fi's been texting, alternately supporting and deriding my decision), but I don't want him to have a heads-up on this.

I ring the doorbell and don't bother smoothing my hair from its play-date with the wind. Tristan's family has a video doorbell. No need for him to see me prepping and preening.

As I wait, I practice what I want to say (I also practice calming my heart rate so I don't defibrillate all over his porch). Nothing I come up with, speech-wise, is Hollywood-worthy, but it's hard to be both romantic and emotionally deep when the wind is blowing your hair in your face. What I really need is a rainstorm. Rain makes everything poignant and romantic.

He opens the door a few seconds later. "Tuna?"

"I like you," I tell him. "I like you a lot and I think you like me."

He steps onto the porch and closes the door.

That's good. At least he didn't flee or slam the door in my face. "And I want you to go out with me. Forget about not-dates and planning for epic dates. I'm asking you on a date-date." And then I shut up, because, once again, I've said "date" a billion times.

He frowns. "Now?"

"What? No, not now." I gesture to my sweatpants and worn graphic t-shirt. "I have a shift at the center today."

"That's what I thought."

"I want to go out with you at a later date." I fish into my pocket and bring out my phone. "There's a home show."

His eyebrows go high. "You want to go to a home show with me?"

"We've been doing a lot of the things I like to do, like the screenplay and trying to get to the movies," I say. "I want you to know that I like you a lot. I like you enough to go to the home show." I push down the grimace that's rising to my face. That was not the greatest line to confess my affection or show him that his interests matter to me. It makes it sound like I'm sacrificing to be with him, or maybe that I think his life choice is boring. But there's no time to edit and in real life, there are no reshoots. "We've been going out on almost-dates and planning an actual date. I'm done. I want to actually date you. Will you go out with me?"

He shakes his head.

Before I can track the heartbreak, he says, "I hate home shows. They're boring and full of overly stressed middle-aged people desperate to renovate their kitchens."

"Oh." The phone returns to my pocket via my shaky fingers. I take a breath to slow my heart. "Something else, then. What kinds of real estate things do you like to do?"

That makes him laugh. "I like real estate, but I don't need to do it on my off time."

Double-oh. "So . . . what should we do for our first official date?"

The laughter in him dies, dimming like a candle flickering to its end.

If I had any doubt this was a pivotal moment in our story, and a negative one, it dies when he says, "We should talk."

Oh, no. *No. Nnnoooo.* I know those words. I've spoken those words. "No, it's cool. I obviously misread the situation. No worries. I'm sorry. This must have been super awkward. I should go." I spin and head for the driveway, but he catches my hand.

"We should talk," he says and pulls me to sit.

I do.

"I really like you—"

"But not in that way."

"No, definitely in that way," he says. "But—"

"My family is too weird."

"No weirder than other families. That's not the problem. It's—"

"My cultural beliefs," I say. "They're too 'out there' for you."

He cocks his head. "Do you want me to talk or just stay quiet while you guess?"

"Is it my fault you don't know how to get to the point?"

"I'm trying to ease into it."

"Well, don't," I tell him. "I've got three seconds before I sweat through my shirt. Is it about my ancestors?" Judging by the look on his face, I've nailed one of the talking points. "You're kidding."

"I don't believe in it," he says, "and I'd be lying if I said I even understand how someone as smart as you can even buy into it—"

I bite the inside of my cheek to stop from defending myself.

"—but these are your beliefs. If they work for you—" he shrugs "—I can learn to live with your quirks."

I catch the words and put them in my back pocket for later retrieval. "We're not that different," I say, trying to push off what I'm a hundred percent sure is his coming rejection. "You look for patterns in math and science. I look for it in everyday life."

"It's not the same."

"Yeah, but it's similar. Science is always changing because our knowledge grows."

"Exactly, that's why superstitions and ancestral interference doesn't make sense."

"But there's always the intangible, the things we can't quantify or touch." There's panic inside me. Not just regular panic that spreads like a pool of spilled water. This one's shooting up and out, exploding in all directions like a geyser. I've liked Tristan since freshman year. This summer was my chance—our chance.

I've worked hard on making this happen, and it seemed like he was, too. Our rom-com can't genre shift into a love story. Rom-com characters end up together, love story characters don't. We're a happy ending couple . . . aren't we?

Aren't we?

Oh, god, I thought Robby and David were a happy ending couple, but they were a love story. How could I be so wrong about them and me?

"I know what you're saying," he tells me, pulling me back to the debate over the ancestors.

I hear the frustration in him, that as much as we're talking, we can't build the bridge over this gulf.

"But we're different, Tuna."

"So what?" I try not to shriek the question.

"So, what do we talk about?"

Okay, I might start shrieking. "Are you kidding? We've been talking all summer!"

"That's now. What about later?"

"We'll find other things to talk about! And anyway, who says people have to share a hundred percent of their worldviews? I don't like you because we're both into Ignaz Semmelweis. I like you because you're likable." Oh, god, the tears are coming. I shove my hands in my pockets and squeeze them into fists so my brain is distracted from the tears. "You're kind, smart, and funny, and you don't let me get away with stuff if you think I'm wrong. I like listening to you talk—" I almost die when my voice breaks "—because you don't look at the world like me, and every time I listen, I see it in a different way. I see it in the Tristan way, and that's a beautiful world to see."

"Me too," he says.

"So what's the problem?"

He doesn't say anything.

A small, cold piece of ice forms in the pit of my stomach and crystalizes out. "What's really going on? Were you just messing around? The not-date—was that so we never had to date and you could just flirt with—"

"No! I love hanging out with you!"

"Then *what*, Tristan?"

"You're moving," he says. "You'll be gone in a couple of weeks." He lifts his hands. "It doesn't make sense to date. I thought I could do it, but I like you too much."

The ice is obliterated by the meteor of anger that slams inside of me. "Yeah, you're right," I say and put my hands to my cheeks, as if he's given me a divine revelation. "Who wants to hang out with someone they think is cool, and have a good time two weeks before school starts? What a horrible idea. Please don't think I'm a monster for suggesting it."

"Don't be smart," he snaps.

"Can't help how I was born," I snap back.

He takes my hand.

I pull away.

"You're going to the other side of the country. Should we be starting anything right before you leave for Georgia? It's not like you're a couple hours away and we can see each other on the weekends."

"We'll have holidays and breaks and video chats," I tell him, annoyed that he's being so obtuse about this. The leaves from the tree in his front yard rustle, and I'm sure I see a butterfly flit past. I push myself to say the thing that hurts to say. "David . . . David's passing made me realize that any moment you can spend with someone you care about is a moment you should take."

"Tuna, I really like you." He takes hold of my fingers.

I let him.

"Even as friends, I'm going to miss you. The whole moving thing—" He squeezes my hand like he knows I'll pull away again. "—Robby made me realize how much it can hurt to lose someone you care about."

The rage meteor is back. The Tyrant strikes again. "I'm not planning on dying!"

"That's not what I mean. I'm talking about texting you, and you don't reply because you're out having fun, and it's cool. But then you're not replying 'cause you met someone you like."

"I can say the same thing about you."

"Exactly. There's going to be all this stuff happening in the next few months. It's not right for either of us to try to hold on to the other person. We should give each other freedom to see this new world."

"But we like each other! Why wouldn't we see where it takes us?" I swing in and kiss him. Not a Hollywood hot and heavy kiss, but enough to make contact, and I feel him connect. There's a bond between us. There's a chance. How can we let it go? I hold his hands and say, "Even if we don't make it long term, even if we drift apart, I'd rather have the memories of being with you than wondering if I should have pushed harder for the chance."

"That sounds nice, but broken hearts suck—"

"Seriously?" I lose whatever hold I have on the meteor. "Broken hearts suck? That's your takeaway? I'm here, asking you out, and you—cold coward—are afraid of a little physical distance between us, so you want to bail before we even start!"

There's a rage meteor in him, and it lights his eyes. "Cold coward?!"

"Ice-cold coward! How can you not take a chance on love and happiness?"

"Because broken hearts suck!"

"Oh my god, are you kidding me? *Are you kidding me right now?* Like I haven't had a broken heart?"

"Of course you have," he bites out. "But—"

"But what, Tristan? Were you at the hospital hearing a doctor tell you that one of the people you loved best was never coming home again?"

"No, but—"

"And were you crying so hard on your porch that you were dry heaving?"

"No—"

"Dry heaving, Tristan! I was crying so hard, I was almost throwing up, and you know what Scott—my *boyfriend of over a year*, the guy who I thought loved me and the guy who I SUPER loved—said to me? That I was too much emotionally! David had been dead for less than three hours, and Scott thought I should be less emotional about it!" I'm shrieking, but I don't even care right now because I'm pissed. I'm pissed at Scott for doing what he did, pissed at David for dying, pissed at Tristan for seeing a chance for love and light and then walking away from it. How can love leave me in the dark like this?

Tristan looks horrified. He also looks like maybe he understands Scott's belief that I'm overemotional.

That just sets me off even more. "I lost two people I loved in less than two years, but I'm still here, on your doorstep, asking you out because I like you, and I know you like me, too. But you—you're just hiding behind words. What does it matter if we call it a 'date' or a 'hang'? We spend time together—we've spent time together! And you kissed me! Oh my god, you kissed me and made me feel like something was happening between us!"

"I'm not a cold coward," he rages. "I'm just trying to do what's the least emotionally damaging for both of us. Something *was* happening between us. I'm trying to stop it before it—"

"By not even trying for it?"

"Long-distance relationships don't work," he says. "The idea of you being with me because you felt obligated, but really, you wanted to be with someone else—" He stops. "I couldn't handle it. I would never want to hurt you like that."

"You're hurting me right now." I spin away, pressing my hand against my mouth, because I'm trying so hard not to cry. Trying so hard not to sob at him not wanting to date me, at him not being the kind of guy I thought he was—the kind of guy who thought being a couple was worth the geographical distance.

And it hits me that while I saw us riding into the sunset, he saw us in the grave. I looked for the happy ending. Tristan just saw us ending.

If that's not a sign, I don't know what is. But I find myself saying, "We're good together."

Now he looks like he wants to cry. "The best together."

And signs are signs, but a heart in love is the loudest sound in the room. My heart won't be denied the last ditch effort; it can't see that this is the moment before the credits roll. I hear myself *begging*—and hating myself for the groveling. "Just think about it, okay? I'm asking you on a date. Please say yes."

He opens his mouth to say something, but I have to go. I'm barely hanging on to my composure. "Just think about it."

I get in my car, and a few blocks away I pull over and bawl my eyes out. By the time I pull into the parking lot, a headache is pounding its way along my temples, my throat is aching, and my eyes are puffy. I'm not looking forward to four hours in the chlorine-scented echo chamber that is the pool.

I spot Mitchell and his mom at the counter and—expert that I am—shove down my pain and smile at them. "Hey, guys, ready for our swim?"

His mom glances at him, then says, "I think we're going to take a break for a while."

"No, why?" I bend to Mitchell. "How come, kiddo?"

He just shakes his head and clings to his mom.

"Some of the kids were teasing him about the accidents and—" She looks at me from over his head. The question is in her eyes: *Am I doing the right thing? Do I pull my kid or push him?*

"Can I tell you something hardly anyone knows?" I say to Mitchell.

After a moment, he nods.

I sit on the floor. "When I first started swimming, I loved the water. I was so happy in it, I used to tell my brother I was a dolphin turned into a human."

Mitchell watches me. He's little, but I see him weighing my words, wary for any false word or tone. Small kids, man. They're lie detectors with jam-covered faces.

"But you know what used to happen to me?" I lean toward him. "I used to have accidents when I was in the water."

His eyes widen, wanting to believe me, but he's already old and cynical enough to know adults tell fibs. "Really?"

"It was horrible. I would cry and promise myself it wouldn't happen again, but it did. I would be in the pool, having fun and swimming, and all of a sudden, accident!"

"What happened?" he asks.

"I was lucky," I say and keep my voice steady. "My brother wanted to be a doctor. He was in school and studying. And you know what he said? That some kids' bodies take a little longer to develop. And that meant sometimes, no matter how hard they tried, they could still have accidents. It didn't mean anything was wrong with them or that they were bad, it was just how their bodies worked."

He comes out from behind his mom.

"You know what else he told me?"

Mitchell shakes his head.

"He wondered if maybe it was a sign I was meant to be a swimmer, because I was so happy and relaxed in the water."

He considers this.

"You know what else? I stayed in swimming and I kept going. My brother was right. After a while, I didn't have any accidents. And I was getting better and better at swimming. Do you know I almost made my college swim team? That wouldn't have happened if I'd let being embarrassed and being different stop me."

"I'm not going to tell you to stay or to quit." I rise. "If you quit, then change your mind, you can always come back the next time the class runs. I won't be here, but I know you'll have an awesome teacher." I make eye contact with his mom. "Maybe you don't have to decide today? Maybe you take a day to think about how you feel?"

"I think that's a great idea," his mom says. "How about if we do something else today and we'll come back to it later?"

He nods, then goes to the window that overlooks the pool and watches the people in the water.

"Don't tell me if it was true or not," she says to me. "I love the story too much."

Mitchell looks back at me as they leave. "Did you really think you were a dolphin?"

"I still think I'm a dolphin."

That gets me a smile and a wave as they walk out the door.

My phone dings as I turn toward the locker room. Tristan. It's not good news. I read the text twice, try not to cry, and cry anyway.

Thanks. Maybe another time.

If I thought telling him the swim story would change his mind about working through tough patches, I'd text him. But his message is definitely a "don't respond." Dark Nights of the Soul are highly overrated as vehicles for character development. Black Moments, too. In fact, if real life could skip from Initiation into the New World and go straight to the Happy Ending, I'd be good.

I push my feelings down into a new space that's next door to all the feelings for David. Then I fake a smile and wave at Penny. I'm just about to head into the back when I hear Robby bellow my name. Everyone in the center hears him. He strides toward me, his face hard with anger.

Penny, who hears him yell, but doesn't see his face, comes out from behind her desk.

"How could you, Tuna. You're the absolute worst!"

Penny does a sharp U-turn that would make car developers weep with envy, and speeds back to her desk.

"Is this about the sweater?"

"No, Tuna." His voice resumes an indoor volume as he comes to a stop by me, but the anger in his voice is a throbbing bass. "I'm talking about this." He slaps down his phone.

I swallow at the screenshot of the Eros and Agape profile.

"This is your doing; don't try to deny it."

"I won't," I say. "It was a private joke; it was an accident that it went live."

"Accident?" His face twists with contempt. "It was live for eight hours."

"That was an accident, too," I say. "I was messing around and Magic jumped on the keyboard—"

"You're blaming the dog for this?"

"I didn't realize the profile was set to live until the next morning, when I heard some people talking about it."

"Right." He infuses the word with Olympic-level disbelief.

"Right. I have to go. Work starts in a few minutes."

He shoves the phone back in his pocket. "Run away. Just like always."

"What's that supposed to mean?"

I don't realize our voices have grown louder until I spot Penny in my peripheral vision. She's running out of her office, her hands moving up and down in a shushing motion, her tunic flapping around her thighs. "I can start your shift," she says to me. "Why don't you and Robby find somewhere quiet to talk?"

Translation: you're scaring the Mommy and Me group, and everyone else in the facility. Please go somewhere else to sort family's dirty laundry. "Sorry, Penny. Robby was just leaving."

"You owe me an apology," he says. "Then I'll leave."

"Okay, okay." Penny's back to hand-flapping. She shoos us outside like a mother hen and gives us a thumbs-up before going back into the center. Smart money says she's locked the door to prevent us from going back inside.

"Nice going, Robby. You totally embarrassed me in front everyone at my work!"

"You're embarrassed? *You're embarrassed!* I'm sorry, are you the one the nurses and doctors are whispering about? Did you go for a consult and have the patient—who will literally be putting their life in your hands—ask if you were 'that online doctor that's trending,' and then wonder if you were mentally fit to perform their surgery?"

"Look, I'm sorry about that, but like I said, it was an accident."

"Right." He scowls. "Act of Dog." He waves his hands at the sky. "No, no. I'm wrong. Act of Ancestors, because somehow you think their ghosts are looking down on us and protecting us."

"Yeah, I do, and you do too—or at least you did—"

"It's garbage, Tuna. How can you not see it's superstitious nonsense to get kids to behave? There are no ancestors looking down on you, there's no one watching out for you."

"That's not true!"

"Oh, yeah!" He gets right into my face. "Then where were they when David—" He stops for a micro beat. "Where was the warning? Where was their protection?"

"From death? Are you totally unhinged? No one gets out of this life alive. It all ends in a body bag, Robby."

"Yeah, and if you're unlucky enough to have a sister like you, it ends in humiliation, too."

"How did they even know it was you?" I ask. "I didn't put your face on there—"

"You think my coworkers can't remember my costume from last year?" He yanks at the collar of his blue sweater and points. "You think they didn't recognize the birthmark?"

The birthmark. How could I forget?

"You're so high and mighty, aren't you? Coming down on me for interfering in your life and saying I'm trying to take over your life because I want to move to Georgia, but where's your accountability? Can you be that selfish to not see what a garbage thing you did?"

"I'm selfish? I'm *selfish*?" Something tight and hard breaks inside of me, and heat spreads.

"David was my husband, and now you're pitching me to strangers like I'm a used piece of furniture?"

"I'm so *sick* of you and your grief for David!" I'm screaming now, but I don't care. "Do you think you own grief, Robby? Do you think you have full possession of his loss?"

"He was the love of my life, Tuna!"

"He was the love of my life, too!" My voice cracks. "He was the love of Mom's life and Dad's life! We all loved him, Robby! We all miss him! We all wish we could have crawled into the cremation oven with him and let the fires take our sadness! But do we get to say any of that? No! Because it might upset poor, sensitive Robby! Do we get to talk about David or have pictures of him around? No! Because that might push Robby further into his mourning!"

"Obviously, you weren't that worried." He gives me a tight, hard smile. "I saw the picture you put in your room a few weeks back."

I can barely see him through the tears, but my laughter holds nothing but contempt. "I've had that picture up since before he died, and you know it. Mom and Dad make me hide it whenever you come over. You know why I hate you being around? Because every time, I have to run through the house, removing anything that might remind you of David. And you were over so often and without any warning that they made me take down everything of his, permanently."

That gives him pause. "They shouldn't have done that," he says quietly.

"*Shut up*, Robby. Don't stand there like you have the moral superiority over Mom and Dad, like somehow they did something wrong. They did it to protect you, because they thought somehow it would help your process. You know why I was playing around with the app that night? Because I'd found Mom in her office, shoved up in a corner, crying until she dry heaved, looking at photos of David. That's what your possessiveness over David's loss has done to us. We're all hunched in the dark, crying by ourselves."

The wind blows his hair and etches the pain on his face. "It doesn't excuse what you did."

"I'm sorry the profile went live, but I'm not sorry I did it. I needed, just for a minute, to feel like I could give you away. David was part of our house before I was even born. I heard his voice when Mom was pregnant with me. I heard his laughter. His existence was woven into my muscle and bone." I wipe the tears from my face. "You took his memory from me, and I'll never forgive you for that, Robby, never."

He swallows hard. "You're too young to understand. He and I were supposed to grow old together. We were supposed to have kids and late nights and early mornings, and I was robbed of it. I'm allowed to be angry."

"We're all angry, Robby. Death is never fair to anyone."

"That proves how immature you are. I lost the love of my life before I was even forty, and all you can give me is fortune-teller readings."

And suddenly, I'm so empty, all I am is a husk of an outer shell. I'm sure if I don't get inside, the wind will pick me up and blow to the end of the earth. "I may be immature, but you're selfish. You met David when you were five, which means you got almost thirty years with him. How many people get to say they were with the love of their life for that long? You may not have grown old with him, but you grew up with him and grew with him, and you're so selfish you can't even be grateful for it."

"You slammed me about the photos," he says, "but have you ever looked at them? Really looked at them?"

"Of course I have."

"Then you must have noticed how often you're between David and me," he says. "You're jealous because I hang out with Tristan every once in a while. But you were there, constantly, with David and me. Constantly. You don't think there weren't times when we wanted it to be just us? Times when your weekly sleepovers were more of an obligation than a hang? But we did it, because family loves and family shares. Except you. You can't share, but by all means, keep calling me selfish."

I want to defend myself, even as the painful truth sears me, but Robby's not done talking.

"You're always going on about your story beats and how life imitates art. God, do you love pontificating about characters and their arc. Do you think you're the good guy in this scenario? Think you're on the side of the angels? You may think you did the brave thing, but what you did was mean."

I don't have time to breathe out the pain because Robby's not done.

"Do you even like Tristan, or are you trying to crowbar him into this fantasy life you built for yourself, where the ancestors talk to you, and David's not really gone because butterflies appear in the heavens."

"I do like him," I say. "I like him a lot."

"No, you don't," he says. "You packed him into your fantasy. You know why you never asked him out? Because it would make everything a reality, and you don't want it. You want Bollywood-Hollywood, where you can play hero in your head and never have to have a real emotion."

"I asked him out," I say, "and he said no. I threw it all on the line for love, and he said 'maybe another time.'"

Robby rocks back in surprise. "I didn't know that."

"Why would you?" The good thing about being mad at Robby is that I'm too pissed off to feel the effect that talking about Tristan is having on my heart and body. "Ever since David, the list of things we can't talk about grows longer every day." It hits me then that he hasn't used any giant, long words with me. I haven't used any long-winded vocabulary with him, either. Which means we're at a level of mad at each other we've never been before. This is our worst fight, and I'm not sure we can come back from it. And the thing that hurts most? I don't care if we never come back from it.

"Maybe posting on the website was mean," I say, "but it was a private vent that got turned public, and I'm sorry for it. I'll be sorry for it for the rest of my life. And maybe it makes me selfish, wanting to sell you off. And maybe it makes me delusional, that I look out for butterflies. But through all of it, I tried to respect you, respect how you mourn. Can you say you did the same for me? I may have been mean, but forcing the rest of us to pretend David never existed makes you cruel. And of all the things you've been, I never thought cruel was one of them." I turn and head for the doors. "I'm done with you, Robby. Stay, leave, come to Georgia, move back home, I don't care. I'm done."

He doesn't say anything as I walk away, and with every step I feel the distance between us growing in my heart and the connection that held us together fraying to a breaking point.

CHAPTER TWENTY-TWO

Dark Nights of the Soul
Are REALLY Overrated

"I CAN'T BELIEVE YOU WENT NUCLEAR WITH ROBBY," FI SAYS. We're lying on her bed. The sun's finally out, but the last few days, I haven't felt any warmth. Mom and Dad are raging because Robby told them about the app. So it's been hours of Tuna the Insensitive and Tuna the Unthinking. He also threw me under the bus with the things I said to him about David and my folks. So I'm doubly the unwanted child for trying to hijack his pain. I never thought I'd hate my brother, but at this moment, if I never see him again, it'll be too soon. Every time I know he's coming over, I book it to Fi's. I'm done with the Robby Show. Thank the ancestors for Fi, because I can't talk to my parents, and I haven't said anything to Tristan since he texted me.

Quick question: How many Black Moments and Dark Nights of the Soul is one life supposed to endure? Asking for a friend. Okay, asking for me, because I'm one piece of bad news away from moving to the hills and living off grass and rainwater. "He deserved it," I say.

"He deserved truth. I'm not sure he deserved it served with a side of napalm."

"Whose side are you on, anyhow?"

"I don't know yet," she says and rolls over. Fi props her head with her hand and smiles. "He lost a lot."

"So did I."

"A brother, but he lost a partner. There's an intimacy he had with David that you didn't."

"Seriously, we're playing the Pain Olympics now?" I stare at the ceiling, at the curling glow-in-the-dark stars we stuck up there in grade seven.

"No. Sorry. Your pain is your pain."

"You're a pain," I say.

"I'm your pain."

I smile. "You are, and I love you for it."

"You should." She lies back on the pillow. "You're still not replying to Tristan's text?"

I shake my head.

"Maybe it was for the best. He never understood your ancestor thing."

"Neither do you."

"Yeah, but he was hetero-male superior about it."

"Truth," I say and try not to get mad about it.

We both stare at the ceiling.

"David and Robby met in pre-K. So did we." She takes my hand and laces our fingers. "It's not the same. They had a partnership love, and we don't. I'm not Tristan, but I love you, Tuna Fish."

I slowly turn to look at her. "It's not like you to get emotional and gushy. What's going on?" I bolt upright. "Is it your back? Do you have to have another surgery?"

"Nah." She waves down my panic. "I was just thinking. You're leaving soon, and I'll be in New York. It's going to be the first time since we were four that we're not together. I won't see you every day, and we won't have sleepovers."

Her words take the air from my lungs. In all the agony over Tristan and the anxiety over Robby, I'd forgotten the obvious part of my move to SCAD. I'm leaving Fi. It's an emotional boulder that rolls over me. I hate it when Robby is right. I was so selfishly focused on silly things (namely, him and Tristan), I missed Fi in all of this. I'm definitely moving to the hills and eating grass. "I can't believe I didn't clock that. How did we not talk about this until now?"

"We tried back in May. Then you started crying, and I—well, I refuse to cry, but my eyes got misty."

"You blamed it on the chlorine in my hair."

"It was a lot of chlorine, but it was a good moment," she says. "I feel like we really shared our feelings then."

"In other words, you've had enough of the mushy stuff?"

"Let's watch something with blood and gore."

"What about Riley? How're you dealing with leaving for New York and your burgeoning—"

She shrugs. "Friends. We're friends, moving toward something more." Fi flashes me a smile that says it's more than friendship. I'm tempted to ask, but she says, "Blood and gore time, Tuna. I've shared enough."

I respect that, so I nudge her shoulder, then turn on the movie.

We're in the middle of watching some D-rated horror flick, *Caw*, when Tristan texts.

You okay?

"It's Tristan," I say and hold the screen out for Fi.

She reads it and her mouth pulls to the side. "How are you going to play this?"

I put down the phone. "I'm not. He said what he needed to say."

"Just because he doesn't want to move past being friends—"

"It's not what he said, Fi, it's how he said it. That he could learn to live with my quirks. It was condescending."

"Tuna, I love you, but your beliefs are in Out There Land."

"Don't start," I tell her. "You love science so much, but it's not infallible. White people used science to prove colored folk didn't deserve an education. And science said women's brains were too small to ever be able to handle things like voting or holding a job. I'm all for science, but it's still held hostage to people's morals and biases. Until scientists can figure out a way around that, then I'm going to embrace facts, science, ancestors, and anything else that helps me make sense of this world."

"That was years ago. Science evolves."

"And intuition can't? You're promising me—one hundred percent— that science will *never* find a way to prove an afterlife?"

"No—"

"So cut me the slack that Tristan couldn't," I snap.

"Was he really that bad, or are you trying to find reasons to stop liking him?"

Before I can answer, Tristan texts again.

I don't want to lose our friendship.

"Oh, no." Fi reads over my shoulder. "Did he just say 'we can still be friends'?"

I don't know if it's the run-off from three days' worth of being scolded by Mom and Dad, or getting the cold shoulder from them, Robby, and Tristan, but I feel unloved, unappreciated, and wildly misunderstood. I'm a wildfire looking for a spark, and Tristan is the match strike that sets me off.

> Much as I'd love to be friends with someone
> who can "learn to live with my quirks," I'm good.

What's that supposed to mean?

> It means my beliefs are my beliefs. They're
> not quirks.

I never said that!

> You did so!

So what if I did? You're a quirky person.
It's one of the things I like about you.

> Don't do that. I'm mashing the keypad so hard,
> I might break the screen. Don't make it out like
> I'm the one with eccentricities.

Right. Because joining my parents' company and
getting a career as a real estate agent is so out there.

> Give the boy credit for being able to ooze
> sarcasm through text. What about your germ
> phobia?

I don't have a germ phobia!

> You wash your hands so much, you could be a
> Bond villain! It's not great as slams go, but this is
> a first-draft fight.

That's not phobia! That's just general cleanliness!!!

> **Yeah? And refusing to take back your bag from
> the lost and found, that wasn't germ phobia?**

"Silence?" says Fi, taking the phone and scrolling the texts. "Who scored the point?"

"I did."

She reads and nods. "That's a good point."

"I have more," I say.

"He's typing!" She hands me back the phone.

**I picked up the sweater because I thought it
was yours.**

> Deflection, the last weapon of the losing team.
> **It doesn't matter. You said what you said, and I
> respect that, even if I don't agree with it. I have
> to go.** I toss the phone on the bed. Then I grab
> it and hit him with one last text. **If you find the
> pink sweater, keep it.**

Why would I keep your sweater?!

> **Because ice-cold cowards always need
> warming up.** I flip to my settings and block him.

Fi watches all of this. "You're going nuclear on everyone."

"I like him," I say, feeling the ache in my throat. "More than a friend. I laid everything on the line for him and he took the coward's route. I don't know why I ever liked him in the first place." *Because he was kind and funny and smart. Because he was a super cute helping of Yummy Boy with a side dish of math puns.* "A couple more weeks and I get to go away.

Then I'll find someone who'll roll the dice on love, and we'll ride off into the sunset on horseback."

Fi puts her arms around me. "I love you, Altuna Kashmir Rashad. You're the worst person when it comes to handling a real-life crisis, but you're never boring." Her voice catches. "And you're my best friend, no matter where you go or who you go with."

I hug her back. I want one of us to say, "At least now things can only get better," but I've learned my lesson. I won't say it because that will just bring the rain down on my head, and not in the cool rom-com way.

"Do you want help with your hair?" Mom stands in the doorway of my room.

"Like I trust you," I say. "You'll probably just cut it off or shave it."

"That's not fair." She comes into the room and starts finger-combing my hair. "What you did was wrong."

"What you did was more wrong. Robby asked you about the photos of David, and you lied to spare his feelings."

She pauses the scalp massage. "I know," she says quietly and sits down. "Sometimes there are no easy answers."

"That's a cop-out."

"Says the girl who tried to sell her brother." Mom sits beside me on the bed. "Grief is a hard thing and—" she shrugs "—I didn't know how to handle your brother and his sadness. You know Robby. Underneath all that obnoxiousness is a sensitive soul. I push too hard and he turtles. I didn't want to add to his sadness."

"So you added to mine."

She winces. "I'm not great in an emotional emergency, I'll admit it."

The doorbell rings and I move to answer it.

"Robby," says Mom. "I—he asked me about the office again."

I stop, ignoring the bell as it rings again. "Did you tell him? About crying? About having to mourn David in the Dark?"

A sad smile flits across her face. "David would have loved that title. David in the Dark."

"He would have turned it into some kind of chocolate dessert with cherries and liqueur. Did you tell Robby the truth?"

"Yes." Tears fill her eyes. "It hurt him to hear." She takes my hand. "But he heard, Tuna. He listened."

The doorbell goes again.

She swipes her eyes and heads down the stairs.

Maybe I did it the wrong way, but at least we're moving in the right direction. Maybe. I don't know. There's no one answer for grief, no one-size-fits-all for families and their dynamics. Especially, not for this family and our dynamics.

I go to the door and open it expecting to see a salesman and find Robby instead.

"I gave at the office," I say.

Magic's in his arms, and she gives me a tongue-out smile that melts my hardened heart.

"But I guess you can come in." I step back.

He steps inside and hands Magic to me.

It's a good sign, but I hide my smile in her fur.

"Where's Mom and Dad?"

I do a slow pivot, look over my shoulder at Mom. "Do we need to run a test on you? Mental faculties dwindling in your age?"

He ignores me, kisses Mom on the cheek, and goes into the kitchen.

"Where are your keys?" I follow him. "Why didn't you just let yourself in?"

"It's called respecting boundaries."

I'm not sure if that's a dig at me or him trying to make amends.

Dad comes from downstairs. "Robby. What's going on?"

"I'm glad you're all here," he says and takes Magic from my arms. "I wanted you to have a chance to say goodbye." He swallows hard. "Mashed Potato's owner contacted me. I take her home tomorrow."

OH MY GOD. HOW MANY BLACK MOMENTS IS ONE PERSON'S LIFE SUPPOSED TO ENDURE?!

His words suck the air out of the room. Mom clutches the edge of the counter and I collapse into one of the chairs.

"Magic's owner contacted you? How is that possible?" Anger overtakes disbelief. "Why now? How are they suddenly calling now? Where were they weeks ago?"

"Out of the country," he says. "They just got back."

"What about the dog sitter or the kennel where they boarded her? Why didn't they have notices up for her? Or answer our notices? Why didn't they at least call to tell us that her family would pick her up when they got back?"

"Does it matter?" Robby's smile is bleak. "She's been found."

"Well, it's not fair—" Mom starts.

"Wake me when life is fair."

"Robby, don't be belligerent."

The entire thing is wrong. Magic was meant for us. I know it. I feel it. Why is this happening?

I know it's superstitious to think the dead watch over me. I know there's no scientific evidence to support any of my beliefs. But it's all I have. If the ancestors watch over us, then the dead are never dead, especially when they send signs.

It means that even though I can't see or hear David, somehow he's still around. Somehow, the connection wasn't broken and the bond between us didn't mean reaching back in my memory. I can look forward to each day, to the surprise of a butterfly or some indication he's still with me. Now, Tristan doesn't want to date me, Robby's mad at me, Fi and I aren't going to be in the same town, and the dog that should have been ours is leaving. I don't know what I think, except the world is cold and bleak and lonely. And maybe I'm the biggest loser in the world for ever believing in happy endings and turning sad moments into joy.

"I made arrangements to meet with them tomorrow and give her back," he says. "But I thought you might want to see her tonight."

This is too much like when we lost David. Too close to the faceless, nameless doctor saying, "You should say your goodbyes."

Magic only has tonight. Tomorrow, we won't talk about donating her organs or a memorial service. She'll live on with the love of her original family. She won't send me signs. I won't look for omens. She'll be nothing but a memory. I'll fade from her existence, but she's going to leave a giant hole in my heart, and nothing and no one will ever fill it.

As plot twists go, this one should be deleted, burned, and forever destroyed.

My world is shaking, the motion stabilizers on life's cameras are broken, and it's all I can do not to hyperventilate. I can't stand still, but the idea of leaving Magic's side undoes me. It's David, all over again.

I need air. Lungs' worth of it. Gallons. I break from the table, run for the front door, fling it open, and slam into a wall.

A warm wall that gives and puts its arms around me.

"Tuna?"

Not a wall. Tristan. *Oh, Tristan.*

"Tuna!" There's urgency in the way he calls my name. "What happened?"

"Magic." I wipe my face and try to focus on his. "Magic."

His face goes white. "Something happened to her?"

"Her owners. They came forward."

His expression crumples, then turns angry. "After all this time? Now they want to look for her? Where were they weeks ago? Why didn't they have signs up? What kind of people are they?"

We both know what kind of people they are. I don't say anything, just shake my head, let his arms fold around me, and accept the comfort he offers.

"What are you going to do?"

"Give her back." I can barely get out the words. "It's all we can do."

"Do you have to?"

I pull away and take a seat on the step. "Why are you here?"

He sits beside me. "You blocked me, didn't you?"

"It seemed the least painful solution."

"For whom?"

"Proper grammar. You've been hanging around my family too much. Why are you here?"

He nudges my shoulder. "Because you're the only one who's allowed to show up at people's doors unannounced?"

I know he's trying for a joke, but I can't find the energy to smile. "Why are you here?" I ask again and hope for a hard pivot from "I don't want to date you, Tuna," to "You're the one for me."

"I came to half apologize."

"Half—?" I don't know what's worse, the painful hope he'd changed his mind or that in my darkest moment (edit: in yet ANOTHER ONE of my darkest moments) I don't warrant a full apology.

"I still think you're quirky, I still think trying to find signs in a chaotic world is ludicrous—"

"Can we get to the apology?"

"You were right. I was condescending and arrogant. And I don't think you're right, but you might have a point about me and germs."

As half apologies go, that's not too bad. "Thanks," I tell him and find my heart taking over my mouth to blurt out, "Anything else?"

His eyes mist over. "No."

"I should go back inside." At the door, I stop and turn. "I'm sorry, too. Especially about blocking you."

"Thanks," he says.

"I'll unblock you," I tell him, "Only . . . don't text me for a while, okay? Like maybe end of September? I need some space."

He nods.

If there's more to his feelings—heartbreak, relief, shrieking pain (like mine)—I'm too emotionally drained to clock it. "Thanks," I say and close the door behind me.

The next morning, I wake up to a sore head and puffy eyes. Robby's in the kitchen, making regular pancakes.

"What happened to no sugar?"

"I have to give her back today. I need all the processed love I can get."

I sit at the table and watch him. "I was thinking, maybe we need some help."

"Giving her back?"

"Coping with giving her back, among other things."

He flips the pancake and turns to me. "A therapist."

"I don't know how to help you," I say. "I don't know the line between enabling and supporting, and I'm tired of resenting you." I blink fast. "I came really close to hating you, and that scares me. I want my brother back."

He slides the pancake onto a plate and hands it to me. "I'm not taking the job in Georgia."

"No, do it," I say. "It wasn't fair of me to—"

"To tell me the truth?" He gives me a small smile. "You were right, Little Fish. I'm just running from myself. I've been running. I have to stop, and

I have to stop dragging you along with me. I'll ask around at the hospital, get some recommendations for individual and family therapy."

"There's a grief group at the rec center," I say, "when you're ready."

He nods.

Just then, we hear the tap of Magic's feet coming down the stairs.

I push away the pancake, not that I was hungry in the first place. "Speaking of grief, let's get this over with."

CHAPTER TWENTY-THREE

Fade to Black

I HOLD MAGIC IN MY ARMS, STARE AT THE DOOR OF THE brownstone, and say, "I don't like this. Let's text them and say we've changed our minds."

"Tuna."

"I can smell the weed from outside. Outside, Robby! Do you know what that means?"

"She has the world's most relaxed owners?" He rings the bell. "She's not ours."

"This is wrong—"

The door opens and a guy a few years older than me, with a surfer's look, peers out at us. "'Sup?"

"Did you call about a missing dog?" Robby asks.

His gaze goes to Magic. "Hey! You found 'im."

"I'll need proof she's your dog," he says, refusing to hand Magic in the guy's outstretched arms.

"For sure, man, for sure. I'll get it—"

"Dwayne—" A woman's voice sounds from within. "What's going on?" The door opens farther to reveal the female version of Dwayne. Just as tall and lean, sun-bleached blond hair, and blue eyes. She looks at us, then Dwayne. Her hard expression softens at the sight of Magic. "What's going on?"

"We think we might have your dog," I say.

Her face goes slack and she does a double blink. "Our dog?"

"Yeah," says Dwayne. "Looks, she's back!"

"That's not our dog," the girl snaps. "We don't have a dog! It's our cat that went missing, you dope head!"

"Oh, whoa," says Dwayne. "Right. The cat. He looks like a dog, though, for real. Acts like one, too."

"God! Just—" She turns and shoves him away. Pushing her hair off her face, she says, "I'm sorry my pothead brother dragged you out here. This isn't our dog."

My brain has fallen apart at this unexpected news. I don't know if it's *deus ex machina* (story-writing speak for the ancestors stepping in), a plot twist, or just the best news I've heard in weeks, but THIS IS THE BEST NEWS I'VE HEARD IN WEEKS! I want to cry and scream and shriek with glee, but I (barely) hold it together and give her a big grin.

Only, the grin might be too big, because she does a double take, like she's memorizing my face in case the cops call looking for an escaped serial killer.

"I'm sorry about your cat." Robby stumbles over his words. No doubt, he's tripping on the same levels of joy that I am.

She looks over her shoulder, steps on to the porch, and closes the door behind her. "He's not missing," she says. "Sam's with my parents. I love my brother, but this whole setup of us living together is a fool's game. I got my own apartment, but Sam was a gift to 'both' of us from my aunt." She jerks her thumb at the house. "Can you see that dumbass being sober enough to take care of him if we weren't living together? Don't get me wrong, Dwayne loves Sam. But he's likely to overfeed him or forget to put out water—or give him too much treats. No, it's better for him to think Sam's missing, at least until he can get clean." She smiles down at Magic. "But that was really nice of you to follow up. What's their name?"

"Magic," I say. "We've been calling her Magic."

"How long has she been missing?"

"I don't know," I say. "We've had her for about six weeks."

She looks at us, incredulous. "Almost two months and no one's claimed her?"

"She doesn't have tags or a chip," says Robby. "We posted on as many online sites as we can think of, local and statewide, but so far—"

"Two months, but no owner has come forward." She looks at Robby as though he's missing a brain. "What do you need, a flashing sign that she has no owner? Take down the notices and keep her!"

"That wouldn't be right," Robby says.

"If she was meant to be found, she'd have been found. If I don't put eyes on Sam every couple of hours when I'm with her, I panic," the girl says. She gives Magic a final head rub and turns back to the house.

"Thanks for your help—uh—" I stop, realizing I never got her name.

"Joan," she says over her shoulder. "Joan."

"Thanks, Joan."

"Keep the dog," she says and closes the door.

My heart is doing some hip-hop, jazz, tap dance inside my chest, and my ribs are keeping rhythm. I'm so happy, I'm light-headed and dizzy. I press my hands against the door because my legs feel like they're going to give out on me. "Oh, man. All the way here, I was running through the possible ways this could end, but I never saw this coming. Of all the scenarios, this was never one of them."

"Of course not, nimrod. This is real life and it's always weirder than fiction."

I give it a two-second count, stare at the framework, then turn to Robby.

He steps back, alarmed. "Why are you staring at me with a serial killer smile?"

I do a two-handed flutter tap on his shoulder. "Did you not hear those names? Joan. Sam."

"So?"

"Robby! Those were the names of the dad and son in *Sleepless in Seattle*. Jonah and Sam! It's a sign that Magic's meant for us." Oh, talk about character pivots and realizations. Why—WHY—did I ever doubt the ancestors?!

"Tuna," Robby's voice is full of condescension.

For once, I don't care, because Joan's right. We've done everything possible under the sun to find Magic's owners. Whoever they are, they don't want her.

"There's no such thing as signs."

"Joan literally asked if you needed a sign to keep Magic, then told you to keep Magic."

"That's not a sign. That's a stranger's opinion."

"Fine," I say. "What about the fact that no one's claimed Magic?"

He steps to the sidewalk. "That might be an indication."

"Did you ever think of where we found her?"

"What do you mean?"

"In the dog park," I say. "People abandon dogs all the time in dog parks, because they figure other dog owners will step in."

Robby's face says more than any words he could come up with.

"She's meant for us. The ancestors sent her to help us."

"There's no such thing as signs," Robby says.

A butterfly, the same shade of blue that David loved, flies down and hovers over Magic's head.

"That's not a sign," he says. "It's a coincidence."

Another one comes to us.

"It's summer," says Robby, "butterflies are everywhere."

Just then, a half-dozen fly our way.

Robby blinks. "Get in the car," he says. "There's no such thing as signs." But he doesn't sound positive.

I belt Magic in, then go to the front passenger seat and do the same for myself. "So? Are you going to take down the notices?"

"I don't know." He puts down the window, then glances back at Magic. "I want to make sure I give the family all the chances to reclaim her."

"You could always out yourself as the guy from Eros and Agape, and post her picture, and ask the Internet to find her original family."

Panic flashes across his face. "No. Too many weirdos will come out of the woodwork and try to claim her. She's not mine yet."

"*Ours.*" I take his hand. "Robby, it's okay to delete the notices. It's not as if—" I don't want to say, *It's not as if her owners are like us. They're not moving heaven and earth to get her back, the way we would for David*, because it feels like too much pain and honesty for our hearts to contain. But I don't have to say anything, because he's already pulled out his phone.

A couple of minutes later, he says, "There. It's all done. The notices are down."

Then he smiles—*really smiles*—at me, and I see Old Robby, Our Robby, My Big and Wonderful Brother Robby. The wind blows through the window and I'm sure it's our ancestors, sighing and crying, and loving every inch of him from their ancestral perch.

He starts the car and heads down the road.

"We need a name for her."

"No way. You're not naming her." He makes a face. "Magic. How reductive."

"You can't keep calling her Mashed Potato!"

"That was last week."

"Dare I ask—?"

"Tater Tot."

"Actually, not a bad name."

He pulls to stop at the red light, and a blue butterfly lands on the windowsill. Robby glances at it, then watches it. He takes a slow breath and inches his finger toward it.

The butterfly's wings flap. It crawls on his hand, stays a moment, then takes to the sky.

He monitors it for a second. Then the light changes and Robby moves on.

CHAPTER TWENTY-FOUR

Let the Credits Roll

'M COMING OUT OF WORK WHEN I SEE TRISTAN. I HAVEN'T seen him in days, and my eyeballs have missed the sight of him. He's a checkered shirt helping of happiness to my heart and soul. I sigh and wish I could do more than feast on him with my eyes.

I also wish I looked half as good. Had I known I'd bump into him, I would have dressed up. As it is, my wet hair's in a bun, my sweats have a mustard stain, and the t-shirt's so old, the collar's gone from a crew neck to a V-neck.

He spots me, too, shifts the messenger bag on his shoulder, and slows. Then looks around as though unsure if he should head my way or avoid me.

I solve his problem by walking up to him. "Hey."

"Hey. I thought you'd be gone by now."

"Almost." I want to tell him about Mitchell and how proud I am of the little dude for coming to class. He's still not sure about getting in the pool, but he's been playing my assistant. The fact he shows up at all is spectacular. I'm sure that next class, he's going in the water. "Class ran late."

"Um—" He blushes, hard, from pink to deep red. "I was thinking about you—" The rest of words are lost in the din of the jackhammer.

I point to the end of the building, where the window washers are cleaning, and hope it might be quieter.

He nods and follows me.

I was right. It's quieter on this end. Mostly. I can hear the guys above us talking as they clean the windows, but their voices are faint. "What were you saying?"

"I was thinking about you, and I wanted to respect your space," he says, the pink tinge creeping back up his face. "But I also wanted to do something to help you celebrate SCAD and the move." He takes a box from his bag and thrusts it at me. "For you. I don't know if it's appropriate or creepy, but—"

"Tell me you don't sell houses like that," I say and open the box. Inside is a pink sweater.

"I tried to find one like the one you lost," he says. "It took a bit, but I think it's close. I was just going to drop it off at your locker, but then I saw you and—and you're not saying anything. This was a terrible idea, wasn't it?"

I stare at the sweater, bubble-gum pink and soft as cream.

"Tuna? Say something."

"I hate pink," I blurt out.

"What!"

"I hate pink and I never lost a sweater. I'm so sorry! I was coming to the field that day to ask you out, and then, I don't know what happened. No, I do know what happened. I got scared. I lost my mind and I lied to you about why I was there—"

"But you described the sweater—wait! Is that why your description matched the one in the lost and found?" he says. "We've been planning a screenplay based on it!"

"I know," I say miserably. "I'm so sorry. I described the one you found. I didn't mean to lie to you about it."

"I guess I should take this back." He reaches for the box.

"No, please, can I keep it? I'll pay you for it."

"But you said you don't like pink. You'll never wear it," he says.

"No, I won't," I tell him, "but I can frame it and put it on my wall. And every time I look at it, I'll think of my friend Tristan." I smile at him and hope he smiles back. I can't quite see from the tears in my eyes, and I have to blink them away.

He doesn't smile back.

"Tristan? I said I was sorry."

"I know, it's not that. Your story's actually kind of cute in that weird, hysterical way of yours."

I decide to log that as a compliment. "What is it?"

"I hate writing," he says. "I hate the screenplay—well, I don't hate it. I just hate working on it."

"Then why—?"

"Because I like you, and you like screenplays. And it seemed like a good way to impress you at the time."

I can't help laughing. "You're as adorably and hysterically weird as I am!"

He grins and rubs the back of his head. "Yeah, I guess I am. In different ways, but yeah, the samesies."

I don't know what else to say, so I go with, "I should head out."

"I'm not wrong," he says quietly. "I've been thinking about us, about you, about everything, and I can't figure out a way this works."

"Because I'll be across the country."

"That too," he says, "but do we really have anything in common? I don't like screenwriting and you're not into math."

"So?"

"So, shouldn't we have some things in common?"

"We do," I say. "You may not like screenwriting, but you like stories."

"Sure, who doesn't like movies—"

"No, I mean, didn't you notice that those houses you help sell, you did it by telling them a story. You gave them a vision of what their lives could be if they bought the house. That's knowing your audience, and that's basic storytelling."

His eyebrows pull down. "I guess, but—"

"And just because science doesn't light me up doesn't mean I don't like it. I get you don't want to date me, but coming up with excuses—"

"That's not true, I do want to date you. A lot."

"So," I say, "date me."

We stare at each other, and I hold my breath.

He takes a slow inhale. Then, "Do you want to go out?"

I'm not letting him go that easily. "Like a hang?"

He relaxes and grins because he knows what I'm doing. "Like a date. Let's go on an official date. I'm asking you out on a date. Will you go on a date with me?"

The world stops. I feel all of my ancestors holding their breath, chewing their popcorn, and watching this in the afterlife's movie theater. "Yes, Tristan Dangerfield, I think we should go on an official date. I'm accepting your offer of a date. I will go on a date with you."

He grins.

"I'm sorry I called you a cold coward."

"You were right, which is what made me so mad. We were spending lots of time together, and I think about you constantly. Pretending it was just a friendship was a fool's game. Pretending it's not going to suck when you leave is a bigger fool's game." He touches my arm. "You make things interesting and fun. It made me realize that I want as much Tuna time as I can get before you leave. Let's go on a billion dates."

I don't know if the ancestors are swooning, but I know I am.

Then he takes me in his arms, double-checks to make sure I'm good with what's about to happen (and YES! SO GOOD WITH WHAT'S ABOUT TO HAPPEN!), and kisses me.

We come up for air and if the ancestors aren't breathless, then I have no hope for them. It's a Hollywood kiss to end Hollywood kisses. Come to think of it, that kiss was definitely NOT PG. I hope the ancestors turned away. I bet they did—well, except Great-Aunt Cecile, but you know how she is.

"What are we doing on our first date?"

"I thought I'd hang up a white sheet in the backyard and stream *Sleepless in Seattle*. We could do a fire pit, blankets, popcorn, whatever you want. What do you think?"

"I think it sounds like an epic first date. I think this moment couldn't be more perfect if—"

There's a shout from above.

Both of us look up to see a wall of soapy water coming down. I scream and gasp as dirty, cold water drenches me.

"Sorry! Sorry!" The apologies come from the washers.

I blink, trying not to get the water in my eyes.

"Tuna?" Tristan says. "Are you okay?"

"Good. Very clean. You?"

"I'm good, too. What were you going to say?"

"That this moment couldn't be more perfect if it happened in a rainstorm." The water dump was Great-Aunt Cecile. I know it.

He laughs. "Maybe signs do exist," he says, then kisses me again.

ACKNOWLEDGMENTS

THE TASK OF WRITING A NOVEL IS A STRANGE ANIMAL. On the one hand, it's a solitary and sometimes lonely activity because, in its early stages, the story belongs solely to the author. It's up to the author to quiet herself, find the patience to hear the characters' voices, and build the story. On the other hand, it's a wildly collaborative effort. There are coffees with friends as we try to sort the voices, talks with our agent as we clarify the story arc and emotional high points, and emails with our publisher as we fine-tune so the story is one that readers will enjoy.

To that end, I'd like to thank my husband for the long walks and early mornings, the teas, patience, cheerleading, feedings, and thoughts as I bounced Tuna's story around in my brain and our conversations. My gratitude extends to Johanna Melaragno, who was willing to pull on her waders and head into the weeds with me on the most trivial of details (that felt so significant at the time). To Katherine Magyarody, as well, for the brainstorming, hurrah'ing, and general shenanigans that ensue when we're together.

Further thanks to The Furious Furies, Kate A. Boorman and Nikki Vogel, for the food shared and time spared, and all the comfort and encouragement that went into these pages and this roller-coaster journey we call "being authors."

I also want to thank the Tall Girls—Alison Hughes, Lisa J. Lawrence, Lorna Schultz Nicholson, and Karen Spafford-Fitz. The stops and starts in creating a novel can be frustrating and bleak. Thank you for the warm hugs and cool shade and for being my rest stop when I needed to catch my breath and refuel.

To my agent, Amy Tompkins, every author should have someone like you in their corner! Thank you for the thoughtful insights on Tuna and for being such a champion of my work.

If I may pause in my grown-up author acknowledgments to squeal in delight and toss (environmentally safe, biodegradable, organic, imaginary) glitter at my Running Press team, I would love that! I am so lucky to have found a home, not once but twice!, with such awesome people. Julie Matysik, Allison Cohen, Amber Morris, Valerie Howlett, Kara Thornton, Dominique Delmas, Michael McConnell, and Joan Roberts, hurrahs, huzzahs, and cupcakes all around! To Stephanie Singleton and Marissa Raybuck, a huge thank-you for such a breathtaking cover.

I'd like to end my thank-yous with a big and grateful thank-you to you, the reader. Of all the books you could have picked up, you chose Tuna's story. Thank you for spending time with her, thank you for diving into the pages. You make the early mornings and late nights, the revisions and page one rewrites, worth every moment.